D0402204

Once upon a Galaxy

Once Upon a Galaxy

Josepha Sherman

August House Publishers, Inc.
LITTLE ROCK

©1994 by Josepha Sherman.
All rights reserved. This book, or parts thereof,
may not be reproduced in any form without permission.
Published 1994 by August House, Inc.,
P.O. Box 3223, Little Rock, Arkansas, 72203,
501-372-5450.

Printed in the United States of America

10 9 8 7 6 5 4 3 2 1 HB
10 9 8 7 6 5 4 3 2 1 PB

LIBRARY OF CONGRESS CATALOGUING-IN-PUBLICATION DATA

Once upon a galaxy: folktales, fantasy, and science fiction /
[compiled] by Jospeha Sherman. — 1st ed.
p.   cm.
Includes bibliographical references.
Summary: Includes fifty folktales from around the world, relating
them to contemporary fantasy, science fiction, and cartoon themes.
ISBN 0-87483-386-8 (hardback): $19.95 — ISBN 0-87483-387-6 (pbk.): $11.95
1. Tales. 2. Mythology. [1. Folklore. 2. Mythology.]
I. Sherman, Josepha. PZ8.1.055   1994
398.2—dc20   94-29478

Executive editor: Liz Parkhurst
Project editor: Rufus Griscom
Design director: Ted Parkhurst
Cover design: Harvill-Ross Studios Ltd.

Star Trek ©1994 by Paramount Pictures. All rights reserved.
Superman and all related elements are the property of DC Comics ©1994.
All rights reserved. "Used with Permission."
Star Wars ™ and ©1977 by LucasFilm Ltd. All rights reserved.
Illustration from *The Fellowship of the Rings* by J.R.R. Tolkien.
Copyright ©1954, 1965 by Christopher R. Tolkien, Michael H.R. Tolkien, John F.R.
Tolkien and Priscilla M.A.R. Tolkien. Reprinted by permission of Houghton Mifflin.
All rights reserved.
Bugs Bunny ©1994 by Warner Bros., Inc. All rights reserved.

The paper used in this publication meets the minimum requirements of
the American National Standard for Information Sciences—Permanence of
Paper for Printed Library Materials, ANSI Z39.48-1984.

AUGUST HOUSE, INC.   PUBLISHERS   LITTLE ROCK

Contents

Notes   215

A Suggested Reading and Viewing List   237

Introduction

Science fiction is all around us. We take for granted the images of strange new worlds we see on television screens and in the movies, and think nothing of playing computer games that let us pilot our own starships and battle alien invaders. Even before the age of television and computers, science fiction was alive in hundreds of books featuring distant futures and marvelous inventions. Readers could enjoy such authors as H.G. Wells with his *Invisible Man* and *War of the Worlds* and Jules Verne, who wrote dozens of thrilling and often scientifically plausible adventures including *Twenty Thousand Leagues Under the Sea* and *From the Earth to the Moon.*

Fantasy fiction is just as widely known in today's world of entertainment. Although fantasy plots are not as popular in the movies as science fiction, stories featuring magical happenings and wondrous creatures are found in every bookstore, frequently outselling the science fiction titles, and often occupying the bestseller lists of both fanzines and mainstream newspapers. Authors such as J.R.R. Tolkien, who wrote of hobbits and human adventurers battling ultimate evil, have awakened a longing for magic in many a reader's heart and mind.

But what few of those readers of fantasy and science fiction realize is that the stories of wizards and starships have much older roots in a world all humanity shares, a world of archetypes, those basic themes and figures that are common to every people. Every culture has heroes who must fulfill great Quests, sometimes for a magic apple that will save a life, sometimes for a Holy Grail that brings spiritual fulfillment; every culture has a Wise Old Man or

Woman who aids those heroes on their quests, whether that wise one is known as Merlin or the Fairy Godmother or even Prophet Elijah. In this shared world of folkloric themes, the gallant adventurers of *Star Trek*'s *U.S.S. Enterprise* find counterparts in the Ancient Greek sailors of the *Argo*, and tricky folk such as Bugs Bunny, whose pranks can beat anyone who tries hunting him, trace their ancestry to such mighty tricksters as Coyote, who shaped the very world.

This book is a collection of those original tales behind popular contemporary books, cartoons, films, and television shows. There's no wonder, after all, that science fiction and fantasy grab us the way they do: they are the children born of the timeless, ageless world common to every race and culture, the world that, even when called by different names, remains a part of all humanity—the wonderful, boundless world that is folklore.

Courtesy of Paramount Pictures

Part One

"To Boldly Go..."

Several centuries into the future, a huge starship speeds across the galaxy. On board, a gallant crew made up of people from Earth and from several allied planets travels on their mission to hunt for yet-unknown interplanetary civilizations. None of them know what perils they may face, but they are all ready for whatever strange new adventures lie ahead.

In 1966, a new television show made its debut—and a whole new universe was born. By now, almost everyone has at least heard of the amazing worlds of *Star Trek* and its TV, movie, and book extensions. The main setting for the first set of these stories was the vast starship known as the *U.S.S. Enterprise*, which was said to house over four hundred people of different races and even different species. Its crew was led by the heroic, clever Captain James T. Kirk, and included his half-Vulcan, half-human Science Officer, Mr. Spock, and the ship's chief Medical Officer, Doctor Leonard "Bones" McCoy. They had been sent out by Starbase Command on a quest to explore the universe.

But the Enterprise's space-faring crew is far from being the first fictional group of bold adventurers who have explored the unknown. The idea of a band of sailor-heroes who set out to find fame, fortune, and adventure is not uncommon in the world that is folklore—a world as vast as human experience. For long ages past, people from every seafaring culture, whether it be the Polynesians or the ancient Greeks, have told their own stories of brave sailors, dangerous quests, and exciting, exotic adventures. Some of these timeless stories, some of them very old indeed, follow.

Jason and the Argonauts

A Tale from Ancient Greece

Jason was born a prince, the son of Aeson, King of Iolchos. But Aeson had been driven from his throne by an ambitious half-brother, Pelias. Since Pelias might well have killed the baby who was the rightful heir, Jason was raised in a far-distant land, ignorant of his true birth. His special tutor was none other than the wise old centaur Chiron, who saw that the boy was given the education fit for a prince. And when Jason grew to young manhood, the centaur told him his true identity, and sent the prince off on his first quest: to gain back his father's kingdom.

As Jason travelled, he came to a river in full flood. On its bank sat an old woman who pleaded with him, "Help me cross this river. Without your aid I shall surely drown!"

Jason was far from sure the flood wouldn't sweep them both away, but when the old woman began to weep, he took her on his back and struggled across the terrible river. At last, he reached the far bank, bruised and weary and missing a sandal that had been torn right off his foot—and found that the old woman was old no longer. So elegant and lovely was she that he fell to his knees in wonder.

"Fear not, Jason," she told him. "I am Hera, Queen of the Heavens. And for the kindness you showed an old woman, I shall aid you whenever you need help most."

Wonder-struck, Jason travelled on and came to Iolchos. King Pelias nearly cried out in horror at the sight of him, for a prophesy had claimed that one day a young man wearing only one sandal would appear, and that young man would be the rightful king. But the wily Pelias smiled and told Jason smoothly, "It is no easy thing to be a ruler. First you must prove your worth to rule Iolchos. Bring me the Golden Fleece that once belonged to our family. Aeetes, the Wizard-King of Colchis, stole it away, and now it hangs in his land, guarded by a terrible dragon that never sleeps."

"I will bring back the Golden Fleece," Jason promised. "And then," he added sternly, "I will claim my kingdom."

And so the prince sent out word throughout Greece asking for brave men who wanted to take part in a great adventure. Soon no less than fifty heroes were assembled, among them the mighty Hercules, son of Hera, and Orpheus, the wondrous musician. While these heroes gathered, their ship was being built by Argos, the finest boatbuilder in the realm. So splendid and swift was the ship he built that Jason named it after its creator: *Argos*. And as they set sail, the heroes called themselves after their ship, becoming known as the Argonauts. As the Argonauts sailed on in quest of the Golden Fleece, they found themselves in a world of strange adventures. Soon after leaving Iolchos, they came to the Isle of Lemnos.

"But there are only women here," the heroes said in amazement. "How beautiful they are!"

"Come, heroes," the women crooned. "Stay with us. Love us."

But Orpheus knew the truth about these women. Beautiful though they were, they had already murdered their husbands, and meant to slay any men who dared fall in love with them. Raising his lyre, Orpheus began to sing of adventure, of the marvels yet to come, of the wonderful, glittering, gleaming Golden Fleece, filling the Argonauts' hearts with such longing to see it that they set sail at once, leaving that deadly island far behind.

But the land of Colchis was far away, and no man knew an easy route. Putting in for food and water, the Argonauts found themselves in a new kingdom.

"It is ruled by King Cyzicus and his beautiful young Queen Clite," the heroes were told.

The king and queen greeted Jason and his men kindly. But the king and his people were so clearly worried that Jason asked, "What troubles you?"

"Savage giants have been ravaging my land," King Cyzicus told him, "and none of my men have been able to put an end to their attacks."

"Ah, but we can!" Hercules said boldly.

Since his mother was a goddess, Hercules had strength far beyond that of mortal men. He was also a deadly archer as well as a mighty fighter, and he led the Argonauts in a fierce battle against the giants. The giants fled the kingdom, never to return, and the Argonauts and King Cyzicus celebrated. Alas, triumph soon turned to tragedy. When the *Argo* set sail, a sudden midnight storm forced the ship back to land. In the stormy darkness, King Cyzicus and his people mistook the returning Argonauts for pirates and fought them. Before the mistake could be corrected, the king had been slain, and his queen died of grief.

Sailing away from that ill-starred visit, the Argonauts pulled briefly in to land to repair a broken oar.

"I'll find us some fresh water," volunteered the handsome young Hylas, Hercules's friend.

He found a clear, lovely pool. But it was the home of water nymphs, who had never seen such a handsome human before. Luring him into the water with their beauty, they drew him down into their watery realm forever.

The Argonauts searched for Hylas in vain. At last Jason told Hercules gently, "He is gone. The wind is changing, and we must sail on."

The grief-stricken Hercules shook his head stubbornly. "Do what you will. I am not going to abandon Hylas!"

He continued to search for his lost friend, ignoring the Argonauts. And at last the *Argo* had to sail on without him.

Days passed, bringing the Argonauts no closer to Colchis than before. They put into land yet again, and were brought before the ruler of that land: blind, prophetic King Phineus, a thin, frail old man who welcomed them to his court with weariness in his voice.

But before the Argonauts could begin to dine, a harsh shrieking filled the air. Monstrous winged creatures, their bodies like birds of prey, their faces those of women, came flapping down, stealing what food they could carry off and fouling the rest.

"It is always this way," King Phineus murmured. "Zeus has set the Harpies on me for my impiety."

"An old man should not be tormented!" Jason said angrily.

And the next time the Harpies came swooping down, they found the swords of the Argonauts waiting for them. The monsters fled in alarm.

"They will return," Phineus said.

"They will not!" cried Zetes, one of the Argonauts. And his brother, Calais, added, "We will see to that!"

The brothers, swift runners both, chased the Harpies, never letting the monsters rest. At last Hermes, messenger of the gods, appeared before them and swore the Harpies would never return.

But neither did Zetes and Calais return. When they abandoned their hunt of the Harpies, they came upon the kingdom of their father, who was no mortal man but Boreas the North Wind. He welcomed the sons he'd never known, and they stayed with him in his kingdom.

Meanwhile, the grateful King Phineus prophesied for the Argonauts, telling them the safest, most direct route to Colchis and the Golden Fleece. Even that route, he warned them, was full of danger for the unwary. "But I shall tell you how to escape that danger."

And so, when the Argonauts set sail once more, they took on board a swift-flying dove. Soon enough they came to the peril of which King Phineus had warned. Towering cliffs rose out of the water on either side of the *Argo*, forcing her into a narrow channel. At the end of the straits, Jason knew, was the Black Sea, on the coast of which lay Colchis. But guarding the entrance into that sea loomed two great rocky islands. Behind him, Jason could hear the Argonauts murmuring in awe, for these were the terrible magical islands known as the Clashing Rocks. Whenever anyone tried to pass between them, the islands crashed together with terrifying force, crushing anything caught between them.

"Now we must follow King Phineus's advice to the word," Jason said. Standing on the *Argo's* bow, he cast the dove into the air. She flew swift as an arrow from the bow between the Clashing Rocks. They came rushing together with a thundering roar, the crash nearly deafening the Argonauts, the waves nearly swamping their ship.

But the dove was swift enough to escape, losing nothing more than the tip of her tailfeathers. The air was filled with a groaning of stone as the Clashing Rocks slowly pulled apart again.

"Now!" Jason shouted. "Row! Row for all your lives! And you, Orpheus, play with all your art!"

Orpheus played music blazing with strength, filling the Argonauts with new power as they rowed and rowed and rowed. "The rocks are closing again!" Jason gasped, but he had no breath to spare to yell a warning. As the Clashing Rocks came thundering together, the Argonauts put on one last, desperate burst of strength. And the *Argo* shot through the narrow opening, escaping so narrowly the rocks grazed the ship's stern.

But now that one ship had safely passed, the spell upon the Clashing Rocks was broken. From that day on, they remained nothing more than motionless rock.

At last the *Argo* reached port in Colchis. Jason knew the Argonauts, brave though they were, would stand no chance in combat against the forces of the Wizard-King. And a magician would surely know if the young prince tried to lie to him. So Jason approached King Aeetes honestly and told him of his quest.

"I can understand why you wish to take the Golden Fleece," Aeetes told him, "but with the possession of the fleece goes a magical blessing that protects me and mine as long as it hangs here. Since we are both of royal blood, we shall settle this matter with honor. But I assure you, Prince Jason, you must prove your worth before I shall give up the Golden Fleece."

He named his tests. Jason must first yoke two fire-breathing bulls. He must then plow a field, the Acre of Ares, and sow it with teeth from the dragon of Thebes. Warriors would spring up from the field, and these Jason must destroy.

Now Jason would never have survived the tests of the Wizard-King without help, and both he and King Aeetes knew it. But Aeetes had a daughter who was a powerful sorceress in her own right. Medea was her name, and she fell in love with Jason almost at her first sight of him. Stealing into the Argonauts' encampment, she whispered to Jason, "Wed me and take me back to Greece with you, and I shall use all my powers to help you win the Golden Fleece."

Medea was beautiful as well as clever, and Jason quickly agreed. In exchange, Medea gave him a small vial of magic potion.

"Rub it on your skin," she whispered, "and you will have no need to fear the bulls. And as for the warriors, if you do as I tell you, why, you shall win over them as well."

When morning came, King Aeetes commanded that Jason

be led to where the two terrible bulls restlessly pawed the ground. Jason saw the flames flickering from their nostrils and felt a tiny pang of alarm. Had Medea played him false? She was Aeetes's daughter, after all.

He strode boldly forward. And to his relief, Medea's magic potion worked. Although he could feel the heat of the flames, the bulls could neither burn nor crush him. Soon he had the fierce, bewildered animals yoked, and he plowed the Acre of Ares and sowed the teeth of the dragon of Thebes as King Aeetes had commanded.

Silence fell. Then the earth began to shake. First the tips of spears tore up through the soil. Then, one by one, warriors rose out of the earth, shaking the dirt from their shining armor, and forming themselves into one great squadron that approached Jason with slow, menacing steps. He gripped his sword with desperate strength, wondering wildly if any one man could defeat so many foes.

But Medea had whispered to him that while these dragon-warriors were mighty, they were also slow of mind. Jason grinned, and threw a stone into their ranks. Sure enough, the warriors couldn't figure out who had hit them. They turned on each other and began to fight. As Jason watched, amazed, they fought mindlessly on and on till at last every one of them was dead.

King Aeetes, who had come to see Jason die, stared in shock at the sight of the smiling prince. "King Aeetes," Jason said pleasantly, "I have done your tasks. I have yoked the bulls, sown the teeth, and defeated the warriors. Now keep your side of our bargain."

Aeetes was furious. He knew Jason could never have passed the tests without help—and he had a pretty good idea who had provided that help. But he only smiled and promised, "Tomorrow morning you shall have the Golden Fleece."

But Jason and Medea didn't wait till then. Medea knew her

father intended to kill the Argonauts and burn the *Argo*. So that night, she, Jason and Orpheus stole away from camp and to the massive tree on which blazed and glittered and shone the wondrous Golden Fleece.

"How beautiful it is!" Jason gasped.

"Like song turned to gold," Orpheus agreed in wonder.

But around the tree curled the dragon that never slept. And if the Golden Fleece were all beauty, the dragon was all ugliness. As it glared at them, and placed one clawed foot possessively against the Golden Fleece, Jason murmured to Medea, "I think this would be a good time for you to use your magic."

"I cannot," she confessed. "Against the dragon I have no spells."

Orpheus, who had never taken his gaze from the dragon, murmured, "But I do," and raised his lyre. "Cover your ears, my friends."

Orpheus sang sleep to the dragon, he sang wonderful, soothing, peaceful sleep. And slowly the creature that had never slept slithered down to the ground. Slowly its eyes began to close. And at last the dragon slept. Jason snatched the Golden Fleece from the tree.

"Hurry," he whispered. "Back to the *Argo*."

Hastily, the Argonauts set sail, and soon Colchis was far behind them. But there were still perils to be faced before the Argonauts could reach their homeland. A mighty storm nearly sank the *Argo*, and the Sirens, flesh-eating creatures who looked like women but lured men to their death with their sweet songs, nearly snared the Argonauts. But Orpheus's music proved stronger than the sweetest of the Sirens' songs, and the *Argo* proved stronger than the worst power of the storm. Medea used her magic against such strange, terrible beings as Talos, a metallic-skinned, seemingly invulnerable giant she tricked into fatally injuring the one vulnerable spot on his ankle.

And at last the Argonauts sailed safely into the harbor of Iolchos with the Golden Fleece gleaming on the *Argo's* deck.

Many more adventures awaited Jason both before he could claim the throne and afterwards, and while some of those adventures were heroic, others were tragic.

But the future was the future. For now, the Golden Fleece was won, Jason had proved his worth as a leader, and the long journey of the *Argo* and the Argonauts was finally over.

The Fool of the World
and the Ship that Flew

A Tale from the Ukraine

Once there lived a farmer and his wife and their three sons. The eldest two were sharp, clever lads, bright as the day. But the third, the youngest son—ah, he was a gentle, friendly soul, the sort who will not hurt a flea. Sometimes, it's true, this youngest son would grow so interested in the way the grass grew that he forgot to change his shirt or so fascinated by the way the clouds moved across the sky that he forgot to eat. Because he acted in such a way, and because he was quiet where his brothers were loud, and friendly where they were aloof, they thought him a useless fool. Indeed, they forgot his name, which was Ivan, and called him mockingly the Fool of the World.

Well now, the two oldest brothers were bored at home and tired of life on a small farm. Word came to them that the tsar had issued a proclamation summoning one and all to a great feast and announcing that he who could build a ship that sailed through the air and arrive at the palace in this ship would win the hand of the tsar's own daughter in marriage.

"We must go to the feast," said the eldest son. "We shall make our fortune there."

"We are going," said the second son to their parents. "All we ask is your blessing."

That they got, and fine food and drink to take with them.

The Fool of the World, who had been sitting comfortably atop the wide, flat stove—which was where folks often sat to get warm in those days—leaped down. "I'm going, too," he declared.

His parents looked him up and down in disgust and gave him no blessing. "Go if you wish," they told him. "Only tell no one you are our son."

And instead of fine food and drink, poor Ivan was given only a stale loaf of bread and a flask of plain water.

"Better than nothing," the Fool of the World told himself, and set out on his journey. He walked and walked and walked. And at last he came upon a white-bearded old man.

"Good day to you, Grandfather," Ivan said politely.

"Good day to you, son. And where is such a polite fellow going?"

"Why, to the tsar's feast at his palace!"

"And are you the one who can build a flying ship?"

"No, I can't," Ivan shrugged, "but I figure going to the palace can't make my life worse. And who knows? It just might make it better."

"Indeed, indeed. Before you travel on, let us rest a bit and eat a bit."

The Fool's face fell. "You do look very hungry, Grandfather, and you are welcome to share what I have. But all I have is some plain water and a loaf of rather stale bread."

"Never mind. Let us share."

And when Ivan took out the loaf, he found it had somehow became two nice, fresh loaves. When he took out the water, he found it had become fine wine. Being the easygoing fellow he was, the Fool of the World simply shook his head in wonder and gladly shared his food with the old man. When they were done with their meal, the old man smiled.

"Instead of going on to the palace, good son, go into the forest. Find yourself a good, sturdy tree, hit it with your axe, and then fall to the ground. Lie there without moving until someone asks you to rise. You will find your ship waiting. Climb aboard and travel on wherever you wish. But remember this: You must take with you everyone you meet."

Well, those were strange words! Wondering, Ivan thanked the old man and entered the forest. He picked out a good, sturdy tree, hit it with his axe, and threw himself to the ground. He lay there so long that he fell asleep.

"Wake up!" said a sudden voice. "Wake up and claim your fortune."

Ivan started up—and found himself facing the most splendid ship he had ever seen. Its masts were of shining silver, its sides were of burnished gold, and its sails were of gleaming, many-colored silk. The Fool of the World climbed into the ship and told it nervously, "Fly."

And the ship flew, more smoothly than a bird. Ivan clung to the rail, staring at all he saw with wonder.

Hey now, but what was this? There below the ship was a man with one ear to the ground as though listening intently to something.

"Good day!" Ivan called down to him. "What are you doing?"

"Good day to you, too. I am called Keen-Ear, and I am listening to the tsar's guests gathering in his palace."

The Fool remembered the old man's words: "Take with you everyone you meet." So Ivan asked, "And are you going to the tsar's palace? Yes? Then welcome aboard!"

They flew on. "Now, who is that?" Keen-Ear asked.

Far below them, a man was hopping along with one foot tied up. "Good day!" Ivan called down to him. "What are you doing?"

"Good day to you, too. I am called Fleet-Foot, and if I didn't have one foot tied up, I would have run straight to the other side of the world. Since I am only going as far as the palace of the tsar, I didn't want to run that fast."

"Come aboard with us," Ivan said, "and you won't have to run at all!"

On they flew. "Now, what is that?" Fleet-Foot asked.

Far below them, an archer had drawn his bow, even though there wasn't a bird or beast in sight. "Good day," Ivan called down. "What are you doing?"

"Good day to you, too. I am called Sharp-Eye, and I am trying to shoot the bird I see on a tree a hundred leagues from here."

"Wouldn't you rather go to the tsar's feast? Yes? Then come aboard!"

On they flew. "Now, what is that?" Sharp-Eye asked.

Far below them, a man was carrying a huge sack of wheat over one shoulder. "Good day to you," Ivan called. "What are you doing?"

"Good day to you, too. I am called Big-Eater, and I am looking for dinner."

"But you have a whole sack of wheat on your shoulder!"

"Oh, this is only a snack!" Big-Eater said with a laugh.

"You will get a bigger dinner at the tsar's palace. Come aboard!"

On they flew. "Now, what is that?" Big-Eater asked.

Far below them, a man stood on the shore of a lake, searching here and there. "Good day," Ivan called down. "What are you doing?"

"Good day to you, too. I am called Big-Drinker, and I am looking for water."

"But there's a whole lake at your feet!"

"Oh, this is only a sip!" Big-Drinker said with a laugh.

"You will have plenty to drink at the tsar's feast. Come aboard!"

On they flew. "Now, what is that?" Big-Drinker asked.

Far below them, a man was hurrying along, hugging a sheaf

of straw. "Good day," Ivan called down. "What are you doing?"

"Good day to you, too. I am called Freeze-Bringer, and I'm bringing this straw to a village."

"But doesn't a village have any straw of its own?"

"But this is *my* straw. All I have to do is spread it around, and even in summer a frost will set in."

"The tsar could use frost to keep his festival food fresh. Come aboard!"

On they flew. "Now, what is that?" Freeze-Bringer asked.

Far below them, a man was hurrying along with a bundle of wood on his back. "Good day," Ivan called down. "What are you doing?"

"Good day to you, too. I am called Wood-Bringer, and I am taking this wood to the forest."

"Surely there's enough wood in the forest already!"

"Not like this. I have only to spread it out, and all the logs will turn into soldiers."

"The tsar would like to see such a wonder. Come aboard!"

On they flew. And this time they flew all the way to the palace of the tsar. In the courtyard, a splendid feast had been set up. Long tables covered with fine white linen stood in rows, crowded with every type of food and drink that ever could have been imagined. Around the tables were gathered every type of person in that kingdom, from elegant noble down to humble beggar.

"There's surely a place in that feast for us!" said Ivan. "Come, let's find a spot to land our ship."

As the flying ship came smoothly to a landing, the tsar saw it and stared at its crew. What was this? A crew of ragged peasants flying a ship of gold and silver? The tsar stared most sharply at Ivan, seeing how poor the Fool's clothing was, how worn and full of patches.

"I promised that I would marry my daughter to the man who brought me a flying ship," the tsar said to his trusted minister.

"But I cannot marry her to a—a nobody! Yet, how can I go back on my royal word?"

The minister thought and thought, then exclaimed, "Aha! I have it! Set the peasant a task, some task that is impossible to do."

"Yes, yes," said the tsar, "I have it. I will tell him that unless he can, before this feast is done, bring me some living and healing water, he will not win the princess—no, no, not only will he not win her, he will have his head cut off!"

As it happened, Keen-Ear overheard this discussion, and went straight to the Fool of the World. Ivan cried out in dismay. "What can I do? How can I ever find such a thing in so short a time?"

"I can," said Fleet-Foot. Quickly he untied his tied-up foot, and was gone. In no time he was at the far side of the world and filling a flask with living and healing water. But even he was feeling a little tired by this point. "I will sit and rest a bit. There's plenty of time before the feast is done."

But there wasn't plenty of time at all, because Fleet-Foot promptly fell asleep! Back in the tsar's palace, the feast was nearly over, and poor Ivan was beginning to see his head on a pike. "I'll find him," said Keen-Ear, putting his ear to the ground. "Curse the man, he's asleep at the far side of the world!"

"I'll wake him," said Sharp-Eye. Drawing his bow, he took careful aim and let the arrow fly. It flew all the way to where Fleet-Foot slept, and brushed his nose as it landed.

Fleet-Foot woke with a start. He sped back to the tsar's palace, and got there just before the feast ended. Ivan handed the flask of living and healing water to the tsar, who pretended to be pleased.

But the tsar was far from being pleased. "He was lucky this time. But I will set the peasant another task, one he shall not so easily accomplish. He and his friends must eat twelve roasted bulls and forty ovenloads of bread in one turn of the hourglass. If he fails, he and they all shall have their heads cut off!"

Keen-Ear overheard, and warned Ivan. The Fool cried out in despair, but Big-Eater only laughed. "A snack!" he said, "a mere snack!"

And he devoured all twelve bulls and forty ovenloads of bread before the other companions could even touch them.

"I could do with a second helping," Big-Eater said cheerfully.

The tsar was not so cheerful. This time, he swore that Ivan and his friends must drink forty barrels of water and forty more of beer in one turn of the hourglass.

"Wonderful!" cried Big-Drinker in delight, and drained the lot without a pause. "I'm still thirsty," he added with a laugh.

Now what could the tsar do? Fuming, he told the Fool of the World that before the young man could meet the princess, he must steam himself properly clean in the bathhouse. This sounded fine to Ivan. But the tsar whispered to his servants that the bathhouse was to be heated till it blazed like red-hot metal. Of course Keen-Ear overheard this threat, and went straight to Ivan.

"My turn," said Freeze-Bringer. He scattered his straw all over the blazing-hot bathhouse, and it grew so cold Ivan hurried up on top of the bathhouse's stove to keep from freezing. There, nice and warm, he settled down for the night.

In the morning the tsar, who had expected to find nothing but ashes, was stunned to find Ivan alive and well. It took him a long, long time to decide what to do next:

"You must muster an army by morning," he told Ivan, "and assemble it before my palace. By morning, do you understand? If you do this thing, I will let you marry my daughter. Fail, and I will most certainly have your head!"

But now it was Wood-Bringer's turn. Hidden by the night, he stole off into a field with a bundle of firewood. He spread the logs about, and each time a log touched earth, it turned to a fine soldier. Soon a whole army of log-soldiers stood in that field.

Morning came. The tsar woke to the sound of a march. "Your Majesty, Your Majesty," servants cried, "the peasant of the flying ship is drilling his soldiers before the palace!"

The tsar stuck his head out the window. Sure enough, there was the peasant, and sure enough, there was his army. And a most terrifyingly large army it looked, too.

The tsar ducked back inside, sure the soldiers were going to attack. But nothing happened. And at last he had to take another look. There was the army, just as before, and the peasant—but this time the peasant was mounted on a shining white steed and was dressed in fine red velvet. He looked quite splendid, and that made the tsar feel just a little better about what he must do. He went down to where Ivan sat on his horse and said, "Welcome, my dear son-in-law."

The tsar sent for his daughter. The princess saw Ivan, he saw her, they smiled at each other, and that was that. They were wed and a great feast was held to celebrate. All of Ivan's companions were guests of honor. And all went well with everyone.

The Children of Puna

A Legend of Hawaii

Once, in the long-ago time, cruel Puna the Sea Demon, he who hated all that lived and breathed and laughed, sent three monsters, the Children of Puna, out into the world to destroy the folk of the warm green Islands. One monster he named Paua, the giant Clam, whose shell held darkness cold as the ocean floor. One was Eke, the Octopus, strong as the sea's crushing force. And the third of the Children of Puna was Mamoa, the great Shark, savage as the ocean storm. So fierce were these three monsters that they slew whoever dared sail the sea. So swift were they that none escaped them.

"My people suffer!" cried Rata, brave young Chief of the Islands. "They starve because we dare not cast our nets or launch our boats. They grieve for lost friends or families. Puna's cruel monsters must be stopped—and I shall stop them!"

So Rata set out in his swift, two-hulled canoe. He took seven men with him, all brave, all heroes. But as they left the land, an eighth man called out to Rata:

"Take me with you!"

"Who are you? I have spearsmen here and sailors, throwers of knives and casters of ropes. What can you do?"

"I am Nanoa, a singer—"

"No, no!" Rata's seven heroes called back. "We have no need of singers!"

They sailed out onto the open sea. But what was this? A calabash, a great gourd, came bobbing and dipping alongside the canoe.

"A floating calabash is good luck!" cried one of the warriors, and scooped it out of the water.

But he dropped it more quickly than he'd picked it up.

"It—it spoke! It called out, 'Rata!'"

The calabash split in two. A tiny man stepped out of it, growing faster than the eye could follow till he was man-tall once more.

"Nanoa!" gasped Rata. "What are you?"

"As I told you: a singer." Nanoa smiled. "A singer of magic. Rata, I am no less brave than any of these warriors. I, too, wish to see an end to the evil Children of Puna. And I think, oh Rata, you may have need of me."

A wizard's wisdom is not to be scorned. So, with Nanoa aboard, they sailed on.

"There!" cried a sailor. "Look at those two great white cliffs rising up out of the ocean."

"Those are no cliffs," Nanoa said grimly. "You see before us the open halves of Paua's shell as he awaits his prey."

At Rata's order, the two-hulled canoe sailed smoothly between the two halves of the huge Clam's shell. The heroes all shuddered to see those tall white walls on either side of them.

All at once, the walls snapped shut! But the heroes did not cower in fear. Oh no, they sprang swiftly from the canoe and hurried down into the darkness to the soft, warm body of Paua, hidden there between the walls of shell. They hurled their spears at it; they cut at it with knives!

The two halves of the shell fell open. The canoe was free again. And Paua, the terrible Clam, lay dead.

"So ends the first of the Children of Puna," Nanoa said softly. "But two remain."

They sailed on. But all at once the canoe stopped dead in

the water. Something—a snake? a vine?—came creeping up across the shining wood.

"No snake, no vine!" cried Rata. "That is a tentacle of Eke the Octopus!"

The monster coiled its tentacle, thick as a man's width, as three men's width, as five men's width, about the canoe. The sailors stabbed at Eke with their knives, but the blades bounced harmlessly off the octopus' hide. And now a second tentacle came curling over the canoe, and a third!

"Wait," Nanoa said. "Eke will keep two tentacles anchored on the sea's bottom, but he will bring his great head up to see what he has caught. And he may be wounded only in the space between his eyes."

Even as he spoke, Eke's fearsome head rose slowly from the sea. The men cried out in horror, for the round, cold eyes of the octopus were wide as pools. Eke's head was vaster than the length of an island!

But Rata was a Chief, and a hero. He leaped up onto the side of the canoe and ran right out onto the tentacles themselves. The cold eyes stared, and the cruel beak of Eke's mouth opened wide to draw him in. But in that moment, Rata hurled his spear—right between Eke's terrible eyes!

Hastily Rata leaped back among his men as the octopus roared in pain and rage. Powerful tentacles tightened about the canoe till its timbers creaked. But they held—the canoe was not crushed! And in the next moment, the tentacles slid away again. The heroes sighed as the dead octopus sank slowly beneath the waves.

"So ends the second of the Children of Puna," said Nanoa softly. "But one remains."

And that one was Mamoa the Shark. Drawn by Eke's death, he came surging up like a monstrous wave of the sea—huge, terrible Mamoa, with his eyes like hungry flames and his teeth like giants' knives.

"Can he be slain?" Rata gasped. "Can a spear even wound him?"

Nanoa shook his head. "Not even you, brave Rata, could hurl a spear with strength enough to pierce *his* hide. No, this task is mine."

The wizard shrank even as he spoke. He sprang into the calabash, and the calabash flew into the water. Mamoa gulped it down and swam for the canoe.

But all at once the Shark leaped out of the water, then dove beneath the waves! There was silence, silence…

And then the body of Mamoa came floating to the surface. The great jaws fell open, and a calabash bobbed free. Rata quickly scooped it up, and Nanoa stepped out onto the deck of the canoe, his proper size once more. In one hand he bore a knife.

"That…that was no easy thing," the wizard panted. "His heart could only be reached from within. But I thought surely he'd swallow me to my death first!"

"You are a hero," the others told him. "The third of the Children of Puna is dead. And now we can go home!"

"No," said the wizard softly. "Oh, don't you see? We slew the three monsters, yes. But Puna himself still lives, Demon Puna of the Darkness, Puna the Evil, who hates all who live and breath and laugh! He knows we slew his Children. And now he will send still crueler monsters into the world to avenge them."

There was silence in that canoe. Then Rata said simply, "Then we shall stop him."

South and south sailed the two-hulled canoe. Puna's barren island lay between the warm green Islands and the coldness of the icy Utter South. The heroes tensed as they saw the island rise, bare and jagged, out of the sea.

But Rata gave no order for his men to land, not yet. Nanoa had warned him. Puna was strong as the sea, but his strength lay in the wind. When it blew from the Utter South, cold and chill, then Puna's power faded till he was no stronger than a mortal man. But when the wind blew instead from the warm green Islands, then his power grew till no one living could defeat him.

The wind ebbed, blowing neither from the north or the south. Rata gave the command for the canoe to be beached. Soon the heroes were on dry land, their hands on their spears and their hearts racing. Where was terrible Puna?

Oh, terrible, indeed! He was there before them. And cold as the sea's dark depths was the demon, cruel as the stormy waves. His teeth were sharp as jagged shells, his eyes were wide and hating, his voice was like the crash of waves on broken rocks.

"Never has mortal man dared step onto this island!" the demon roared. His chill, chill eyes stared at Rata. "You are the leader of these fools. Who are you?"

"No fool! I am Rata, Chief of the Islands. And I have come to save my people from your evil!"

Puna threw back his head and laughed, his sharp teeth gleaming. "We shall indeed fight, oh Rata, without magic, hand to hand as honorable warriors fight. We shall wrestle—and I shall slay you!"

Without another word, he threw himself at Rata. They battled hand to hand, and their strength was even. They wrestled once more, and now Rata was the stronger, for he fought not only for himself, but for the safety of his people. Oh, surely he would win!

But Puna, fearful, pulled away. He forgot his vow. Hastily, the demon called the wind to him, the warm wind from the Islands! And Puna's strength grew with that wind. Terrible in his sorcerous power, he hurled Rata to the ground.

"Now, little man, you shall die!"

"Oh, liar!" cried Nanoa. "You swore to use no magic, yet you called up the wind! Well then, so shall I! This shall be a fair fight, this I vow!"

And the wizard began to sing. Before Puna could stop him, he sang forth the cold, chill wind form the Utter South! The warmth fled before the coldness—and Puna's strength fled with it. Now he was once again no more than a mortal man, even with Rata. And Rata, brave young Chief of the Islands, caught the demon by the waist and cast him down on the rocks, cast him dead upon the rocks.

It was done. The people of the Islands were freed from danger.

And Rata, their Chief, Nanoa the wizard, and the seven warrior-heroes smiled at one another, and set sail for home.

The Seven Semyons

——————— A Folktale from Russia ———————

Once, long ago, there lived seven brothers, and each and every one of them was named Semyon. Now, when these seven brothers were still very young, their parents died, leaving them alone in the world. But as it happened, Tsar Alexei rode by one day. The tsar was still a very young man himself, and when he learned that the boys were orphans, he remembered his own childhood, and pitied them.

"I will be as a father to you," he told the brothers. "I will apprentice you to whatever trade you wish."

"I will be a smith," said Semyon the First, "and forge a mighty iron pillar that will almost reach the sky."

"And I," said Semyon the Second, "will climb that pillar and see what is happening in all the foreign lands."

"Very good," Tsar Alexei murmured. "But what of you other Semyons?"

"I," said Semyon the Third, "will become a shipwright and build a fine, swift ship."

"Yes," agreed Semyon the Fourth, "and I shall be the ship's helmsman."

"And I," said Semyon the Fifth, "shall, when needs be, hide the ship at the bottom of the sea so no foe may find her."

"And I," added Semyon the Sixth, "will be the one to safely

bring the ship back to the surface again."

The tsar shook his head in wonder. "These are all strange but useful crafts. But what of you, the youngest Semyon? What will you become?"

"Why, I shall become a thief!" exclaimed Semyon the Seventh.

"A thief in my lands?" Tsar Alexei shouted. "Never! You must pick another trade."

Semyon the Seventh bowed, but he secretly refused. A thief he meant to be!

And so the swift years passed. Tsar Alexei had the seven brothers brought before him and asked them to display their crafts.

Semyon the First, Semyon the Smith, tapped his hammer on his anvil and one, two, three, forged an iron pillar that towered into the sky.

Semyon the Second, Semyon the Climber, scurried up that pillar as swiftly as a squirrel up a tree. He began calling down to Tsar Alexei what was happening in all the surrounding lands. "And in the thrice tenth land I see," he told the tsar, "I see the Princess Elena the Fair walking alone and lonely in her garden. So lovely is she that I—I have no words to say."

Tsar Alexei had secretly loved Princess Elena the Fair for years. "Oh, I long to see that princess," he cried. But what could he do about it? Princess Elena's lands were so far away. And so the tsar shook his head sadly, and asked Semyon the Third to display his craft.

Semyon the Third, Semyon the Shipwright, hammered, one, two, three, and before him rose a ship as beautiful as a swan. Semyon the Fourth, Semyon the Helmsman, sprang onto the ship and showed that she sailed as lightly as that swan.

"Now, watch what I can do," cried Semyon the Fifth, Semyon the Hider. He caught the ship in full sail and dragged it down under the waves.

"Now, watch what I can do!" added Semyon the Sixth, Semyon the Revealer. He leaped into the sea and brought the ship safely back to the surface.

"This is all wonderful!" the tsar exclaimed. "But there were seven brothers. What of the seventh? What has he become?"

Semyon the Seventh stepped out from hiding. "A thief, Your Majesty. Wait, wait," he added to the guards who tried to seize him, "don't be so hasty. Your Majesty, I am a good thief who hurts no one. Order me to steal Princess Elena the Fair for you. Send me and my brothers for her in our ship, and I promise you, the princess shall be yours."

The tsar nodded, hardly daring to hope.

And so the seven adventuring Semyons set sail on their quest. They sailed near, they sailed far, and at last they reached the thrice tenth kingdom where Elena the Fair lived. Semyon the Thief slipped ashore and saw how things were in that land.

"They have no cats," he told his brothers. "Think of that!"

"But what good is such a thing?" asked Semyon the Smith.

"First we must sail to the thrice ninth land and find us a nice little kitten. And then ... wait and watch, watch and wait," Semyon the Thief said with a laugh.

And so the seven Semyons returned to the thrice tenth land. Disguised as a merchant, Semyon the Thief went ashore with a pretty little kitten. Petting the little cat till it purred and purred, he carried it past the window of Elena the Fair. The princess saw the pretty kitten, and wished to buy it.

"I am a wealthy merchant," Semyon the Thief told her, "come to trade in this land. I will not sell you this kitten—but I will give it to you as a token of good will."

He and Elena the Fair spoke together. Semyon the Thief told her wonderful stories of the lands he'd seen and the people he'd met. He told her even more wonderful stories of the riches he'd gathered on his journeyings. "But these riches are simple things," he added, "mere gold and jewels, the sort of things anyone can see. But you, Princess Elena, would you like to see a treasure beyond all price?"

"What treasure is this?"

"No, no, I can't speak of it here, where anyone might overhear! The treasure is aboard my ship, under heavy guard."

"But what *is* it?"

"I cannot tell you, save to say that it is a wonder brighter than the sun and more glowing than the moon. But now that I have it, I cannot be rid of it!"

"Whyever not?"

"Oh, surely everyone would want to possess the wonderful treasure, and my life would be in peril!"

"I would not let you be harmed!" Princess Elena said indignantly.

Overwhelmed by curiosity about this marvelous treasure, she agreed to go with Semyon the Thief to his ship. Of course, as soon as she was aboard, Semyon the Thief called to his brothers, "Cast off!"

Off they sailed. Quickly, Semyon the Hider pulled the ship beneath the waves. They hid there, safe, while overhead, on the surface of the sea, the Princess Elena's people searched in vain for her.

At last they all gave up the search. Semyon the Revealer pulled the ship safely back to the surface of the sea.

And what of Princess Elena? Semyon the Thief had spoken truth in a way: the treasure he had brought her was a portrait of Tsar Alexei. As she looked at it and looked at it, seeing how handsome he was, seeing how kind and gentle he appeared, the princess began to forget about being angry at the seven Semyons.

Tsar Alexei was overjoyed at the sight of Princess Elena. "I never thought to be able to welcome you to my home!" he cried.

"I accept your welcome," she said with a smile.

And what of the seven sailing Semyons? Well now, when Tsar Alexei and Princess Elena were wed, as wed they soon were, the seven Semyons were, as can well be imagined, honored guests at the feast. The tsar saw that they went home from that feast happy, wealthy men. And after that, the seven Semyons went sailing only when they wished.

The Story of the Sampo

A Tale from Finland

Once in the ancient days, the old wizard Vainamoinen, he who had lived for many years in the womb of his mother the Earth and who was born an old man, sat wondering about how to best bring prosperity to the land. At last he went to Ilmarinen, who was as wise in the ways of smithing as Vainamoinen was in magic.

"I know exactly what the land needs," the smith said, "and that is a wondrous creation known as the Sampo, which will grind flour endlessly for whoever owns it. I built the Sampo for Louhi, the Witch-Queen of Pohjola in exchange for her daughter's hand. Well, I won a bride for only the shortest of whiles— but Louhi kept the Sampo, and it grinds flour for her every day."

"Since you no longer have a bride and since Louhi has not truly earned the Sampo, let us go and take it back from her," said the wizard.

"That would be no easy thing. The Sampo has become lodged deep within a copper mountain, and is bound fast with nine locks. One of its three legs is held fast by the Earth, the second has grown into the mountain itself, and the third is embedded in the sea."

"Be that as it may," said Vainamoinen, "we shall free it. But first we need a mighty ship to carry us swiftly there and take the

Sampo swiftly out of Pohjola. And I shall need a mighty sword, because I doubt that Louhi will let the Sampo go without a fight."

So Ilmarinen set to work forging a sword, a mighty sword, a hero's sword, a sword sharp and keen enough to cut a rock in half. "This is a wondrous blade," Vainamoinen said with pleasure. "Now let us see about that ship."

But as he and Ilmarinen rode along the shore to where a ship might be built for them, they heard the sound of plaintive weeping. It was no woman who wept, but a ship lying abandoned on the beach.

"Why do you weep?" the wizard asked.

"I weep because I am fairly made and swift-sailing—yet here I lie abandoned on the beach while coarser, clumsier ships lumber freely over the waves."

"Are you strong as well as fairly made and swift?" asked Vainamoinen.

"Oh, I could carry a hundred men and all their gear and never feel the weight!"

"Then I think you shall serve us," said the wizard, "and serve us well."

With that he sang a song of magic, a song of Power, a song that conjured up a full crew for the new-found ship. Only he and Ilmarinen were not conjurations aboard that ship, they and one other, the mighty hero Ahti, who chanced upon them and asked to come along on their adventure.

So Ilmarinen, the master smith, launched the ship, and they set sail, gliding swiftly over the waves to Pohjola. Vainamoinen cast spells to ward off those who would threaten them, all the many beings of Power of the sea, and for a time all went very well.

But with a sudden jar, the ship stopped fast in the water. "A pike!" Ahti cried. "We're caught on the back of a giant pike!"

Drawing his sword, the hero attacked the enormous fish,

hacking it to bits. All aboard the ship ate well of the succulent flesh, but after they were done, Vainamoinen sat for a time studying the pike's white bones, turning them this way and that.

"I wonder..." he mused. "I wonder to what use these could be put."

"To no use, surely," Ilmarinen said. "Cast them overboard."

But Vainamoinen shook his head. Soon he had turned the bones into the world's first *kantele*, the musical instrument of Finland, and coaxed wondrous, magical music from its strings.

They sailed on. And at last their ship reached the strange, chill, far-northern land of Pohjola. The Witch- Queen Louhi was waiting on the shore, her terrible eyes hard as ice. "Why have you come?" she asked.

"We have come," Vainamoinen said coaxingly, "to share the Sampo with you. For surely there is magic enough in it for all to use."

"What nonsense is this?" Louhi snapped. "What fool would share a wonder? The Sampo is mine, and mine it will remain."

The wizard sighed. "If you will not share, then I fear we must take the Sampo from you."

The Witch-Queen laughed coldly. At a snap of her fingers, armed warriors came running from every side. But Vainamoinen raised his *kantele* and began to play. He sang rest to those warriors, he sang ease, he sang such gentle, gentle sleep to them that one by one they sank snoring to the ground. Even Louhi, though she fought the sleepy music with all her sorcerous will, fell victim to its power.

"Come," Vainamoinen whispered. "Let us take the Sampo."

Ilmarinen, that wonder-smith, found no difficulty at all in opening the nine locks. But when Ahti tried to lift the Sampo, to tear it free from its moorings, he could not move it for all his heroic strength. Only when all the heroes pulled at it together were they able to free the Sampo and carry it away to their ship. And in a short while they were sailing back over the waves.

"Play for us," Ahti told the wizard. "Play a song of triumph."

But Vainamoinen refused. "Not yet. I do not wish to break my sleep-spell by mischance."

"Then I will sing," cried Ahti.

But his voice was so loud and harsh that the sound of it echoed all the way back to Pohjola. Louhi woke with a start. "The Sampo!" she shrieked.

Sure enough, it was gone. The Witch-Queen shouted out to Uutar, Ruler of the Fog, "Send me a fog! Blind the way of Vainamoinen. Trap his boat for me!"

But what if the wizard found a way to destroy that fog? "Iki-Turso," Louhi cried, "Lord of the Sea, if Uutar fails, drown Vainamoinen and all his men in the sea, saving only the Sampo!"

But what if the wizard found a way to conquer Iki- Turso? "If Uutar and Iki-Turso fail me," Louhi pleaded, "then you, mighty Ukko, Lord of the Clouds, must send a storm to destroy Vainamoinen and all his men!"

Uutar, Lady of Fog, granted Louhi's prayer with a fog so dense that for three long days and night neither Vainamoinen nor any on that ship could find their bearings. But at last Vainamoinen slashed at the fog with his sword, the sword forged by Ilmarinen, master smith, and the bright blade cut the fog to fading ribbons.

But now Iki-Turso, Lord of the Sea, answered Louhi's prayer, sending great waves crashing up over the ship. Yet Vainamoinen was swifter than he. Seeing the being in the waves, he caught Iki-Turso by the ears, raising him with painful force from the water.

"Let me go!" Iki-Turso pleaded, squirming helplessly to free himself.

"Only if you promise not to do us any further harm." the wizard said.

"I swear it! Now let me go!"

Vainamoinen agree, and Iki-Turso disappeared beneath a

suddenly tranquil sea.

But now Ukko, Lord of the Clouds, deigned to answer Louhi's prayer. He sent a terrible storm shrieking and swirling down upon the ship, tearing the *kantele* from Vainamoinen's hands and sweeping it into the sea. Vainamoinen hardly noticed, so busy was he casting spells to fight the storm.

Meanwhile, Louhi was prepared for battle, setting sail with her warriors in a swift warship. As the storm died, she and her men gained and gained on the heroes' ship. "Look!" cried keen-eyed Ahti aboard that ship. "We are surely being followed."

"Louhi," Vainamoinen said grimly. "Row, all of you. Row with all your might."

Snatching out his tinderbox, he whispered magic over it. "May you become a hidden reef in the sea!" the wizard willed, and threw the tinderbox overboard. At once, it became a sharp-edged rock on which Louhi's ship struck and broke apart.

Louhi was ready. Quickly the ship's sides became her wings, its helm became her tail, its scythes became her talons. Fierce as a mighty eagle, her warriors riding on her wide wooden wings, she took flight and came thundering down upon the heroes' ship, landing on the mast with a terrible groaning of wood. Vainamoinen snatched the helm from Ilmarinen, sweeping it about with all his might, severing all but one of Louhi's taloned fingers. With a shriek, she fell, dropping her warriors into the sea, snatching blindly at whatever she could catch to try to slow her fall.

And what she caught in that mad plunge was the Sampo, dragging it down into the sea with her, where the waves smashed it into a thousand fragments. There at the bottom of the sea what remained of the Sampo lay forever. And as it lay there, it ground on and on. But since there was no grain for it to grind, it ground salt, and ever more salt. And so at last all the water in all the seas was turned from fresh to salt.

"We have failed," Ilmarinen said sadly.

"Not quite," said Vainamoinen. "Wait."

They came back to Finnish land. Vainamoinen walked along the shore, watching with his keen eyes. Tiny fragments of the Sampo had washed ashore, and these he gathered, casting them over the land the way a farmer casts seeds. And so the voyage to seize the Sampo was not a failure after all. Even though the wonder of the Sampo was lost, the magic in those fragments was just enough to keep Finland prosperous forever.

The Journeys of Maeldun

— A Tale from Ireland —

Once, in the days when the ways of the druids were being challenged by those of the Christian priests, a baby was born, young Maeldun, only to be given to a queen to raise as the companion of her three princely sons. And so the baby grew to be a boy and the boy to be a young man, never knowing a word about his true birth. But he began to show greater skills than the princes, in the hunt and in games. And after being defeated by Maeldun once too often, one prince challenged:

"Fine deeds from a fellow who doesn't even know who he is! Fine deeds from one who has no father!"

Off Maeldun went to the queen. "Tell me who I am," he insisted. "Tell me of my parents."

The queen sighed. "Your mother was a nun," she told him. "It was she who left you here to be fostered by me."

"And my father? What of him?" Maeldun asked.

"Your father was the mighty warrior known as Ailill Edge-of-Battle."

"But where is he? Why has he never come to see me? Is he ashamed of me?"

"Never that." Reluctantly, the queen told Maeldun, "He was slain by the men of a foreign clan, the Laighis."

Angry and grieving, Maeldun went to the druids for advice.

They told him what he had already decided: He must sail after the Laighis and avenge his father.

"However," warned one druid, "have your ship built only on the correct day. And take with you seventeen men, seventeen heroes, no more, no less."

Maeldun agreed. And as soon as a ship had been built, he selected seventeen brave men and set sail. But when his three princely foster brothers learned that he was going off on an adventure without them, they swam after the ship and climbed aboard. There was nothing for Maeldun to do but take them with him as well.

And at first all went well. When they put into a small island for fresh provisions, even before they could disembark, they heard some of the Laighis feasting there as well. And one of the Laighis warriors boasted of having helped slay Ailill. But before Maeldun could attack, a terrible storm swept up and carried his ship back out to sea. By the time the storm let up, it was morning.

"Where are we?" Maeldun wondered, staring about at nothing but open sea. Not one of the heroes could tell, and Maeldun sighed. "It is your fault," he told his foster brothers. If you hadn't disobeyed the druid's warning, I would have already avenged my father. And we wouldn't be lost in the middle of nowhere!"

There was nothing to do but sail on, hunting for land. For three days and nights they saw nothing but water, but on the morning of the fourth day one of the crew cried, "That's the sound of waves breaking on land!"

But no sooner had they put ashore on the small island than the men saw great hordes of ants larger than any horse rushing towards them, plainly set on eating both crew and ship. Hastily the men all leaped back on board and cast off. For a time, Maeldun was sure the monstrous ants meant to follow them right into the water. But then the ship's sail caught the wind, and soon the Island of the Ants was left far behind.

They sailed on for three more days, and Maeldun began to

worry about provisions, which were running dangerously low. But then, much to the crew's relief, they put in at a second island, so full of lovely birds that the air was bright with the colors of their wings and rich with the beauty of their song. As the men reprovisioned their ship, they smiled with delight. But there were no traces of the Laighis to be found here. Regretfully they left the Island of the Birds and sailed on.

The next island they reached was inhabited by nothing but a huge monstrous beast, like no creature any of the crew had ever seen before. It seemed friendly enough, but since there was again no trace of the Laighis here, they sailed on from the Island of the Monster the short distance to the next island.

"Horses," one of the crew said suddenly. "Large ones. Look at the size of these hoofprints. They were galloping about here as though on a racecourse."

"Never mind that!" another man gasped. "Look at the size of the racegoers!"

Were they giants? Or were they demons? They were vast, misty beings who ignored the humans completely, watching a horserace only they could see. Nervously, Maeldun and his men slipped back aboard their ship and sailed away from the Island of the Horseraces.

They reached many other islands after that. "Too many islands," the men murmured wearily.

There was the Island of Solitude, on which stood an empty palace filled with a wondrous feast; the Island of the Wonder Tree, which bore a magical apple tree that fed the crew for fully forty days; the Island of Demon Horses, terrible beasts that fought each other endlessly; the Island of the Magic Queen, who fell in love with Maeldun and did her best to so entangle him in charms he very nearly stayed with her forever. When he tried to sail away, she cast a magic thread after him to catch the ship, and only one quick-thinking hero, who slashed the thread with his sword, set them free again.

There were so many more islands that Maeldun admitted wearily, "I am growing thoroughly sick of the very sight of marvels."

But nowhere in all this wandering from wonder isle to wonder isle did he or his men catch even the slightest sign of the Laighis.

"It's your fault," the men told the three princely foster brothers. "If we had allowed only seventeen of us on board we would have ended our quest long ago. We should never have permitted you to stay aboard."

Maeldun held up a hand. "We've sailed as comrades in arms all this while. Would you destroy that friendship now?"

They put in to a small, green island that, for once, bore no signs of wonder. But one of the men pointed up at a falcon, crying eagerly, "See that bird? It looks just like a falcon from home!"

Maeldun sprang to his feet. "Watch him closely! See which way he goes!"

The falcon flew straight southeast, and southeast Maeldun and his men sailed. The wind died; they rowed on. And they sighted land at dusk. As they put in to shore, Maeldun gasped. "This is the island on which we first landed, the Island of the Laighis."

He and his men stole silently up to the hall in which the Laighis were gathered. But deep in his heart, Maeldun realized he no longer burned for revenge. He had sailed so far and travelled so widely he had completely lost the edge of his rage. And so, instead of attacking, he waited, and heard the Laighis men talking about him.

"What if Maeldun were to attack us now?"

"Nonsense. Maeldun was drowned long ago, during his travels. Everyone knows that."

"But what if he did appear? What should we do?"

"I know what I would do," said a richly-dressed man who was plainly the chief of the Laighis. "It was I who slew his father, yes, but it was in fair and equal combat. And if Maeldun, who is surely worn and weary from his journey, were to enter now, I would, though we were enemies once, greet him as a hero and a friend."

"So be it," Maeldun said, and entered.

The chief of the Laighis was as good as he'd sworn. He greeted Maeldun and his crew like old friends, and feasted them like heroes. There was peace between them all.

And so the weary journey was finally over, and the long-held enmity was at last put to rest.

Courtesy of DC Comics

Part Two

"It's a Bird, It's a Plane..."

The girders of the bridge are giving way under the weight of the storm. A busload of children rolls over it—and the bridge gives way, sending the bus plummeting down to the gorge below. Just when all hope seems lost, a figure soars into sight. Is it a bird? No, it's a dark-haired man in a cloaked costume. He catches the bus as though it were a feather, and carries the children easily to safety before flying away again.

Superman, that gallant hero of alien origins and super-human strength who tirelessly fights against wrong-doers and injustice, first appeared in Action Comics in 1938, and since then has gone on to star in comic books, television shows, and movies. Whether in his true identity as a costumed super hero or in his disguise as the mild-mannered reporter Clark Kent, he's a character who is easily recognizable around the world.

But not as many people might recognize Superman as a modern incarnation of an ancient type of folk hero as well, one who is amazingly popular and is found in the traditional stories of almost every people in the world. This folkloric hero is the young man who is born of noble or royal blood but who—usually because of some terrible trouble that will mean his death if anyone learns his true identity—grows up ignorant of who he really is. Eventually, though, he does find out about his true origins, and goes on to gain his proper place in the world and become his people's—or his adopted people's—protector.

But the story of Superman also belongs to an even more specific folkloric archetype, one that turns up in literally dozens of folktales and legends. In these stories, the hero isn't merely taken away from his roots, but is actually cast adrift in a boat or box as a baby, and is rescued from certain death by a foster parent. Superman definitely fits this description. He was sent as a baby from Krypton, his dying native planet, in a small space capsule that sailed the sea of space and was cast "ashore" on Earth. Rescued from the capsule by the Kents, a Midwestern couple who became his Earthly parents, he was raised in humble circumstances, and remained ignorant of his true origins (except, of course, for his super powers) until adulthood. But there are, indeed, a great many tales of earlier heroes—both historical figures such as Sargon and Moses and fictional folkloric characters—who were said to have been rescued from small boats or boxes.

Sargon the Mighty

A Tale of Ancient Akkad

Once, in the long-ago days in the faraway land of Akkad, a priestess fell in love. Alas, such a thing was not permitted for her or for other priestesses of her belief. She must, the laws all stated, remain chaste and aloof from love.

But love is often stronger than law, and soon the priestess, whose name we know not, realized that she was going to bear a child. What could she do? The law would have her, and her baby with her, put to death!

There was only one thing for her to do. She must cast away the child and pretend it never existed.

"But I will give my baby at least a chance to survive," the priestess thought.

And so, when the baby, a strong, healthy little boy, was born, the priestess secretly stole down to the banks of the Euphrates River. She placed her baby into a little reed boat she had woven and made waterproof by smearing it with bitumen. Weeping, she pushed the little boat out into the river and hurried away.

The mighty river carried the boat and the baby safely on its surface, smoothly as a mother's arms. The boat floated along till at last it was snared in some reeds at the river's bank. A gardener named Akki happened to be working nearby.

"What's this?" he wondered. "What could be hidden in

such a tiny boat?"

He waded into the river and fished out the boat. The baby woke and began to gurgle. Akki stared down at him in wonder.

"I have always wished for a child," he told the baby in delight. "And now the gods have sent me one. I shall adopt you, little one, and raise you as my son. And your name, I think, shall be Sargon."

So it was that Sargon won a name, a family, and a profession. Akki taught him all the ways of plants as the boy grew, and by the time Sargon had reached young manhood, he was a fine gardener in his own right.

Now, it happened that the goddess Ishtar, goddess of love and war both, enjoyed the sight of well-kept gardens and often wandered among them, unseen by mortal folk. She liked the sight of Sargon, too, and when she searched into his mind, she liked what she found there, too.

"This is far too fine and noble a man to be wasted as a gardener," Ishtar decided. "I shall love him and set my seal upon him."

She whispered in his ears. She set ambition in his mind. And Sargon was no longer content to be merely a gardener. With the goddess watching over him, he learned weaponry and statecraft. With the goddess loving him, he rose from being the nameless son of a nameless priestess as high as a man might rise. Now known as Sargon the Mighty, he fought and conquered the king of the land of Kish, and founded the land of Akkad. And King Sargon and his descendants ruled wisely and well.

The Story of Moses

A Tale from the Old Testament

There was a cruel Pharaoh in Egypt who enslaved the Jews who were living in that land. Fearing that they might become too numerous and become a danger to him, he ordered that all newborn male babies born to the Jews should be drowned.

Soon after this cruel decree, one Jewish woman, Jochebed, gave birth to a fine, handsome son, and refused to have him put to death. She managed to hide her baby for three months. But at last, knowing she could keep him safely hidden no longer, the desperate mother built him a little ark out of bulrushes. Making it proof against the water with pitch, Jochebed put her baby into it and set the ark into the Nile, hiding it among the rushes. The baby's older sister, Miriam, kept watch to see what would become of her brother.

Now, this was where Pharaoh's daughter often came down to bathe. As she strolled along the riverbank with her handmaidens, she spotted the little ark hidden among the bulrushes. Curious, the princess had it brought to her, and was amazed to find the handsome little boy within it. But he was weeping from fright and loneliness, and her heart was filled with love and pity.

"This is surely one of the Jewish children," she said, and determined that he should not be drowned.

Miriam, meanwhile, had seen what was happening, and came running up to the princess. "I know a Jewish woman who would make a perfect nurse for the baby," she said. "Shall I go for her?"

Pharaoh's daughter, holding the baby to her, said, "Go."

Miriam went running to her mother, who hurried to the princess. Pharaoh's daughter told Jochebed, "Take this child and nurse it for me, and I will pay you."

Jochebed showed not the slightest sign that this was her son, but of course she nursed the baby with her heart full of joy. As the baby grew and thrived, the princess's heart was filled with joy as well.

"He shall be my son," she proclaimed. "And his name shall be Moses, because I drew him out of the water."

And so Moses grew to be a man, not knowing who he really was until the day he saw an Egyptian man beating a helpless Jewish slave. Furious at this injustice, Moses struck down the Egyptian and slew him. As a result, Pharaoh ordered that Moses, too, be slain. But the young man fled and hid among the Jews. And gradually he learned their ways, which were his ways, and came to know their faith as well. And when the Jews cried out against their unjust slavery, it was Moses, once a baby in danger of being drowned, then the foster son of an Egyptian princess, and at last a true hero of the Jews, who led his people out of bondage and after many hard trials into the sanctuary of the Promised Land.

The Two Babies
Cast into the Water

A Tale from Poland

Once, long ago, three sisters sat wishing for husbands. The eldest sister decided, "I shall marry a baker. Then I shall never want for bread."

The middle sister decided, "I shall marry a cook. Then I shall never want for nice, hot soup." But the youngest sister said, "I would like to marry no one but the prince. I dreamed that we should have two wonderful children together. The bathwater of our son would turn to purest gold, and as for our daughter, why, roses would bloom when she smiled and pearls fall when she wept."

What the three sisters didn't know was that the prince himself had overheard them. He married the eldest sister to the royal baker and the middle sister to the royal cook. Ah, but the youngest sister—Well now, he married the youngest sister himself.

Things should have been happy in the royal castle. But soon enough, the eldest and middle sisters grew jealous of their princess-sister. And when she gave birth to two lovely children, a boy and a girl, the evil sisters stole those babies away while she slept and put a puppy and a kitten in their place. Putting the two human babies in a box, the sisters threw them into the river, then went weeping and wailing to the prince.

"Alas, alas, our sister, our own sister, is a—a witch! She has given birth not to children but to animals!"

The prince didn't want to believe such a tale, but there was the proof, the puppy and kitten, before him. "You promised me a son whose bathwater turned to purest gold!" he shouted. "You promised me a daughter whose smile would create roses and whose tears would create pearls. And yet all you give me are monsters!"

Refusing to listen to his wife's pleas, he locked her away in a dark cell.

Meanwhile, a poor fisherman saw the box float by and pulled it from the water. Opening it, he was delighted to find two lovely babies inside, for he had no children of his own.

"I shall raise you as my own," he promised the babies. "You," he told the boy, "I shall name Simon, and you," he said to the girl, "shall be Wanda."

The fisherman was quite amazed to see that Simon's bathwater turned to gold and Wanda's smiles to roses, but soon he had accepted that what was, was. He built his adopted family a lovely house of gold. Rose bushes grew all around it. And the fisherman and the two children lived together happily for several years.

But one night Simon and Wanda both had the same magical dream of a crystal spring, a singing tree, and a talking bird. The next day, the boy told his sister, "I am going to look for these wonders."

Wanda sighed. "Then I will stay home and help our father."

So off the boy went into the forest on his quest. But on the way, he met an old, old man who asked Simon where he was going.

"I'm hunting for a crystal spring," said the boy, "and a singing tree. Oh, and a talking bird as well."

"All three of those wonders are together," the old man told him, pointing out the way. "But be wary. As you draw water from the spring, you will hear a terrible roar behind you. If you so much as look over your shoulder, you shall turn to stone."

The old man looked as though he were about to say more, but Simon was too eager to reach the spring to wait. He hurriedly thanked the old man for the warning and went on his way.

Soon enough Simon was at the crystal spring, and bent to catch some of the water in a flask. But as he did so, a terrible roar shook the forest. It so startled Simon that he forgot the old man's warning and looked back over his shoulder.

And he was turned at once to stone.

Meanwhile, back at home, Wanda was worrying and worrying over her missing brother. At last she sighed and went looking for him. She, too, met the old man in the forest. He gave her the same warning he had given her brother. But when he looked as though he might say more, the girl, even though she was in a hurry to reach the spring, waited to hear what he might say.

"When you take the water from the spring," he told her, "be sure to sprinkle some of that water to the right and left as you leave."

Wanda thanked him for his kindness, and hurried on. She came to the spring, and gasped to see how beautiful it was. As she bent to catch some of the water in her flask, the terrible roar so startled her that she began to look over her shoulder. Just in time, Wanda remembered the old man's warning, and refused to look until she was sure it was safe to leave.

As the girl left, she sprinkled some water to the left. And

a tree began to sing! As she stared in wonder, a beautiful little bird flew out of it and cried, "Thank you for freeing us! Now sprinkle some water to the right as well."

Wanda did—and her brother turned back into flesh and blood and came running to her. "And thank you for freeing *me!*" he cried.

They started happily for home, and the singing tree and the talking bird came with them.

Ah, but meanwhile their father the prince still mourned for his wife, locked away in her dark cell. He longed to free her—but he still believed she was a witch. To take his mind from his grief, he went hunting.

The two children heard his hunting horns. "Listen!" cried Simon. "Who do you suppose that is?"

"Let's go see what's happening," added Wanda.

As they peered through the bushes, the two children saw the hunters. "How splendid they are!" Simon whispered. "I—I will show them how well I can hunt."

So the boy shot a hare with his own little bow, right in front of the prince.

"Well done, child!" the prince said with a laugh. "I award you the hare. What's more, I will come and help you eat your prize!"

"G-give us time to prepare, please," Simon stammered, and he and his sister hurried home.

"How can we possibly make a meal fine enough for a prince?" Wanda wondered.

"No fear, no fear," chirped the talking bird. "Your house of gold is pretty enough for a prince. Take down some of the branches of the singing tree. Roast the hare on them and garnish it nicely with some pearls. I shall do the rest."

Well now, the prince was astonished to see a little golden house surrounded by rose bushes there in the middle of the forest. But the talking bird chirped, "Why should you be surprised? These pearls come from your daughter's eyes, those roses come from her smiles, and that gold comes from your son's bathwater."

The prince cried out in wonder and hugged the children to him. "Oh, how could I ever have believed the lies told about my wife? How will she ever forgive me? How, ah, how has she fared all these long years?"

"She has fared very well," the bird chirped. "Since she was unjustly accused, time refused to harm her, so she is just as pretty and healthy as the day you two first wed."

The prince and his two children rushed off to the palace, where the princess was soon freed, looking just as pretty and healthy as though she had never been imprisoned. A great feast of rejoicing was held, and the fisherman was made Royal Fisherman.

Only the two evil sisters were not there. They had paid the price for their sins with their lives. Everyone else, of course, lived long and happily together.

Grandfather Wisdom

—————— A Tale from the Czech Republic ——————

Once, in long-ago times, there lived a cruel and selfish king who cared only for himself and his pride. One day he went hunting in the forest, and soon became quite lost. He stopped for the night at the hut of a poor peasant, whose wife had just given birth to a son.

That night, the king woke to see three old women standing around the newborn child, and realized they were the Fates who decided the future of each soul.

The first Fate said softly, "This babe shall undergo grave peril in his life."

The second Fate added, "But he shall pass through that danger in safety."

And the third Fate whispered, "He shall come to marry the daughter of the king and rule in his place."

The king nearly cried out in anger. What, the child of a peasant marry his daughter? The child of a peasant rule in his place? Never!

In the morning, alas, the peasant found that his wife had died. "What am I to do?" he wailed. "How can I possibly raise a baby and work at the same time?"

"Give me the child," the king said. "I shall send a servant to bring him to my court, and I shall see that the babe is well-treated."

What could the peasant do? If his son grew up at court, the child would surely live a happy, wealthy life! So he eagerly agreed.

The king went home. Sure enough, his wife the queen had given birth to a fine baby girl. "She will not marry the son of a peasant," he muttered, and sent for a soldier. Telling him where the peasant's hut stood, the king commanded, "You will take the child—and toss it into the swift-running stream!"

The soldier did as he was told. He took the baby, which was nestled in a woven basket, and tossed the basket and baby both into the swift-running stream.

And so the prophesy of the first Fate was fulfilled.

Ah, but the basket was strongly made and finely woven. It rode on the water as nicely as a little boat, rocking the baby sweetly to sleep.

A fisherman sat on the shore. He saw the basket, and drew it out of the water. "Well now, look at this!" he cried to his wife. "The waters have brought us a son! Let us call him Jirik."

And so the prophesy of the second Fate was fulfilled.

The years passed and the baby grew to a boy and the boy to a fine, handsome young man. One day the king went hunting again, and came to where Jirik stood by the stream. "Bring me water," the king commanded, never recognizing in this fine fellow the baby he'd ordered drowned. As Jirik politely obeyed, the king asked the fisherman, "Is this handsome young man your son?"

"Ah well, not exactly," the fisherman admitted. "I found him floating downstream in a basket when he was a babe. Some cruel soul must have tried to drown him, but that was clearly not his fate."

The king grew pale with shock. The baby he had ordered drowned! The baby who was going to marry his daughter and take his place on the throne! Right away the king began a second plan to kill Jirik. "There is an important message I must have delivered to my queen at court. I shall send your son as messenger."

But what the king wrote was this, "Have this young man slain at once. This is my will." Then he neatly folded and sealed the message and handed it, smiling, to Jirik.

Now of course Jirik had no reason not to trust the king. Off he went. But the forest was very thick, and darkness overtook him before he could reach the royal court. As the weary young man looked for a place to spend the night, a voice asked, "Where are you going?"

An old woman stood before him. Jirik bowed politely. "I am going to the king's court to deliver this message, but night has overtaken me."

"Stay at my house, then, till morning. We met once, when you were newly born."

It was one of the three Fates, the one who had prophesied that he would bypass all danger, but Jirik didn't know that. He went with her to her cottage and soon was fast asleep.

The old woman opened the king's message and frowned, then replaced it with a message of her own and smiled. In the morning, Jirik went on his way, never guessing what she had done.

And the message the queen read was this: "Marry this young man to our daughter as soon as possible. This is my will."

The queen was puzzled, but she had no intention of risking her husband's terrible anger. So Jirik was married to the princess, and though both young people were equally puzzled, they weren't at all unhappy.

The king returned. To his horror, he found Jirik married to the princess. But there was his message, written in what looked like his hand, so what could he do? The king brooded and plotted, plotted and brooded. And at last he said, "Young man, now that you are my son-in-law, you must prove your worth with a brave deed."

"Anything," Jirik said.

The king pretended to think long and hard about it. "I know," he said suddenly. "I want you to bring me three golden hairs from the head of Grandfather Wisdom."

Who was Grandfather Wisdom? No one really knew, except that he lived in a faraway realm and was very, very wise—but very, very perilous. He had no love at all for visitors. Indeed, some stories said he even ate any man foolish enough to bother him.

What could poor Jirik do? Off he went on his long journey. The princess wept, the queen wept—but the king smiled.

Well now, whether Jirik travelled long or far, at last he came to the shore of a sea of black water. An old ferryman stood on the shore.

"God's blessings to you," Jirik said politely.

"And to you," the ferryman replied. "Where are you going?"

"I go to the realm of Grandfather Wisdom to take three golden hairs from his head."

The ferryman laughed. "For twenty weary years I have labored here without rest. But I was given a prophesy that a young man on such a quest would come to me, and that he would learn from Grandfather Wisdom when my work here would be done. If you promise to ask him that, I will ferry you across for no fee at all."

Jirik agreed, and the old ferryman took him across the dark sea. Soon enough, the young man came to a great city—but a city in sad ruin. A man sat sadly in the broken gateway.

"God's blessing to you," Jirik said.

"And to you. But where are you going, young man?"

"I go to the realm of Grandfather Wisdom to take three golden hairs from his head."

"Aha!" the man cried. "Listen to me, young man: I am the ruler of this sad city. Once we were strong and happy, for in the marketplace stood an apple tree that kept us all young. But for twenty years the tree has not borne fruit, and we have all become sick and old. If you will ask Grandfather Wisdom how to make our tree bear fruit, I will reward you richly."

Jirik agreed, and went on his way. Soon he came to another city, and if the first one had looked a ruin, this one looked worse. A second man sat sadly in the broken gateway.

"God's blessing to you," Jirik said.

"And to you," the man replied. "Where are you going?"

"I go to the realm of Grandfather Wisdom to take three golden hairs from his head."

"Aha!" the man cried. "I am the ruler of this poor city. Once we were all happy and full of life. In the marketplace was a well of Living Water that kept us all that way. But for these twenty years, the well has been quite dry. If you will ask Grandfather Wisdom how to make the water return, I will reward you richly."

Jirik agreed. Off he went again, through forest and field, till at last he came to a castle of gold so bright it blazed like fire in the sun. To Jirik's surprise, the gates stood open and unguarded, so he warily entered. In the topmost room in a golden tower, he found an old woman working at a spinning wheel.

"Welcome," she said with a smile, and Jirik saw to his amazement that it was the same old woman he'd met in the forest. "What has brought you here?"

Jirik sighed. "I have married the princess, and we are very happy. But her father the king wants me to prove my worth, so he's sent me here to take three golden hairs from the head of Grandfather Wisdom."

"Is that so?" the old woman said. "Grandfather Wisdom is my son. In the morning, he is but a babe, in the afternoon a grown man, and in the evening old enough to be a grandfather, indeed."

"B-but how can that be?"

"Oh, easily, young man. You see, he is the Sun."

Jirik stared. How could he ever hope to gain three golden hairs from someone that fiery? The old woman smiled. "Don't be afraid. I shall get those hairs for you. Ah, but you must hide! When he comes home at night, he is so weary he will destroy any man he sees. He would roast you with his fire and eat you!"

Hastily Jirik hid inside an empty wine cask. But before he pulled the lid over his head, he told the old woman about the questions of the ferryman and the two rulers.

"I will ask my son those questions," the old woman agreed. "Listen well."

Just then, the Sun came home in a blaze of light, an old, old man with bright golden hair and beard. Jirik hurriedly pulled the lid over his head.

"I smell a man in here," Grandfather Wisdom said shortly. "Does a man dare come here?"

"Oh, my dear, shining son, you fly over the world all day," the old woman answered quickly, "and the world is full of men. It is no wonder that you carry the smell of the world and of men back with you."

Grandfather Wisdom sat down at his table without another word and began eating the dinner his mother had prepared. Then he lay down to sleep, his head in his mother's lap. Quickly she plucked a golden hair from his head. Grandfather Wisdom stirred. "What was that?"

"Nothing, my son. I only had a strange dream. I dreamed

of a city which held a well of Living Water, a well that had sadly dried up. How, I wonder, could the water be made to run once more?"

"What an easy riddle! At the bottom of the well, a great toad sits, blocking the spring from which the Living Water flows. All the people need do is remove the toad and clean the well, and the water will run free."

He sank back down into sleep. The old woman plucked a second golden hair from his head.

"What was that?" Grandfather Wisdom asked.

"Oh, nothing. I merely dreamed of a city in which grew a wondrous apple tree with magical fruit. But for years the tree grew no fruit at all. I wonder if it could be made healthy once more."

"A simple thing! At the roots of that tree is a great serpent gnawing away at them. If the people kill the snake, the tree will recover and bear fruit."

He sank back down into sleep. The old woman plucked the third golden hair from his head.

"What are you doing?" Grandfather Wisdom cried. "Why will you not let me sleep?"

"Hush, my son. I but dreamed of an old ferryman who has been working for long and long. When, I wonder, will his labor be done?"

"What a fool he is! All he needs do is hand his oar to another man and jump ashore. Then the other man will become ferryman in his place. Now, let me sleep!"

The night passed. Jirik slept as best he could in that cramped wine cask. When morning finally came, he peeked warily out of the cask, just in time to see Grandfather Wisdom turn into a young boy who leaped out of the window and flew away. As Jirik climbed out of the wine cask, the old woman gave him the three golden hairs.

"Now you have the answers to your questions and the

goal of your quest," she told him, and sent him on his way.

Jirik returned to the city with the dried-up well. "Have you found the reason the Living Water no longer flows?" the people asked.

"A great toad sits at the bottom of the well," he told the people, "blocking the water. If you remove the toad and clean the well, the Living Water will flow freely once more."

The people hastily removed the toad and cleaned the well and, just as Jirik had said, the Living Water flowed freely once more. The ruler of the city was the first to drink of it, and instantly became a youthful, healthy man once more.

"You have our endless gratitude!" he cried to Jirik. Giving Jirik twelve white horses loaded with gold, he sent the young man on his way with a blessing.

On Jirik went, and returned to the city with the dying apple tree. "Have you learned what ails our tree?" the people asked.

"A great serpent is coiled about the roots of the tree," Jirik told the people, "and gnaws at them. If you kill the serpent, the tree will recover and bear fruit."

The people hastily slew the serpent, and the tree at once began to put out blossoms. Soon wondrous fruit hung from the branches. The ruler of the city was the first to taste the fruit, and instantly became young and healthy once more.

"We are forever in your debt," he told Jirik. Giving Jirik twelve black horses loaded with gold, he sent the young man on his way with a blessing.

Soon Jirik came to the shores of the black sea. The old ferryman was waiting. "Did you speak to Grandfather Wisdom?" he asked eagerly. "Did you find out how I may be freed?"

"I did," Jirik said, "but I will not tell you till we are on the far side of the sea."

The ferryman hurriedly carried Jirik and his horses

across the sea. "Now tell me, how may I be freed?"

"The next time a man asks to be taken across," Jirik told him, "wait till he is in your boat, then hand him the oar and leap onto the shore. Then he will be the ferryman in your place."

Soon enough, Jirik was home. The king stared at the twenty-four gold-laden horses in wonder. "Where did you find such riches?" he asked greedily.

"Here and there, there and here," Jirik answered.

"But you have not brought me that which I ordered," the king said.

"The three golden hairs from the head of Grandfather Wisdom? Here they are."

The king stared at them. How had the young man done this? How had he succeeded? "You must tell me all that has happened to you!" he commanded.

And so Jirik told of all his adventures. When he mentioned the Living Water and the wondrous apple tree, the king's eyes brightened. When he mentioned the gold, the king sprang to his feet. To be forever young and strong and wealthy! Before Jirik could tell him about the ferryman, the king had called for his fastest horse and ridden away.

Soon enough he came to the ferryman. "Take me across!" the king ordered.

The ferryman gleefully agreed. Halfway across, he handed the king the oar and jumped overboard, swimming quickly back to shore.

"Free!" he laughed. "Free at last!"

"Wait!" the king cried. "Come back!"

But of course the former ferryman never even turned his head to look back. And the king found that he could not leave the boat, no matter how hard he tried.

And so the third prophesy was fulfilled. The king was now a ferryman. And Jirik, happily married to the princess, ruled wisely in his place.

The Children of Ahmed Aga

—————— A Tale from Turkey ——————

Once there was and once there was not a rich man who, as the law in Turkey permitted, married a second wife since he and his first wife had no children. This second wife was younger than the first, prettier than the first, and far, far more kind-hearted than the cruel first wife.

Soon enough, the second wife became pregnant and gave birth to twins, a boy and a girl. But the cruel first wife had already made a pact with a sorceress, who posed as a midwife. The sorceress stole away the newborn twins, dumped them into a jar, and tossed the jar into the sea.

"Alas!" she cried, rushing to the rich man and pretending to weep. "Alas!"

"What is wrong?" the rich man asked in alarm.

"Your wife, your second wife—aie, I know not how to say this!"

"What of my wife? Tell me!"

"She has given birth—but not to human children, no, no, she has given birth to a—a monster, a snake!"

"No!" the rich man cried in horror. "This cannot be!"

But the sorceress had conjured a dead snake to show him. The rich man had no choice but to believe that his second wife was a witchly creature, and had her thrown out of his house.

Ah, the poor young woman! She wandered here, she wandered there. At last she came to the house of a shepherd and his wife, kindly people who took her in and made her their adopted daughter.

Meanwhile, the jar holding the twin babies did not sink, but floated sweetly on top of the waves, rocking the babies to sleep as nicely as though they were in a cradle.

Not far from where the jar was floating along lived a second rich man, Ahmed Aga, and his wife. They loved each other very much and so he had no wish at all to take a second wife, but they, too, to their despair, were childless. The very night the twins were born, the woman woke with a cry.

"What is it, my wife?" Ahmed Aga asked.

"I just had a such strange dream," she told him. "I dreamed a mermaid rose up out of the sea with a jar in her arms. She told me that Allah has granted our fondest wish."

"For a child?" the man asked in wonder. "Can this be?"

Urged on by his wife, Ahmed Aga hurried down to the seashore. And there, sure enough, he found a jar floating on the waves. Wading into the water, he drew it forth.

"Wife! Wife! Look what I've found!" Ahmed Aga cried in delight, rushing home. "Here are two beautiful babies for us to raise."

And so the childless couple was childless no more. The boy and girl grew up as happy youngsters do, knowing they had been rescued from a jar but never guessing anything about their true parents.

But then one night both twins dreamed the same dream. They saw a lovely young woman living with a shepherd couple.

"This is the mother who bore us," said the girl.

"I shall look for her," said the boy.

And off went the son of Ahmed Aga on his quest. At last, after many weary days he reached the hut of the shepherd. His mother was overjoyed to learn that her children were alive and happy, and visited often with them and their foster parents.

And what of the rich man who was the true father of the twins? For his folly, he never found his wife again or his children. He lived unhappily from then on.

But the children of Ahmed Aga, their foster parents, and their true mother lived happily all their days.

Courtesy of LucasFilm, Ltd.

Part Three

"In a Galaxy Far, Far Away . . ."

It is far into the future, far away, and the cause of freedom looks all but lost. An evil Empire rules over a network of captive worlds, and only a few desperate rebels hold out against the forces of Darkness. But far from the scene of action, a young man is growing up as a farmer on a backwater planet. Little does he suspect, for all his dreams of adventure, that soon, with the help of a wise old man and daring friends, he will leave his dull life and become a hero.

In 1977, a new science fiction movie opened that became one of the most successful of all times and that had a tremendous impact on American popular culture. The movie chronicled the perilous adventures of a young hero from a backwater planet who, with the aid of a wise old man, a daring princess, and a swashbuckling mercenary, fought against the forces of an evil Empire. It is, of course, Star Wars, and by now there are very few people who haven't heard of Luke Skywalker, the young man who rises from obscurity to heroism, or his friends and allies.

Luke Skywalker is yet another modern-day fictional hero who has ties to numerous heroes and heroines out of folklore.

Like Superman and his predecessors, Jason of ancient Greece and Maeldun of Ireland, he is a young man born of noble or royal blood (Luke is, of course, the son of a murdered Jedi Knight) who grows up not knowing his true birth.

But Luke belongs to a more specialized category of hero. This type of hero does find out who he really is, often through his own cleverness or a sense of inner worth, and actively seeks to gain his rightful place in the world. Of course he often needs the assistance of a supernatural helper of some kind, whether a magical animal, a ghost, or a wise old man—such as Luke's mentor, Obi-Wan Ben Kenobi, master of the Force, or King Arthur's wizardly advisor, Merlin—who not only gives him vital information about his true origins, but aids him with his heroic deeds. Variants on this popular folkloric theme are found in stories from all over the world

The Story of King Cyrus

A Tale of Ancient Persia

Once, long ago, King Astyages ruled over the prosperous Persian land of the Medes. He was respected by all and challenged by none, and should have been content with his life. But Astyages was not.

And one night King Astyages dreamed that his daughter, Mandane, was the fount of wondrous water that spread out over all his lands. What could this strange dream mean? The king hurriedly summoned his Magi, his sages wise in the ways of magic, and commanded, "Interpret this dream for me!"

The sages thought for a time and studied the omens, and at last told the king, "Great Astyages, your dream means that a son shall be born to your daughter who shall conquer your lands and put an end to you."

Horrified, Astyages decided he must have Mandane slain. But no, he could not take his daughter's life!

Mandane was secretly in love with a commoner—or at least she and her young man *thought* their love was a secret. But her maidservants came rushing to the king with their gossip. To their surprise, Astyages only smiled. Here was the answer to his problem! He would marry Mandane to her commoner love, and any son Mandane might bear would never be able to inherit the throne, because he would not be of the highest blood.

"Thus I shall forestall the prophesy," he decided.

And for a time, King Astyages slept sweetly. But after Mandane had been married for a year, Astyages dreamed a second strange dream. And in it, he saw a vine spring from Mandane to cover all his lands. Astyages woke with a start.

"I have not put an end to the threat," he realized. "I must send someone to my daughter's home. If she bears a girl-child, it shall live. But if she bears a son, I shall have it taken away and slain. And *then* the threat of the prophesy shall be ended!"

Sure enough, Mandane was with child. And soon she gave birth to a fine son who was named Cyrus. When he heard the news of this birth, King Astyages sent for his steward, Harpagus.

"You must steal away Mandane's son," he told Harpagus. "Take the boy home and kill him."

Harpagus bowed low in obedience. His men silently stole away the baby in the night and brought it to him. But as he looked down at the small, sleeping face, Harpagus winced. Surely, he told himself, it was not wise for the royal steward to do such a foul deed. Surely the killing of the child should be done by someone so lowly he would have no honor to be stained. So Harpagus sent for the royal cowherd.

"I order you in the king's name," he said sharply, "to take this child and slay it."

What could the cowherd do? He could hardly refuse. Then Harpagus might have *him* slain! Sadly, he took the baby and went home, trying to find some way to save the poor child's life.

But when the cowherd reached his house, he found sadness. His wife had given birth to a stillborn child.

"I have already lost one child," she told him, weeping. "I will not let you kill another."

"What choice have I?"

"Our baby never had a chance to live. Take his poor body to the king, and let us raise this child in his place."

The cowherd gladly agreed. The stillborn baby was buried in the casket that was to have held Cyrus's body. King Astyages was satisfied that the prophesy had, at last, been blocked. And Cyrus grew up as the son of the cowherd and his wife, never suspecting he was anyone but their child.

But as Cyrus grew into a fine young man, he became impatient with the life of the cowherd. Even though his foster parents begged him not to wander, he visited the court again and again.

The sons of the court nobles sneered at him. "Look at this peasant!" they jeered. "How dare he think himself our equal?"

That stung. "I am not your equal," Cyrus agreed coolly. "I am your better."

The nobles' sons cried out in fury. But when they would have all attacked him, Cyrus shook his head. "Is *this* how noblemen behave?" he asked. "Attacking in a pack like lowly beasts?"

Instead, he challenged them all to a game of skill and strength known as "king." So strong and agile was Cyrus that he won over each and every boy who came against him. But in the struggle, he accidentally injured one of the noblemen's sons. All the other boys attacked him. The noise brought the palace guards running. They quickly broke up the fight, and separated Cyrus from the others.

"What is this riot?" they asked. "Who started it."

"He did!" the boys shouted. "See? He attacked this boy without warning and hurt him!"

"They're only angry because we were playing 'king' and I won," Cyrus argued. "I did not mean to harm anyone."

The guards wouldn't listen to him. Those were the sons of noblemen, and this was surely only the son of a peasant! So they brought Cyrus before King Astyages to be punished.

Cyrus stared at the king without any fear. And Astyages stiffened in shock, seeing in the boy's proud face echoes of Mandane, echoes of himself. "Who are you?" he gasped.

Puzzled, Cyrus told him. Astyages summoned the cowherd and soon learned the truth. But as he looked at his fine young grandson, the king told himself, "The prophesy must have been fulfilled when Cyrus won that game of 'king.' Surely I am safe. Surely I can let my grandson live."

And so Cyrus finally received the training due a prince of the Medes.

But, alas, as the years passed, Astyages again began to suspect his grandson. The young man was becoming too wise, too clever and far, far too popular with the people! And at last Astyages again tried to have Cyrus slain.

But Cyrus escaped. He called followers to him, and at the head of a rebel army, overthrew Astyages and took the throne. He reigned long and wisely, far more wisely than had suspicious Astyages.

And so the prophesy was at last achieved in full.

Percival: The Backwoods Knight

A Tale from Great Britain

Once, in the days when King Arthur ruled from Camelot, that splendid court, there lived a lady who had suffered great wrongs at the hands of he who was known as the Red Knight. This false knight had slain in treacherous battle both her husband and her elder son, leaving her with only her younger son, a baby. Sickened after these tragedies at the very thought of knighthood and fearing to lose this last child to battle as well, the lady fled to a humble refuge deep within the forest. And there she raised her son, whom she named Percival, as a simple boy unaware of the world of courts and combat.

For years, Percival ran free in the woodland, growing to be a well-made, kind-hearted lad, innocent of harm, knowing nothing of his true heritage. But one day, when he was nearly grown, he chanced to see a company of knights riding through the forest. So wonderful did they seem, all glittering in the rays of sunlight filtering down through the leaves, that Percival ran home to tell his mother about these strange, splendid beings.

"They were so very wondrous," he cried, "so bright and brave and—and who were they, Mother? What manner of beings?"

A pang of fright stabbed the lady to the heart. She knew these could only be knights of the Round Table. But she answered quickly, never showing a trace of her sudden alarm,

"Angels, Percival. They were angels, my son. Do not seek to bother them."

Angels! The thought only filled Percival with further wonder. He followed the glittering strangers, tracking them silently through the forest until at last he could stand the weight of his curiosity no longer and burst out from hiding to ask, "Are you angels, good sirs?"

The beings laughed. "No, lad. We are but knights, knights of good King Arthur's Round Table."

Percival stared blankly at them. "What are knights?" he asked, and the knights laughed again.

"An innocent!" one said. "A true innocent!"

But another knight looked kindly at Percival and told him, "A knight is one who is well trained in weaponry but who has sworn an oath to use his skills to defend the weak and helpless. We have sworn such an oath to Arthur, King of the Realm."

"I, too, will be a knight!" Percival cried in delight, and rushed home to tell his mother the news.

The lady, when she heard her son and saw the eagerness blazing in his eyes, nearly wept. Wearily, she admitted, "You are of noble birth, my son," and told him a little of why she had hidden them in the forest. Only the name of her husband's slayer did she keep secret. For surely one as terrible as the Red Knight would think nothing of murdering an untrained boy. "I sought to keep you safe here, Percival, far from the world. But now I see an eagle cannot be caged. Go forth, my son, and do what you must. Only remember my words: Act always with honor. Help those in need and treat all women with gentle reverence. It is no shame to take a single kiss from a maiden, but no more than that. And always remember to return a gift with another gift. Now go, with my blessing. Go, Percival, before I change my mind!"

So Percival went out into the wide world. Over his simple goatskin tunic and leggings he wore a coat he'd made of woven branches in imitation of knightly armor, and he had woven a blanket of similar armor for his pony as well. He had no sword, but stuck a hunting javelin in his belt to serve as weapon.

After several days of riding, Percival came to a silken tent as blue as the heavens, so lovely that at first he thought this must surely be a church, and knelt to pray, asking the Lord to let his dream of knighthood come true.

As Percival got to his feet again, he saw that in the tent a table had been set with roasted meat and fresh bread. Percival looked about, but saw no one. Since it had been over two days since he'd last had a full meal, the young man gladly went inside and ate his fill. As he finished, Percival saw with a start that a young woman was quietly watching him, her eyes more blue than the silken tent, her hair more golden than the sunlight. Overwhelmed by her beauty, Percival kissed her gently, but only once, remembering his mother's warning. He took the golden ring from her finger and, since he knew he must return a gift for a gift, replaced it with his own.

"I am known as Percival," he said, a bit unsteadily.

"What is your name, my lady?"

"I am known as Blanchefleur," she began, then stiffened in alarm. "But you cannot stay here! I hear my brothers returning."

"I don't wish to leave you, not —"

"Go!" the lady insisted. "I will not see you harmed!"

Sadly and reluctantly, Percival obeyed, and rode swiftly away. But now a second prayer had been added to the first: that he might someday meet the Lady Blanchefleur again.

At last, after a long and wandering journey, Percival arrived in his wooden armor at glittering Camelot. As he rode in all innocence right into the royal hall, all the knights burst into laughter at the sight of this ragged fellow. Only Arthur did not laugh. Tall and golden-haired, he looked so majestic Percival stared in wonder. And to his astonishment, this wondrous king greeted him kindly.

"Welcome to Camelot, young man. Why have you come?"

"I wish to be a knight!" Percival cried, and the knights all roared with renewed laughter.

"He wishes to be a knight!" they cried. "This this *peasant* wants to be a knight!"

Arthur held up a hand for silence. "The young man is our guest. And I will have courtesy for any guest."

But no sooner had these noble words been spoken than a knight in blazing red armor strode into the hall. A little page boy who stood in his path was hurled aside with one mailed fist, and the wine cup the boy held went flying so that the wine splashed Queen Gwenivere. In the confusion, the Red Knight snatched up the queen's own goblet and strode away, shouting over his shoulder, "Let any who dare follow and give challenge!"

This was too much for Percival. Had not his mother taught him to treat all women with gentle reverence? "I will take up that challenge!" he shouted, trying to ignore the rush of laughter that followed. "I will! I shall avenge the queen's honor, and then I shall come back to Camelot to be knighted."

He rode out of the hall before any could stop him. Beyond the walls of Camelot, he saw the Red Knight waiting for him, sitting astride a powerful warhorse.

"Is *this* the best champion Arthur can host?" the Red Knight sneered. "This ragged peasant?"

With that, he charged, his mighty horse sweeping Percival's little pony off its feet and sending the young man tumbling to the ground. But Percival had grown up in the forest; he knew how to defend himself against dangerous beasts. Quickly he snatched up his javelin and hurled it right through the Red Knight's eye and into his brain. With a clashing of armor, the Red Knight fell dead. Scrambling to his feet, Percival took back the queen's golden goblet.

"Now I shall also have proper knightly weapons, and a proper knightly horse, as well."

But Percival had not the faintest idea of how to unbuckle

armor. As he struggled with the heavy body of the slain knight, he became aware of someone watching, and looked sharply up to see an old man, straight-backed with knightly pride for all his age.

"If you are willing to stop that foolish struggle, I shall show you how to unbuckle that armor. It is only fitting that you take it—for this Red Knight is the man who murdered your father and brother."

"How—how would you know that?" Percival gasped.

"Your mother is my younger sister. I am your uncle. And," he added, eyeing Percival's ungainly armor, "your tutor in arms, I think."

"I would greatly like that," Percival said.

And so he spent several months with his uncle, learning the ways and rules of knighthood, the mastery of arms and study of proper manners. He must always show courtesy in deeds and speech, and never ask foolish questions or make idle boasts. Many times during that training Percival blushed to think how ridiculous he must have looked when he'd first ridden into Camelot.

At last his uncle said, "Now you are ready to seek honor and adventure. Go, ride out into the world, my young hero."

So Percival set out on many a brave adventure, seeing many a wonder and defeating every knight who came against him, bidding them to return to Camelot and tell who had vanquished them.

Queen Gwenivere's golden goblet he kept hidden in his gear.

At last Percival's riding took him to a beautiful little castle. Entering, he left his horse tethered in the stable, then entered the great hall. A table had been set for chess, and Percival idly moved one of the white pieces. To his amazement, the red pieces moved to block him. Magic! Lost in wonder, he played three games, and each time was defeated.

The softest of laughs made Percival glance up.

"Blanchefleur!" he cried. "And you wear my ring!"

"I do, indeed."

"Oh, my lady, how I have longed to see you again! You are surely the most beautiful woman in all the world, and I vow to love you and be faithful to you for all my days. Will you—will you be my wife?"

But Blanchefleur only sighed. "I would, dear Percival. But our time together is not yet come."

With that, the most miraculously clear light filled the hall. Percival, breath catching in his throat in wonder, saw a silent procession of white-veiled women, the first of whom carried a cup that, even though it, too, was veiled, bore about it such an air of solemn joy that Percival, for all that he knew no knight asked foolish questions or made idle boasts, could no longer remain still.

"I must follow that cup!" he cried.

And as soon as the words left his lips, all vanished, procession, castle, all, even his beloved Blanchefleur, and Percival found himself alone in the wilderness. Dazed and wondering, he found his way back to Camelot.

There, Percival recovered his stunned senses. "I have returned, Sire," he told King Arthur. "And I have avenged the wrongs done here. I have slain the Red Knight who would have dishonored your queen."

With that, he placed the queen's golden goblet down on the Round Table.

King Arthur knighted Percival that very day, and gave him permission to bring his mother from the wilderness back to her own castle. And in the days that followed, Sir Percival proved himself fully worthy of his honor.

But the memory of his lost love, Blanchefleur, lingered in his mind. Someday, Percival vowed, he would see her again and wed her, and then they would live together in endless joy.

The Boy with the Straw

A Tale from Japan

*I*n the long-ago days there lived a poor woman and her young son. Because they were so very poor and could not afford warm food or decent shelter, the woman soon became ill. Knowing she was about to die, she told the boy, "Alas, my son, I have nothing to leave to you except these three bundles of rice straw. If you take it to the *miso* shop, you will at least be able to exchange it for some *miso*."

Miso was a type of bean paste, and the woman was hoping her son would at least be able to make a good meal out of it.

"Now," she added, "I shall tell you the story I have told no one else, the story of these bundles of straw. You see, my son, once I was much more than a poor woman. Once I was wife to the king himself."

"The king!" the boy cried. "Then—then what are we doing living like beggars? Why are we not in the royal palace?"

The dying woman sighed. "Alas for me, alas for us both, my husband was a grim man, intent on whatever job he had ordered be done. And that fatal day, he was overseeing the building of a fine new ship. So fine was that ship that I cried out, 'Oh, how beautiful it is!' I startled the ship builders so much by my cry that they damaged a beam of the ship and had to cease work until the beam could be replaced the next day. My husband was so angry that a whole day of work would be wasted that he ordered me cast out from his palace. The only thing I was given to take with me were these three bundles of straw."

With that, the poor woman died. When he had finished mourning, the boy went to the *miso* shop with the three bundles of straw, as his mother had told him. Sure enough, he was able to trade the rice straw for a bowl of *miso*.

But the clever boy was after more than one brief meal. He took the *miso* to a tinker's shop. "I will trade you this fine *miso*," he said, "if you will give me one of your kettles in exchange."

The tinker shrugged. In exchange for the bowl of *miso*, he gave the boy a cracked old kettle. Off the boy went to the blacksmith's shop. "I will trade you this kettle," he said, "if you will give me a sword in exchange."

The blacksmith shrugged. He could always melt the kettle down and use the metal for something better. So he gave the boy a dull old sword.

"Now I'm getting somewhere," the boy said to himself. "But I'm not yet finished."

Off he went to the seashore. A fine ship was putting into port, but it would be a good while before it docked. The boy sat down, and soon drifted into sleep. A thief snuck up to him and tried to steal his sword. But every time the thief attempted to touch the hilt, the sword turned into a snake and frightened him away.

The captain of the ship saw what was happening. "Boy!" he called, and the boy woke up. "Come aboard my ship with that sword of yours."

As soon as the boy was aboard, the captain asked, "Won't you sell the sword to me?"

"No. But I will trade it for one of the folding screens I see on board."

The captain shrugged. Taking the sword, he gave the boy a broken old screen. The only pretty thing about it were the birds painted upon it. As soon as the boy was back on land, the captain tried to get the sword to turn into a snake. But it would not turn into a snake for him. It remained a dull old sword no matter what he did.

Meanwhile, the boy traveled on with his screen to the palace of the king. There he set up the screen and lay down to rest. As soon as he was asleep, all the painted birds began to sing so sweetly it caught the attention of the king.

"Sell me that wonderful screen," he commanded.

"I am sorry, but I cannot sell it," the boy replied. "However, I will trade it for this: all the waves of the sea and all the water in your realm."

The king was sure the boy was a madman, but he had a scroll made out certifying that the boy was now the owner of all the water in the land and in the sea.

Ah, but a law, no matter how lightly made, was still a law. Soon the king learned that every time his people wanted to use any water, the boy collected a fee from them. The people went to the king to complain about this ridiculous new tax.

"What can I do?" the king wondered. "I made the law myself!"

So he sent for the boy and tried to buy back the rights to his land's water.

"I'm sorry," the boy told him, "but I will not sell them. I will, however, ask you two questions. And if you can answer them correctly, I will give up all rights to the water. My first question: Who was it who was so easily distracted by painted birds that he bargained away something of such price?"

"I was," the king muttered. "What is your second question?"

"Who was it who had no pity on his wife, on my mother, because his workmen, even as was the king, were distracted?"

The king's eyes widened. "You are my son!" he gasped. "I have regretted my cruel, foolish deed all these years. Now, if you will let the water run freely, I will give up my throne, and you shall rule in my place."

"The water is free to all," the boy said. And from that day on, he ruled, and ruled wisely and well.

The Boyhood of Finn

A Tale from Ireland

In the long-ago days of the druids, the warrior Cumhail, who was the leader of the Fianna, the royal war-band, fell in love with the maiden Murna, and she with him. Alas, her father most certainly did not approve of the match and her father was a druid, powerful in the court and in magic. Cumhail and Murna fled, but Murna's father went straight to the warrior Goll mac Morna, who was of a clan that was enemy to Cumhail's own.

"Cumhail has stolen away my daughter," he told Goll, and a druid's will was behind the words. "Avenge my honor. Avenge her honor. Show yourself a true warrior of your clan and slay Cumhail."

Goll mac Morna could not resist the will of the druid. He went after Cumhail and slew him. But Murna was already bearing Cumhail's child. When her father's magic told him this, he was furious that any trace of Cumhail's blood should survive. Murna fled into the forest, and there she bore her child, a son.

"I dare not let the world know about him," she knew, "or my father will surely kill him."

So she gave her son, whom she named Demne, into the safe-keeping of two wise women, Bodhmall and Liath Luachra. Some say they were of the druid class, others merely that they were clever in woodscraft and weaponry. Whatever the way of it may be, little Demne grew up in the forest, secure under their never-

94

flagging watch. It was no easy schooling they gave him, training him as sternly as ever warriors were trained in hunting, swimming, running after prey, with never a moment of pity shown to him but never a blow given to him without reason.

And Demne grew under that harsh, just rearing—grew and thrived, a tall, agile youngster with hair so fair it was nearly white. One thing only he knew nothing about, and that was his true name and origin, for Bodhmall and Liath Luachra meant to keep him safe as long as possible. Restless with his lonely forest life, the boy wandered out from the woodland to play with others of his age.

It was not the best of things for him to try. But then, what could Demne know about the jealousy of others? Once he found a lake where a group of noble boys were swimming and greeted them cheerfully.

"I shall swim with you," he told them.

But the boys saw only his rough clothing. "Go away, you peasant!" they shouted.

Demne only jumped in with them and began swimming. The two wise women had taught him to swim as swiftly as a trout. And when the other boys saw his skill, they were so jealous they tried to drown him, nine of them to his one. Demne ducked them all and vanished into the forest, shaking his head at the stupidity of them.

But he was still lonely. Demne tried again to fit in, travelling all the way to the plain of the Liffey, where another group of noble boys were playing that rough game of ball known as hurling.

"Let me play," Demne said.

But the boys only shouted, "Go away, peasant!"

Demne joined in anyhow, and defeated one and all. But his fine, fair hair caught the sunlight—and the attention of an older man who had been watching the boys play.

"What is your name?" he asked Demne.

"Why, I am called Demne," the boy replied.

"No, no, with that fair hair your name should best be Finn," the old man proclaimed, and Finn, which means "fair," or "fair-haired," Demne was from then on.

But all this while the druidical father of Murna had not forgotten about his grandson. Bodhmall and Liath Luachra realized he had found out they had been sheltering Finn, and they sat him down and bluntly told him who and what he really was. Then they sent him forth into the world to find his fortune at the High King's court.

But before he reached the court, Finn came upon a second Finn, this one an aged man fishing intently on the banks of the River Boyne.

"What are you hunting so fiercely?" Finn asked him.

The old man glanced sharply up at him. "The Salmon of Knowledge, boy, the Salmon of Knowledge that swims in this river. For seven long years I have been trying and trying to catch the creature and Aha! You have brought me luck!"

Soon the old man had netted the Salmon of Knowledge and set it to cooking. But he was so weary from his long trial that he quickly fell asleep, warning Finn just before his eyes closed, "Keep a stern watch. Do not let the fish burn. When it is done, wake me at once. And do not, do you hear me, do not take even the tiniest bit of a taste of that fish!"

"I will not," Finn agreed.

But as he cooked the salmon, Finn let out a yelp of pain. He'd burned his thumb! Without thinking about it, he stuck the burned thumb into his mouth to soothe it—and a strange new flood of wisdom rushed into his head.

The old man woke with a start. "What is it? What happened? Did you eat the fish?"

"I did not," Finn said sharply. "But I did burn my thumb and stuck it in my mouth. I guess a little of the juice from the salmon was on that thumb, because—"

"No, no, no!" the old man screamed. But then he sighed and

started to walk away. "By that taste, you have won the wisdom of the Salmon of Knowledge," he called over his shoulder. "You'd might as well eat the whole fish."

And from that day on, whenever Finn had need of special wisdom, all he needed to do was place his thumb in his mouth as though he'd just burned it.

On went Finn on his journey. For a time he tarried with a smith, learning the art of working iron, the one art the two wise women who had raised him had never taught him. He went away from that smith with a powerful spear, one so hungry for blood it needed to have its point hidden in a hood like a hunting falcon.

At last, Finn reached the court of High King Cormac mac Art, where he boldly declared, "I am Finn mac Cumhail, and I have come to take back the leadership of the Fianna."

All the assembled warriors roared with laughter at the thought of this untried boy making such a boast—all but two. Goll, he who had slain Cumhail and led the Fianna, did not laugh, but watched Finn with a speculative eye.

Nor did the High King laugh. Tomorrow was the autumn solstice, and he was saddened by the thought of what happened every autumn solstice evening. Each year on that very night, an otherworldly creature known as Aillen would appear, playing such magical music that even the fiercest of warriors had no choice but to sleep. As soon as all the human folk were asleep, Aillen would burn down the royal fortress by his sorcery.

"I shall put an end to this creature," Finn promised. "And thus I shall prove my worthiness to you and the Fianna."

That night, Finn stood guard alone, watching and waiting, his blood-hungry spear at his side. Soon a strange, shadowy shape appeared out of the darkness, and Finn knew this must surely be Aillen. The creature coaxed the softest, sleepiest of music from his harp, and even Finn, tense and alert though he was, found himself starting to yawn. Hastily, he pulled the hood from the head of the blood-hungry spear, pressing his head against the cold iron. And the blood-hungry song the spear hummed shattered his sleepiness and kept him awake.

When Aillen saw that one human had not fallen under his sleep-spell, he started in angry surprise. With a great blast of air, he breathed a sudden blaze of fire at Finn. The young man just barely managed to dodge the worst of that fiery attack, and hastily beat out the flames with his cloak. Then, before Aillen could draw another breath, Finn snatched up his spear.

What was this? Aillen stared in disbelief. In all the time since he'd first discovered the humans, never had he come under attack, never! Shocked to the heart of him by this sudden reversing of events, Aillen turned and fled.

"I can't let him get away," Finn told himself. "If the creature escapes me now, this will all need to be done over again next year."

And next year Aillen just might win. So Finn raced after him like a famished wolf after a deer. Just as Aillen reached the hollow hill out of which he had come, Finn drew back his spear, his blood-hungry spear, and hurled it with all his strength. And that blood-hungry weapon pierced Aillen through and slew him.

Finn returned to High King Cormac with the head of Aillen. Holding up his gristly trophy, he asked the king, "Am I not worthy of the honor I claim? Am I not worthy of leading the Fianna?"

"You are, indeed," the High King said with a touch of wonder in his voice. To Finn's amazement, Goll mac Morna, whom he'd thought to have to fight, solemnly agreed with this royal verdict.

And so Finn mac Cumhail at last came into his inheritance. Many brave deeds were performed by him and the Fianna, and some darker deeds as well, but those were still in the future. For now, he had proven himself a worthy leader of the Fianna, and Finn mac Cumhail was satisfied.

Cap O'Rushes

A Tale from England

Once upon a time there lived a wealthy lord who was as foolish as he was rich. He had three daughters, Mary, Margaret, and Ann, and one day took it into his head to test them to see how much they loved him. So he called the first daughter, the oldest, Mary, to him and asked, "How much do you love me?"

"I love you as my life," she replied quickly.

"That's good, that's very good," the lord said with a smile, and called the second daughter, the second oldest, Margaret, to him and asked again, "How much do you love me?"

"I love you more than all the world," she told him quickly.

"That's very, very good," the lord said with a smile, and called the third daughter, the youngest, Ann, to him and asked yet again, "How much do you love me?"

"Why, I love you as meat loves salt," she told him.

"What manner of answer is this?" the lord roared. "You don't love me at all! And you shall not stay here, no, not a moment longer!"

With that, he drove the poor girl right out of his house.

Well now, there she was, a girl used to fine things and kind words, out in the cold, rough world with not a penny to her name. Did she weep? Did she bemoan her fate and plead to be forgiven?

Oh, most certainly she did not! "If my father will not have

me," Ann said to herself, "then I must earn my fortune for myself."

But she knew the cold, rough world was no place for a pretty young woman to wander alone. So off Ann went to a nearby fen, and picked herself rushes, which she wove into an ugly hood and cloak that hid her face and form and fine clothing. On the girl travelled till she came at last to a fine mansion, and went around back to the servants' entrance.

"Do you have any work for a willing pair of hands?" she asked.

"We have a place for someone to wash the pots and scrape the pans," they told her.

"Good enough," Ann said cheerfully. "At least I will have food and shelter," she added to herself. "And as for more than that, well, we shall see what we shall see."

They asked the girl her name, but she would answer to nothing but Cap O'Rushes. And Cap O'Rushes she became, cleaning pots and pans without complaint, doing whatever kitchen work was asked of her.

Now, the young lord of the mansion, the master's son, loved to dance. And one day news came down to the kitchen that he was going to attend a grand ball, and all the servants were allowed to come along and see all the fine, noble people. Only Cap O'Rushes refused.

"I am too tired," she told the servants. "I will stay at home."

But as soon as everyone was gone, she hurriedly removed her rushy disguise, washed her dirty face, and went off to the ball in her fine noblewoman's gown.

Well now, what should happen but that she and the young lord should see each other, and dance with each other, and look deep into each other's eyes. "What is your name?" the young lord asked. "Where are you from?"

Cap O'Rushes only smiled and said nothing. Seeing that smile, the young lord decided then and there that he would dance with no one else.

But as soon as the dance was done, Cap O'Rushes slipped away. Hurrying back to the kitchen, she was dressed in her rushy disguise once more, curled up as though asleep.

Next morning, she listened to all the servants gossip about the ball, and about the beautiful stranger with whom the young lord had danced. "No one knows who she was! Even the young lord couldn't learn her name. But she was very beautiful, indeed."

"I should like to have seen her," Cap O'Rushes said with a smile.

"Well now, there's to be another ball next month. Perhaps she will be there."

On the night of the ball, Cap O'Rushes again pretended to be too tired to see the fine nobles. But once more, she threw off her rushy disguise and hurried to the ball. Once more she and the young lord danced happily together. "What is your name?" he asked again. "Please tell me."

But Cap O'Rushes still wouldn't tell him. And once more she slipped away after the dance was done, and hurried back to the kitchen. Once more she pretended to be sound asleep by the time the servants came home.

Next morning, she listened to all their gossip. "And the beautiful stranger was there again!" they said. "But once more she slipped away before the young lord could even learn her name."

"I should like to have seen her," Cap O'Rushes said with a smile.

"You have one more chance," the servants told her. "There is to be a third ball a month from now."

But on the night of the ball, Cap O'Rushes once more pretended to be too tired to see the fine nobles. Once again, she left her rushy disguise and hurried to the ball in her noblewoman's gown.

The young lord was overjoyed to see her again. "Please, please, tell me your name," he begged.

Cap O'Rushes only smiled and shook her head. The young lord pulled a ring from his hand and gave it to her. "Keep this so you will not forget me," he told her, "for if I don't see you again, I think I shall die."

"No one yet ever died of love," Cap O'Rushes said.

And before the dance was quite over, she had slipped away yet again, and was back in the kitchen and pretending to be asleep long before the servants returned.

Well now, the young lord tried this and that, looked here and there, hunting any clue as to his mysterious lady, but look where he might, try what he would, he could find not the slightest hair from her head. He grew wan and weak for love of her, and at last he took to his bed.

Down in the kitchen, the servants heard of the young lord's illness.

"We must make some gruel for the young lord," said the cook. "He is dying for love of his lost lady."

"No one yet ever died of love," Cap O'Rushes said. "Let me make the gruel. I have a secret recipe that will return his health to him."

So the cook let her make the gruel. Cap O'Rushes slipped the young lord's ring into it and waited as the cook took the gruel upstairs.

The young lord drank the gruel, and found the ring at the bottom. "Who made this gruel?" he cried.

The cook was sure something had been wrong with the gruel. Now the young lord was going to punish her! "I—I did."

"You did not. Come, tell me who did. I promise you shall not be harmed."

"Oh, then, it was Cap O'Rushes. We call her that," the cook added. "Don't know her real name."

"Send for her. Now."

So Cap O'Rushes stood there in that fine room in her ugly, rushy disguise, staring at the young lord.

"Did you make my gruel?" he asked.

"I did."

"Where did you get this ring?"

"From him that gave it to me."

The young man trembled. "Who are you, then?"

"Don't you know me?" Cap O'Rushes asked, and took off her rushy cap. The young man gave a cry of joy and caught her in his arms, rushy cloak and all.

Well, the young lord was soon quite healthy again. He and Cap O'Rushes, now finely dressed Ann once more, were to be wed in a grand ceremony. Noble folk from all over the land were invited, and one of those who accepted the invitation was Ann's own father.

"I want you to prepare his meat without a single grain of salt," she told the cook.

"That'll be a nasty thing," said the cook.

"So it will," Ann agreed, "but just for a short while."

She and her young lord were wed, and at the wedding banquet everyone rejoiced all save for Ann's father, who took one bite of his meat and began to weep.

Ann pulled her hood forward to hide her face. "What is wrong?" she asked.

"Once upon a time I had a daughter," he told her, "and I, fool that I was, asked her how much she loved me. She told me, 'As meat loves salt.' And I, fool that I was, thought that meant she didn't love me. I threw her out of my home, the finest, truest of my daughters, with nothing more than the clothes she was wearing. By now, for all I know, the poor, miserable girl may even be dead!"

"No, Father. She is not dead or miserable at all. She is alive and here, and very, very happy."

With that, Ann threw back her hood. Her father gave a great shout of joy, and he and she embraced.

And from that day on, they all lived quite happy ever after.

Donkey-Skin

———————— A Tale from France ————————

Once, long ago, there was a nobleman whose wife was very beautiful. But, alas, she died soon after giving him a daughter, whom they named Marie. As she died, the lady caught her husband by the hand and told him, "Marry no one save someone as beautiful as I."

Who can tell why she said such a thing? But those were her dying words, and the nobleman took them to heart.

Years passed. As the young girl grew, she came to look more and more like her mother. And at last she was of the age her mother had been when the nobleman had first met her. And since Marie looked so very much like her mother, the nobleman decided she and she alone was the one he must marry.

Marie was horrified. What, a father marry his daughter? It must never be! But her father would not listen to her pleas, so off she hurried to her godmother. A strange woman was that. Some said she must surely have the gift of prophesy. Some even called her a fairy godmother.

"What am I to do?" Marie asked her godmother. "I cannot marry my own father!"

"Don't hurry to decide," her godmother told Marie. "First you must ask your father for the three most beautiful gowns in all the world, and see what he does."

Strange advice. But Marie went to her father and told him, "I cannot think of marriage unless I own the three most beautiful gowns in all the world."

Her father sent his men out hunting through all the markets near and far. They returned with a gown that glowed as softly silver as the moon.

"This is only one gown," Marie said. "I must have three."

Her father sent his men out hunting through all the markets yet again. They returned with a gown that blazed as brightly golden as the sun.

"These are only two gowns," Marie said. "I must have three."

"You are bringing me to ruin!" her father cried. "These gowns are worth the ransom of a prince!"

"I must have three," Marie insisted, "or I shall never agree to wed."

With a sigh, her father sent his men out hunting through all the markets once again. Days passed, weeks passed. And at last they returned with a gown that sparkled like a field of diamonds.

Poor Marie went hurrying off to her godmother. "He has found me the three most beautiful gowns in all the world!" she cried. "Now what can I do? I cannot marry him!"

"And you shall not," her godmother said firmly. "Instead, you shall run away from him. You shall take with you this little magic chest, which shall, at your command, hide underground so none shall see it, and this little wand, which shall, at your command, bring it back to you, wherever you are. In the chest you shall hide away the beautiful gowns till you need them."

"But where shall I go? What shall I do?"

"You shall go where fate takes you, and do what you must do. But a beautiful girl must not travel the world without disguise. You must dress in rags like any beggar, and wear an ugly donkey-skin over that."

So Marie ran away from her father and her home dressed in rags, with the donkey-skin flapping and flopping around her and the ears waggling down over her face. The only things she took with her were the magic wand and the little chest with the three beautiful gowns inside.

She wandered here, she wandered there. And at last she showed up on the estate of the king himself, and asked to be allowed to work for her keep. Since she looked so ragged and dirty in her donkey-skin, she was given the lowly task of tending the turkeys. And soon Marie was even more dirty-looking than before, so very dirty that she caught the eye of the prince.

"Who are you, you ugly creature?" he called from his window.

"I am Donkey-Skin," she told him.

"A pretty name for a pretty girl!" the prince taunted and laughed.

Now, it was usual for a servant who watched over this type of animal or that to do something else as well to pass the time. Some would knit, some would sew. Donkey-Skin made lace, just as she had when she was Marie living in her father's house. Such fine lace she made that the steward of the farm saw it and granted her a little room of her own in which to sleep. As soon as she was alone in that room, Donkey-Skin called up the little chest from underground and tapped it with the magic wand.

"Open," she said, and open it did, revealing the three most beautiful gowns in the world. That night, and every night, Donkey-Skin would bathe and dress in one of her beautiful gowns.

But every morning, she was no one but the lowly, dirty Donkey-Skin again.

One cold winter's day, Donkey-Skin stopped in the royal kitchen to huddle on the hearth for warmth. The prince passed by and frowned.

"Keep away from me, you ugly, dirty creature," he said, and gave her a poke with a poker to keep her from soiling his fine clothes.

That night was the first of a three-night royal ball. When

everyone else had gone off to attend it, Donkey-Skin called up the little chest and tapped it with the magic wand.

"Open," she said, and the chest opened. Donkey-Skin bathed and combed out her hair and dressed herself in the gown that glowed like moonlight.

Off she went to the ball. As she entered, everyone turned to stare, the prince most of all. He went straight to her and asked her to dance with him. When the dance had ended, he asked her name.

"I am called Poke with a Poker," Donkey-Skin told him.

The prince laughed. Surely this lovely lady was joking with him! "A goodly name!" he said. "I'll remember it!"

But Donkey-Skin slipped away before he could ask her anything else.

The next morning, the prince wandered over the estate, telling everyone he saw about the lovely stranger he'd met at the ball.

"No more lovely than I," murmured Donkey-Skin from where she huddled on the hearth.

"Be still, Donkey-Skin!" the prince snapped. Grabbing up the bellows, he blew a blast of air at her and stalked away.

The second night of the royal ball arrived. Again, Donkey-Skin waited till everyone else was attending it, then bathed and combed out her hair and told the little chest, "Open." Dressing herself in the gown that blazed like the sun, she went off to the ball.

Once more everyone stared at her, the prince most of all. Once more he asked her to dance. And when the dance was over, he asked her for her name.

"I am called Bellows Blast," Donkey-Skin told him.

The prince laughed. How this lovely lady jested! "A clever name," he said. "I'll remember it."

The next day, the prince wandered once more all over the estate, telling everyone about the lovely stranger.

"No more lovely than I," muttered Donkey-Skin.

"Be still, Donkey-Skin!" the prince shouted, and struck her with a stick.

The third night of the royal ball arrived. Donkey-Skin waited till everyone else was gone, then bathed herself, combed out her hair, and told the little chest, "Open." She dressed in the gown that sparkled like a field of diamonds and went off to the ball.

Once more, everyone stared at the lovely girl, the prince most of all. Once more, he asked her to dance. When the dance was over, he asked for her name.

"And this time, please, no jests."

But Donkey-Skin only smiled. "I am called Struck with a Stick," she said.

Before the prince could know what had happened, she had fled. In the days that followed, the beautiful stranger never appeared again. Ah, and what a change there was in the haughty prince! Haughty no longer, he wandered the estate like a ghost, sick for love of the one he could not find. At last he took to his bed.

"Poke with a Poker," he murmured. "Bellows Blast." And then the prince stopped short. "I wonder . . . no, it it couldn't be. And yet: 'Struck with a Stick'. I have been so cruel to poor Donkey-Skin. Dirty and ugly though she is, I had no right to poke her with a poker or blast her with a bellows or strike her with a stick. Could it be? Could it be?"

He grew so ill with worry he could eat no food, drink no drink. At last his frightened servants asked him what he *would* eat.

"Soup," the prince said. "But soup made by Donkey-Skin, and Donkey-Skin only."

So off the servants went to the kitchen to tell Donkey-Skin she must make some soup for the poor, sick prince.

"So now, he is figuring out my little puzzle," Donkey-Skin

realized. "But I can hardly make any decent soup as dirty as I am."

She hurried off to her little room to bathe and change into one of the beautiful gowns, since they were the only clean clothing she owned. But the prince, weak and sick though he was, stole after her. Peering through the keyhole, he saw her tell the little chest, "Open," and take out the beautiful gowns.

"Open the door, Donkey-Skin!" the prince cried. "Open the door, Poke with a Poker, Bellows Blast, Struck with a Stick. Open the door so I may say how sorry I am for what I've done—and how much I love you!"

Donkey-Skin opened the door. "I forgive you," she said. "And I love you, too."

Together they ate the soup she had made. Together they wed. And together they were very happy.

Here is written in the Feänorian characters according-
ing to the mode of Beleriand: Ennyn Durin Aran
Moria: pedo mellon a minno. Im Narvi hain ech-
ant: Celebrimbor o Eregion teithant i thiw hin.

Courtesy of Houghton Mifflin

Drawing by J.R.R. Tolkien of the Doors of Durin in *Lord of the Rings*.

Part Four

"One Ring to Rule Them All . . ."

In a faraway world where humans and the small folk known as hobbits share a wary truce and ancient, magical peoples such as elves linger in the forests, a being of total evil dwells in his dark fortress. He hunts the one great Ring of Power that will allow him to complete his conquest of all that is good. Against him stand the merged forces of those who refuse to let evil triumph. But unless the ring itself, with its chill, seductive call, can be destroyed, no army will be able to withstand the darkness. And no army can hope to pierce the terrible fortress. Only by stealth can two brave hobbits fulfill their quest to return the ring to the fire that forged it, and with that fire, destroy it.

When J.R.R. Tolkien's fantasy trilogy, *The Lord of The Rings,* and its "prequel," *The Hobbit,* were first published in the United States in paperback editions in the 1960s, they were devoured by thousands of readers hungry for tales of epic heroes, magic, and wondrous adventures. Up till then, such tales had been all but totally missing from bookstores and libraries.

But Professor Tolkien, who was thoroughly familiar with Anglo-Saxon and other Northern European cultures and their folk literatures, was deliberately drawing on such earlier sources when he created Middle Earth and its inhabitants. Many books have been written that discuss his various inspirations, but three of the most basic, most universal folkloric themes that turn up in *The Lord of the Rings* are "The Quest," "The Magic Ring," and "The Broken Sword, or the Sword in the Stone."

I.

The Broken Sword
or
The Sword in the Stone

Swords of various types and enchantments turn up in the folklore of every sword-wielding people. Some blades, such as Durendal, the weapon said to have belonged to the French hero Roland, are famous for their owners' deeds but have no actual magic of their own, while other swords bear enchantments to keep their owners safe or destroy their enemies. All folkloric blades, enchanted or not, grant their wielders great fame, particularly if the sword has been given to a hero by his deity.

The motif of a broken sword that must be reforged is less common in world folklore, but it does turn up in Northern European tales. There's an obvious symbolic value to such a broken blade: the hero's honor has been similarly damaged (not always through his own fault), and must be restored by the sword's reforging, either by him or his heir.

The Sword in the Stone:
The Coming of Arthur

A Tale from Great Britain

When Uther Pendragon was King of England, he fell madly, mindlessly, in love with the Lady Igraine, wife to the Duke of Tintagel. When Igraine refused the king's suit, he turned to magic to win the lady for him. Calling upon Merlin, the mightiest—if most mysterious—magician in the land, he said, "If I may not have that lady, it shall be the death of me."

Merlin agreed to help the king, but for his own reasons. His magic had already told him the son of Uther and Igraine would prove to be the greatest ruler the land had ever known. So, whatever private misgivings he might have felt about using his Art for trickery (if, indeed, he had any such misgivings at all, being the son, some said, of a nun and a devil), Merlin transformed Uther into a likeness of Igraine's husband.

"You must promise me this first," he told Uther, his eyes wild with Power. "You must give me your firstborn child for me to do with as I see fit."

Uther laughed. A child was in the future, and his longing for Igraine was here and now. "I agree," he said shortly.

And when the disguised king came to the lady's chambers, she let him enter.

Not long after, the Duke of Tintagel died in combat. Uther's deception was revealed to Igraine, but when he offered her his hand in honorable marriage, she agreed, for she was already with child. When the child, a fine, healthy boy was born, Merlin appeared from nowhere and everywhere, and claimed him.

"His fame shall be wide-spread," he promised the grieving parents. "And his name shall be Arthur."

Merlin was not as cold-hearted as he might have seemed, carrying off the newborn babe. He had already seen that Uther had not much longer to live. With the king dead, what man would dare support the claim of a mere child—and one who had been started outside of marriage?

So Merlin carried the baby Arthur safely away, and found him fosterage with an honest friend, Sir Ector. But the magician told no one, not even Ector, of the parentage of the babe, only bade the nobleman raise the boy like his own son.

"I promise," Sir Ector agreed, then looked about in surprise, for Merlin had already disappeared.

So the years passed. Sir Ector was true to his word, and raised Arthur along with his own son, Kay, proud to see them both grow into strong, tall, handsome young men. Kay, however, was an arrogant youngster, one who never quite let Arthur forget that he was a nameless nobody while Kay was Sir Ector's flesh-and-blood.

Meanwhile, as Merlin had known, many factions of nobles fought for the empty throne. So the magician sent word to the Archbishop that all the noblemen in the land should come to London at Christmastide. "And then God will show us who shall be the true King of England."

The Archbishop may have had his doubts: no man knew if Merlin was a good Christian, or indeed any sort of a Christian at all. But he agreed that anything that brought peace to the troubled land was a fine thing.

When the nobles all assembled in London to attend the grand church there, they found a wonder waiting in the churchyard: a huge stone that seemed to have appeared there by magic. Set into this stone was an anvil, and embedded in this anvil was a naked sword. And on that sword, in blazing golden letters, were the words, "Whosoever pulleth this sword from this stone is rightly King of England."

Oh, there was not a one of those nobles who didn't promptly try his hand at pulling out that sword! But not a one of them could budge it as much as a hairsbreadth. There was much grumbling about that, and not a few mentions of that dark word, sorcery. But what sorcery could be worked within a churchyard?

New Year's Day came around, and with it, the great winter tourney. Sir Ector was there, with Kay, already newly dubbed knight, and Arthur, serving as Kay's squire. It was just before the tourney was to begin that Kay discovered to his shock that he'd left his sword at the inn.

"Hurry!" he cried to Arthur. "Fetch it for me!"

Arthur set off with a will—only to find the inn bolted shut while everyone was at the tourney. What could he do? Kay could hardly take part in a tourney without his sword!

Hardly stopping to think about it (after all, a mere squire hadn't been near enough to the sword in the stone to read the wondrous words, or even see the useless attempts to free the blade), Arthur hurried to the churchyard. He would borrow this sword, he told himself, and replace it after the tourney with none the wiser. So the young man closed his hand about the sword's hilt and pulled.

It came free without the slightest hesitation.

As soon as Kay saw the sword, he recognized it and hurried to his father. "Here is the sword from the stone. I must be King of England!"

Sir Ector paled. "How did you come by this sword? The truth, on your knighthood."

Kay sighed. "Arthur brought it to me."

If it were possible for Sir Ector to pale still more, so he did.

"Arthur, tell me the truth as well: How did you come by this sword?"

"Why, I pulled it from the stone. Have I done wrong?"

"Were you seen by anyone?"

"No, my lord, no one was about."

Ector took Arthur by the arm. "Hurry, back to the church-yard. Put the sword back in the stone, then show me that you can draw it forth again."

"No easier thing," Arthur said.

But when he drew the sword from the stone a second time, he cried out in dismay to see Sir Ector and Kay kneel before him. "You were a father to me, and you, a brother!"

"But now we know your true father," Sir Ector said. "He was surely Uther Pendragon—for you are most surely King of England." There were yet the nobles to be convinced. But after many trials, they saw that Arthur and Arthur alone was the only man who could pull the sword from the stone. And all the people cried, "We will have Arthur for our king!"

It was then that Merlin appeared, as mysteriously as ever, to tell how Arthur was, indeed, the son of the late King Uther, and the rightful heir to the throne. The Archbishop, glad to see the end of civil strife, crowned Arthur king that very day.

And so began the wondrous reign, the fame of which was to echo down throughout the ages.

The Sword is Broken:
The First Part of the Volsung Saga

———— A Tale from Norse Mythology ————

In the dark, ancient days when gods and men often met on mortal soil, there lived King Volsung and his nine children, the youngest of which were the twins, Sigmund the warrior and his sister, Signy.

As time passed and Signy grew to lovely young womanhood, she was betrothed by Volsung to Siggeir, lord of the Goths, a cruel, cold man but a powerful one: a valuable ally, or so Volsung thought. Alas, no one thought to ask Signy how she felt about such a wedding. But a princess grows up knowing she must wed whomever is chosen for her. And a daughter of Volsung would hold true to her marriage vows and her husband even if there would be no spark of love between them.

The wedding feast of Siggeir and Signy took place in the Goth lord's great hall, which had been built around the support of the mighty oak known as Branstock. As the festivities were at their highest (and perhaps no one noticed that only Signy and her twin, Sigmund, lacked for genuine joy), a poorly clad stranger entered the hall, his one eye glittering from beneath his slouch hat. In one hand he bore a sword that blazed with light, dazzling all who saw it. Everyone within that hall froze in wonder as the stranger approached Branstock. Without a word, he thrust the gleaming blade so deeply into the trunk of the vast oak that the sword was buried up to its hilt.

"The sword belongs to he who can draw it forth," the stranger said shortly, and strode off before a man could think to block his path.

"It was Odin," ran the whispers. "Who else could it have been?" Everyone knew the one-eyed king of the gods often roamed the earth in such a guise. "And the sword must surely be Odin's sword!"

The hall erupted with excitement then. What warrior would not wish to bear the weapon of a god? First to try his hand at the wondrous prize was Siggeir himself. But to his red-faced rage, he could stir the blade not at all. Nor could any of his men best his effort, or any of Volsung's sons—save one. When Sigmund closed his hand about the hilt, the gleaming sword pulled free from the tree as sweetly as though from a scabbard.

"Odin's sword is mine," Sigmund said, and perhaps there was a note of surprise mixed in with the pride.

Siggeir said nothing. But envy tore at his heart till he could think of nothing else but the sword. At last the lord of the Goths vowed to himself that Odin's sword would be, *must be* his, no matter how high the cost.

And so Siggeir set a treacherous ambush for Volsung and his sons. All fell to the fatal trap save Sigmund himself, who was taken alive and spared from being slain on the spot by Signy's desperate pleas to her husband.

"He is my twin brother, now my only brother, my only kin! I beg you, let him live."

After a long moment of silence, Siggeir agreed, "He shall not meet his death at my hands."

But the Goth lord, even while he was pretending mercy, secretly had Sigmund bound to a tree in the forest and left him there for the wolves to devour. Odin's sword he took for his own, and sat alone in his chambers, studying its gleaming length and gloating.

When Signy learned from a maidservant what her husband had done, she knew there was no time to waste in mourning her lost kin. Instead, she rushed out into the night-dark forest, seeking the only brother who might still be alive.

And she found Sigmund torn and exhausted but alive. He had managed to free himself from his bonds just in time to fight off the wolves barehanded, his determination to survive as his father's last heir granting him strength. For several years he lived on in the wilderness, visited secretly by Signy, looking for a chance to take back Odin's sword.

At last the chance came. Sure none of Volsung's race remained save for his wife, Siggeir let down his guard. Sigmund, fierce as a wolf, stole into the Goth lord's fortress, narrowly escaping imprisonment and death, and closed his hand about Odin's sword with the slightest, gladdest of sighs. Then he slipped back outside, bolting the doors fast behind him, and set fire to the fortress to avenge the deaths of his father and brothers. Siggeir died in that blaze—but so, alas, did Signy. Bound by her honor and marriage vows, she rushed back into the fortress to die with her husband.

Grieving, Sigmund went his way, returning at last to his father's land. There, last of King Volsung's heirs, Sigmund became king in his own right, and Odin's sword served him well in all the years that followed.

But Sigmund's tale was not yet done. One thing only did he lack, and that was most vital for a king: an heir. His first wife had left him without a child. So Sigmund wooed and won a second wife, the wise young Hiordis, who was pleased to wed so famed a warrior, even if he was no longer young.

But Hiordis had another suitor, a king named Lynge. Lynge was young and handsome and could hardly believe any woman could refuse him. When he learned that Hiordis had spurned his suit, had actually dared wed another, he shouted with rage.

"I shall claim her. I shall claim Hiordis as my own even if it means war!"

And war it was. Sigmund went against Lynge in single combat. And although Sigmund was no longer young, he was wise in the ways of battle, while Lynge, though he was young, was yet untried. And so Sigmund, Odin's gleaming sword in his hand, would surely have won. But just when the victory seemed most certain, just when Lynge was staggering back from his foe's attack, eyes wild with panic, Sigmund froze, staring at the sight of the one-eyed stranger standing quietly to one side, watching the combat, leaning on a spear. Sorrow glinted in that single eye.

But Lynge, puzzled by his enemy's sudden pause, was gathering himself for the attack. Ignoring the stranger as best he could, Sigmund lunged. But the stranger pointed with his spear, tapping Sigmund's blade—and the gleaming sword, Odin's sword, shattered. It was at Odin's will he had survived so long, but now the god had come to take Sigmund with him to Valhalla.

And so, at Odin's will, death came to Sigmund, last king of the Volsungs.

The Sword Reforged:
The Second Part of the Volsung Saga

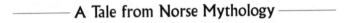

───── **A Tale from Norse Mythology** ─────

King Sigmund, last of the Volsung rulers, was dead, slain by his rival, King Lynge in the battle over Queen Hiordis, Sigmund's wife, and the sword of Odin lay in fragments.

But Hiordis, who was bearing Sigmund's child, refused to be Lynge's prize. Taking the shattered sword with her, she fled across the sea to Denmark, where she wed Prince Alf and bore her baby, Sigmund's son, whom she named Sigurd.

Sigurd grew to be a strong, handsome boy who was apprenticed to the nonhuman Dwarf, Regin, a subtle, mysterious being but a master blacksmith. Regin taught the boy the many ways of iron and steel, of music and hunting. But Regin's heart was dark, his thoughts bitter. Deliberately, never letting any know his secret plots, he stirred in Sigurd the longing for battle and brave deeds, the longing, too, to find his own land, his own kin.

"Remember," Regin whispered to him, "you are not Alf's son; you can never inherit his throne nor be other than a servant to his sons." And, "Remember," Regin whispered to Sigurd, "you are the son of Sigmund the King, and as such are destined for great deeds."

"What deeds are there for me to do?" Sigurd exclaimed in despair. "There is nothing left for a hero here!"

Regin smiled a slow, subtle smile. "Ah, but there is," he said. "There is one deed that would in one stroke right an ancient wrong and win you a wondrous treasure."

"Tell me more!" Sigurd cried.

But for a long while, Regin was silent, on his face the look of one remembering ancient, bitter days. At last he said, "I am the son of no human man, as you know, but of Reidmar the Ancient, of a race less than the gods but far, far older than your kind. Three of us sons there were: Fafnir, Otter and myself. To Fafnir, our father gave the gift of a fearless spirit but a stone-chill heart."

Sigurd shuddered. "That last hardly sounds like a gift to me."

"You are human," Regin snapped. "Listen. To Otter was granted the gift of hunting and snaring whatever he hunted. And to me, the youngest of his sons, he gave the skill in every craft to which I choose to turn my hand. But he gave me as well a bitter gift, for my heart may never know peace, nor may I take pleasure in my skills.

"To all three of us he gave the power to shift shapes at will, though that is not my strongest art."

Once more he was silent for a long, long while. Then Regin roused himself and added, "That shape-shifting gift was the doom of Otter. One day the gods Odin and Loki, that fiery trickster, came to earth. Otter had taken the shape of his namesake and was hunting fish in a stream. Loki saw only Otter's sleek fur, and cast a stone that slew him, slew Otter."

"Ah, what a terrible mistake!"

Regin grinned without humor. "Was it a mistake? Who can say with one like Loki? But it was Loki who was forced by my father, by Reidmar, to bring him ransom for Otter's death. So the Fire God stole away the treasure of Andvari the Dwarf, including a ring on which there lay a terrible curse that brought disaster to whomever owned it.

"The tale of the curse was true. It was Fafnir who won the

ring, and Fafnir who was seized with lust for the treasure. At last he could bear it no longer and struck down his father, our father, and slew him. Before I could even try to stop him (and what could I do, I, the smallest, the youngest, the weakest?), Fafnir had carried off the treasure. Turning himself to a terrible dragon, he coiled around his loot, his breath hot as flame, his eyes cold as death."

Regin paused, watching Sigurd. Sigurd eagerly waved him on. "That treasure was won by murder. It should surely be mine. You, Sigurd, Sigmund's son, are young and strong and fearless. You can win the treasure and end the curse. Will you dare to do this thing?"

"I will, oh, I will! This is truly a hero's deed. But you, Regin, must forge me a sword worthy of that hero."

So Regin set about forging Sigurd a sword cold and sharp as winter ice.

Sigurd took up the sword with pleasure, but when he brought it down against the anvil on which it had been forged, the sword shattered.

"This is a toy!" Sigurd cried in dismay. "Make me a hero's sword."

So Regin set about once more to forge a sword. This one was keen as the winter wind. But when Sigurd smote it against the anvil, it, too, shattered.

"You are no smith," he said in disgust, and stalked off to his mother. "Grant me the shards of Father's sword," Sigurd said, and Hiordis carefully unwrapped them from their protective furs and gave them to him. Sigurd caught his breath at the way the broken sword still gleamed and glittered.

"You have faithfully kept my father's trust in you," he told Hiordis. "And now I take up the responsibility. These shards shall be reforged into a bright new blade. This I promise."

And so Sigurd and Regin together reforged the sword of Odin into a blazing new blade. It flashed like the sun as Sigurd raised it, and when he brought it whistling down upon the anvil, it was the anvil that shattered.

"The sword that was broken is now made whole!" Sigurd cried in triumph. "I name it Gram. And now I shall do deeds worthy of it!"

So Sigurd set out in search of Fafnir with Regin as his guide, travelling for three days through terrible, barren land. But a strange guide was Regin, now there, now gone. And Sigurd was quite alone when he met a strange old man, a one-eyed man who stared at him with awesome power.

"Where are you going, Sigurd?" the old man asked, and Sigurd started at the sound of his name.

"To the lair of the dragon and his stolen treasure," he answered honestly.

"Do you mean to slay that dragon?" asked the stranger.

"Of course, with Gram, my father's sword reforged."

"Then heed my advice. No man may approach the dragon face to face and live, for he breathes fire. You must be subtle. Find yourself the deep track in the desert that marks the trail the dragon has cut on his way to drink. Dig yourself a hole in that trail and wait with drawn sword till the dragon passes over you. Only then can you hope to pierce him to the heart."

"My thanks to you, old one!" Sigurd cried and would have hurried on.

"Wait. When you have slain the dragon, bathe in his blood. Then no weapon will have the power to harm you."

Wonder-struck, Sigurd would have thanked the stranger again—but the stranger had somehow faded into mist and was gone.

"Odin," the young hero murmured in wonder. "That was surely Odin."

He set off on his hunt, and soon had found the deep track the dragon's passing had cut into the desert floor. Sigurd dug himself a pit as the stranger had said, and hid, naked sword in hand. Soon the earth shook and the air grew thick and smoky with fumes from the dragon's fiery breath as Fafnir made his slow, heavy way down to the water. The sky darkened from the mighty shadow he cast, and Sigurd, hidden there in the pit, clutched the hilt of Gram more tightly, his heart racing, knowing he must wait for his one, his only, chance to strike.

Ha, now! The dragon was fully overhead, cutting off all light and air, and Sigurd lunged up with all his might. Gram pierced Fafnir's tough scales and thrust fully into the dragon's heart.

Fafnir reared up with a roar, thrashing about in agony. And then the dragon came crashing back down to the ground and lay still, covering the pit and bathing Sigurd in a reeking shower of his blood. Sigurd endured it, remembering the stranger's words, and the blood covered him totally—save for where a leaf clung to a small patch between his shoulders.

He could stand the hot, choking air no longer. Cutting his way up, Sigurd at last squirmed his way out to freedom. For a time he stood panting, drawing wonderfully clean air into his lungs.

But suddenly Regin was at his side. "You have slain my brother."

Sigurd glanced at him, surprised at the grief in the dwarf's voice. But no grief at all glinted in Regin's eyes. "I have done as you begged me to do," Sigurd said shortly. "But there is treasure enough for two. Take what you would of it as blood-ransom."

Regin gave a long, sad sigh. "He was my brother, no matter how evil his heart had turned. But that heart contains great knowledge as well. Use that sharp sword of yours to cut it out, then roast it for me. Meanwhile I—I must rest."

As though overwhelmed by what had happened, Regin sank to the ground and seemed to fall into weary sleep. Shaking his head, Sigurd cut out the dragon's heart and began roasting it. The sizzling fat spat at his hand, and with a startled oath, he stuck his burned finger in his mouth.

But then Sigurd let his hand fall again, staring about in wonder. As soon as the dragon's blood had touched his tongue, the cries of the eagles circling overhead had become clear as speech.

"Regin has brought a hero here," they called.

"Regin has brought a Volsung-son here."

"Regin has brought a Volsung-hero here to kill him so he alone may claim the treasure."

Sigurd whirled, catching Regin in the act of lunging up with a knife, and brought Gram whistling down. The dwarf crumpled lifelessly to the ground.

"Lie there with your brother," Sigurd muttered. "Treacherous Regin, I would have shared the treasure freely."

He followed the dragon's tracks back to Fafnir's lair. The treasure of Andvari lay there, glittering, glinting, a wondrous mound of gold. As Sigurd stared in amazement, one gleaming ring caught his eye. Not realizing this was none other than the cursed ring of Andvari itself, he slipped the handsome thing on his finger, grinning at how fine it looked on his hand.

But the cries of the eagles made Sigurd look sharply up at them.

"The gold is nothing," they called.

"The gold is cold and hard."

"There is a finer treasure, far finer, to be found, a treasure for a true hero, waiting there on Hindfell. A warm and vibrant treasure, there on Hindfell."

What treasure could this possibly be? Sigurd left the gold where it lay and hurried on, following the eagles. Far he travelled till he came to a great, rough mountain, its peak swathed in eerie reddish light. This was Hindfell, and Sigurd, overwhelmed by curiosity, climbed up and up, till he had reached the very peak. For a moment he paused, looking in wonder at the ring, the ribbon of fire that surrounded the peak like a fiery wall. Beyond was—was what? The treasure must surely lie behind that blazing guard. Taking a deep breath, Sigurd rushed through the flames— but they never burned him, never even scorched his skin. As he passed, they settled down into ash, then vanished altogether.

Before Sigurd stood a smooth marble bier, on which lay a warrior clad in full mail. What could this be? A memorial to some long-dead hero? No, now Sigurd could see that the warrior was very much alive but deep in slumber. Wondering, he approached, then gently removed the warrior's helm.

"A woman!" Sigurd breathed.

She was young and fair, and Sigurd knew in that first stunned moment that he loved her. He touched her, called to her, but she never stirred. At last Sigurd bent and softly kissed her.

The woman's eyelids fluttered open. For a long moment she stared up at Sigurd in wonder, then slowly sat up. "Who are you?" she asked. "Where are you from?"

"I am from the world of human folk," Sigurd answered. "And my name is Sigurd, son of Sigmund, son of Volsung."

"I am Brynhild," the woman said, getting to her feet, then standing joyously enfolded in sunlight. "I have not seen you, oh sun, for far too long!"

Then she turned back to Sigurd, and to his great joy he saw the same love he'd felt for her shining back at him from her eyes. "I am Brynhild," she repeated, "and I was once one of Odin's Valkyries, Choosers of the Slain whose souls were to be taken to Valhalla. I was sent to see that a certain man died in combat. But I pitied him and let him live, and for that disobedience, Odin set me on this mountain peak, here to lie in enchanted slumber till a hero should wake me. Him should I love. And you I do love. Even without the magic spell, I do love you, Sigurd."

And so the sword that was reforged led Sigurd to a hero's deed, a golden treasure, and a wondrous new love.

II.

The Magic Ring

Magic rings, those wondrous creations which, according to their nature, grant wishes, contain or imprison fabulous beings, or control the very forces of the Earth itself, are at least as common in world folklore as tales of swords, and almost as common as quest tales. Magic rings can be found in the tales of every culture that has rings. In some cases, such as in *The Lord of the Rings* or the Norse sagas, the ring may be accursed, an object of darkness or death, but a magic ring is much more likely to be a force for good or an enchanted tool, something to be used by whoever wears it, neither good nor evil in itself.

The Curse of the Ring:
The End of The Volsung Saga

—— A Tale from Norse Mythology ——

Sigurd, last of the Volsung line, and Brynhild, once a Valkyrie
beloved of Odin and now a mortal woman, were joined in
love, living in bliss on Mount Hindfell. But heroes cannot live in
obscurity forever; that is not their fate. And Brynhild was very
much aware of this.

"Your father's slayer still lives," she reminded Sigurd. "There
are still heroic deeds you must do before we may share our happiness in peace."

Sigurd agreed, not without a sigh. Slipping the ring of
Andvari off his hand, never realizing it was the cursed ring of
which Regin had spoken so long ago, he gave it to Brynhild.
"Keep this for me as token of our love, and as a reminder that I
shall return. For that, I swear, I shall do."

Brynhild sank back into slumber so she would more easily
pass the time till her love returned. Sadly, Sigurd left Hindfell,
and Brynhild behind. His search for King Lynge, the man who
had slain his father in combat took him far from his love. At last,
weary and alone, Sigurd came upon the fortress of Queen
Grimhild and asked for hospitality. He was ushered inside, and
brought before the queen herself.

Fair was Grimhild, and friendly to a stranger—or so it

seemed. What hid behind that fair face was a cruel, cold mind full of cunning. She had children, did Grimhild, a son, Gunnar, and a daughter, Gudrun, and she wished this heroic young Sigurd woven into her family's lives. So the welcoming drink she gave him from her own slim hand bore a strange potion within it, and a spell was in her eyes.

Sigurd suspected nothing. He drank . . . and the potion seized his mind, destroying memory. He forgot Brynhild, forgot all but his name and lineage. And when Grimhild brought her daughter, her Gudrun before him, he was seized by the witch-queen's spell and declared his love for the maiden. Soon Sigurd and Gudrun were wed.

But Grimhild was not yet finished with her dark work. Her magic had told her of Brynhild waiting for her love's return, and she thought that this woman, with her strange past and alliances with Odin himself would be a most valuable addition to her family. And so she had Sigurd and her son Gunnar brought before her.

"There is a maiden waiting for you, Gunnar, atop Hindfell. No, do not interrupt, no matter how strange the tale may sound. She waits surrounded by a ring of magic flame, but you and you, Sigurd, may safely pass if you are brave enough."

Sigurd shrugged. He knew he was brave enough, but Gunnar, decent enough but soft and willing to be led, was another matter. "We will do what we can."

"Ah, but wait," said the cunning Grimhild. "A disguise is necessary as well. The maiden wears a magic ring that must be taken from her, and for that, you must not be who you truly are."

And so she changed their likenesses so that Sigurd wore Gunnar's face and form, and Gunnar his. Off they rode to Hindfell, and there Sigurd passed easily through the flames, which died down to ash for him. Gunnar followed more warily, but he was the first to see Brynhild where she lay asleep once more. And he fell instantly in love with her. But the fiery circle had already stolen away his courage, and he dared not wake her.

Sigurd was not afraid. With Grimhild's magic still fogging his mind, Brynhild meant nothing to him. Wearing Gunnar's shape, he woke her by taking the ring, the cursed ring, from her hand. And she, caught in the spell and the curse, could do nothing but agree to wed Gunnar.

And so two couples matched by sorcery lived in Queen Grimhild's fortress, and discord lived with them. So did the curse of the ring.

Gunnar's two other brothers hated him for winning Brynhild. But they hated Sigurd more for being all the heroic things they were not. That hatred burned and burned within them, the flames of it fanned by the evil of the queen and the darkness of the ring. And at last, pretending friendship to lure Sigurd off his guard, they murdered him, striking by chance—or perhaps not really chance—the one spot, the fatal spot, between his shoulderblades where the dragon's blood had not touched him.

And so died the last of the Volsung sons.

As Sigurd's body was brought to the funeral pyre, the spell holding Brynhild's mind captive snapped. At once she knew who she was—and knew what sorrow lay before her. Before any could stop her, she snatched up Gram, that shining blade, and plunged it into her heart. Together she and Sigurd lay upon the funeral pyre, the sword between them, together they lay amid the flames. And together they left the mortal world behind and travelled on to Valhalla.

But the ring, the cursed ring, remained behind. In a short time it was the death of Grimhild, who perished from the breaking of her spell over Sigurd and Brynhild, then Gunnar, who was slain by an envious rival lord, Atli. But Atli held the ring for less time than any, and it was Gudrun who finally took it in her hands and, realizing what evil it had caused together with the evil wrought by her own witch-mother, walked quietly into the sea and put a final end to the curse.

And so, in grief and resolute peace, ended the final chapter of the Volsung Saga.

The Fairies' Goddaughter

— A Tale from Estonia —

Once there was a young woman who went into the dark, mysterious forest to pick strawberries. The berries were very ripe, and soon she had filled her basket. But as the young woman was turning for home, she stopped with a gasp. The loveliest girl she had ever seen was lying wounded amid the bushes.

"Oh, the poor thing! I must help her."

Hurriedly the woman dumped the berries out of her basket and filled it instead with water from a nearby stream. She gently tended the lovely girl till at last the girl's eyelids fluttered open. The young woman gasped again, because the girl's eyes were as green as the leaves and full of strange, strange light. This wasn't a human at all! No, no, this could only be one of the fairies who lived in the wild wood.

"Don't fear me," the fairy told her softly. "I fell afoul of an enemy who wounded me. But you have helped me, and for your kindness, I thank you. Tell no one of our meeting, but take this ring so you shall not forget me. And when the child you are bearing is born, my two sisters and I shall be her godmother."

With that, the fairy vanished, and the young woman hurried home. When she looked in her basket, which seemed far too heavy for an empty basket, she found the bottom covered with silver coins.

Sure enough, half a year later, the young woman gave birth to a lovely little girl.

"But how can I invite the fairies to the christening?" she wondered. "I have no idea where they might live!"

The christening day drew near. The sleighs of the guests stood all about the church. But as the young woman and her husband stood in the doorway of the church, the chiming of sweet bells rang out. A beautiful sleigh, white as moonlight and drawn by gleaming horses arrived. And in the sleigh were three maidens so lovely the young woman knew they could only be the fairy and her sisters.

"Welcome, godmothers," the young woman called, even though her husband frowned.

"Who are these maidens?" he whispered.

But the young woman only shook her head.

The christening was done. The only strangeness about it was the insistence of the three maidens that the baby be named not Mari, not Maret, not any normal human name, but Maasikas, which means Strawberry.

The years passed, and Maasikas grew into a pretty, happy little girl. Alas, though, when Maasikas was seven, her mother died, and her father prepared to wed a second wife, a cruel, cold woman.

But that night, three beautiful maidens appeared to the little girl. "We are your godmothers," they told her gently, "and we will take care of you."

So Maasikas, taking with her only the ring the fairy maiden had given her mother, went to live with the fairies in their magical palace that stood hidden by spells within the forest. She grew up in that palace from a little girl to a fine young woman.

"You are human," the fairies told her sadly, "and the time has come for you to live as a human. You must go forth and seek your fate. But the ring you wear shall help you. You need only touch your ring and make the wish, and whatever you need shall appear."

So Maasikas went out into the world in a carriage pulled by
fine horses. She travelled for a long, long time, all alone, till she
came to an old wizard who was a friend of the fairies. He recognized by her ring that Maasikas was a friend of the fairies as well,
and warned her, "Be careful. Soon you will meet a monstrous serpent, the Serpent King himself, who will try to devour you. Use
your ring to escape him; you will find a way. He will, however,
devour your horses and carriage."

"Oh!"

"Don't fear. That shall be his last meal; they are magical
things he cannot swallow. When the Serpent King dies, the horses and carriage shall come trotting safely out of his mouth again.
And with them shall come three animals, an elk, a wolf, and a
bear. You must find a way to mark each of them with your sign."

"B-but how shall I do that?" Maasikas asked.

"Put your silk ribbons about the elk's neck and your leather
belt around the wolf's neck. But you must put your magic ring
on the bear's claw."

More than that, the old wizard would not say, but hurried
her on her way.

And sure enough, suddenly the great, terrible head of the
Serpent King loomed up before Maasikas. Hastily, the girl did
the only thing she could think to do: Touching the ring to a pebble, she commanded it, "Turn into a giant eagle!"

The pebble turned into a giant eagle, just like that, and
Maasikas soared safely up on its back, out of the serpent's reach.
But, just as the old wizard had warned, the serpent devoured her
carriage and horses.

Ah, but just as he had predicted, that magical meal was the
end of the Serpent King. He roared once, writhed once, then lay
still. Out of his open mouth trotted the horses and carriage, with
not a mark on them. Out of his mouth dashed an elk, a wolf, and
a bear as well.

Warily, Maasikas approached the elk. "Don't be afraid," she told it, "I won't hurt you." The elk stood still as stone, and Maasikas tied her silk ribbons about its neck.

Warily, Maasikas approached the wolf. "Don't be afraid," she told it, "I won't hurt you. And—and I hope you won't hurt me, either." The wolf stood still as stone, and Maasikas tied her leather belt about its neck.

Now for the most frightening beast of the three. Very warily, she approached the bear. "D-don't be afraid," she told it, struggling to keep her voice from quivering, "I won't hurt you. And p-please don't hurt me, either."

Ah, but now she must give up her precious ring. Maasikas hesitated a moment, then slipped the ring onto the bear's claw.

All at once, there was no elk, no wolf, no bear. Instead, Maasikas found herself facing a richly clad older man wearing a leather belt about his neck, a richly clad older woman wearing silk ribbons about her neck, and a handsome young man, on whose hand glittered the ring Maasikas had put on the bear's claw.

"Thank you, my brave young woman," said the man who had been a wolf. "You have saved us from long imprisonment. Once, I was King of the South. Then the evil Serpent King caught me, my wife, and my son, and kept us trapped as you saw us."

"But now you have freed us," added the queen.

As for their son, the prince, he said nothing, but he smiled as he looked at Maasikas, and she smiled back at him. "Come," Maasikas said, "my carriage shall see us to your home."

Later, once they had settled in the palace, the prince gave her back her ring—as they were being wed.

The Ring of the King of the Djinn

A Tale from Egypt

Once there was or was not a poor man named Ali who had nothing left to his name but a few copper coins. Throwing himself into the hands of God, he went to see if there was work to be had anywhere in the world.

But Ali had not gone very far before he came upon a man who had snared a bird and was beating it with a stick. "Stop!" Ali cried. "Let the poor bird go!"

"This bird has been stealing my figs!" the man cried. "I won't let it go unless you pay me to do so."

"I have nothing but a few copper coins," Ali admitted.

The man snatched up three of them. "Done. The bird is yours."

He dropped the bird and Ali caught it and cut the snare from its legs. The bird ruffled itself so a few feathers fell free. "If you ever have need of me," it said, "burn one of these feathers and I shall come to you."

Now, the owner of the figs hadn't seen that the bird was magical. But he realized he had a chance to make a little extra money easily. So he began to meanly kick a stray dog.

"Stop that!" Ali cried.

"The dog has been chewing at the bark of this fig tree," the man lied. "Pay me and I will stop."

So Ali gave him three more of his precious coins. The man

thanked him, then promptly began smothering a little cat.

"Stop that!" Ali cried.

"This cat has been clawing at the bark of this tree," the man lied. "Pay me and I will stop."

So Ali gave him yet three more of his precious coins. The man thanked him, then pounced on a mouse and dangled it by the tail.

"Stop that!" Ali cried.

"This mouse has been gnawing the roots of the tree," the man lied. "Pay me and I will stop."

So Ali, with a sigh, gave him three more of his precious coins. "These are the last I have," he admitted.

"What a shame," the man said with a laugh and swaggered off.

Ali sat down in despair. Oh, he didn't regret having save the poor creatures' lives. But now he had no job, no money. What was to become of him?

He looked down at the magical feathers. "I can hardly be in worse difficulties," Ali said, and burned one of the feathers.

All of a sudden, the air was filled with a thunder of wings. The sky darkened, and Ali saw not the little bird he had saved but a huge monster of a bird. "Tell me your trouble," it commanded.

Trembling a bit, Ali told the huge bird what had happened.

"Climb onto my back," the bird said, "and be not afraid. I am not truly a bird, just as I was not truly a bird when that fool of a man snared me, but one of the sons of the King of the Djinn."

"W-where are we going?" Ali asked, looking nervously down at the ground now so far below them.

"I am taking you to my father's court. There, he will offer you the richest of gifts. But you are to ask for only one thing: the ring he wears on his little finger."

So they came at last to the court of the King of the Djinn, and Ali gasped in wonder at its shining marble splendor. Most splendid and terrifying of all was the King of the Djinn himself, but he smiled kindly at Ali and told him, "You have helped my son. Take what you will as a reward."

Ali swallowed drily. "If—if it please you, Your Majesty, I need nothing much. Nothing save the ring on your little finger."

The King of the Djinn laughed. "My son has counseled you, I see. Very well, take it with my goodwill. It is a granter of wishes: Use it wisely."

Back the great bird flew to the world of men, with Ali clinging to it. He was left exactly where he'd started.

Ali looked down at the ring he wore, the ring of the King of the Djinn. "I wonder," he said, and rubbed the ring.

Suddenly a great smoky Djinn was there. "I am Subbek Lubbek. Ask and I shall obey."

"Take me to—to the city of the Sultan," Ali said. Almost before the words had left his mouth, he was there, staring about in delight at the busy streets and the wonderful things there were to be bought. But, alas, he had no money!

"But I do have the ring!" Ali quickly rubbed it, and when the Djinn appeared, commanded, "Subbek Lubbek, I would like a fine house surrounded by pleasant gardens."

"Nothing easier."

"Make it a—a very fine house, as fine as that of the Sultan. And make the gardens very beautiful indeed."

"It is done," said Subbek Lubbek, and vanished back into the ring.

Now, when the Sultan saw this fine new estate that had appeared so suddenly, he was struck with wonder. Surely its owner must be very rich . . . and very powerful. Maybe he was even a magician!

"A valuable ally," the Sultan mused.

He had a daughter, Salima, who was as yet unwed. Ali had no wife. "You will wed my daughter," the Sultan told Ali, "and all will be well for the three of us."

Salima was pretty and sweet of heart, and Ali, now that he had enough food to eat, was handsome and kind of heart, and neither minded at all being wed to the other.

But one day, after they had been married for several weeks, Salima noticed the odd ring her husband always wore. "What a lovely thing it is," she said. "May I have it?"

"I dare not take it off," Ali told her.

"I know!" Salima cried. "Let me only borrow it, and I'll have the goldsmith make me a copy. Then you can have your ring back, and I'll have a pretty ring of my own to wear."

That sounded fair enough to Ali. After all, what danger could befall the ring in so short a time?

Unfortunately, the goldsmith was a badly overworked man. It happened that while he was holding the ring in his hand, wondering where he could possibly find the time to copy it, he cried out in despair, "I wish the whole palace and its gardens were all in the middle of the sea!"

Sure enough, in the next instant, the palace and its gardens had vanished.

Ali had been visiting the Sultan at the time. When he saw that his home, with his wife within it, had disappeared, Ali hastily felt for the ring on his hand—and only then remembered that he had given it to Salima.

"No, oh no," he moaned.

"What is this?" the Sultan cried. "Where is my daughter? Bring her back to me or I shall have your head cut off!"

"I will bring her back," Ali assured him. "But I must be left alone to think."

Once he was alone, Ali paced and paced till at last he remembered he still bore the second feather from the magical bird who was the son of the King of the Djinn. Hastily he set it on fire, and as soon as the huge bird appeared, stammered out what had happened.

"Never fear," the bird told him. "Now is the time for your kindness to animals to be repaid."

The son of the King of the Djinn summoned to him the cat,

dog, and mouse Ali had saved and told them what had happened. At once, the mouse leaped onto the cat's back, the cat leaped onto the dog's back, and off they ran. They reached the seashore, and the dog sprang into the waves and began to swim. When he grew weary, the cat and even the mouse helped him by paddling with their legs.

At last, just when all three animals were about to give up from hunger and weariness, they came ashore on an island in the middle of the sea. And there was the palace and its gardens. The animals hunted until they found the goldsmith and the princess sitting together. Since they could not find a way off the island and because the goldsmith had no idea the ring could help them, they were doing the only thing they could: they were having dinner. The animals could not speak to the humans to tell them how to use the ring. So they waited patiently until the goldsmith had fallen asleep, then searched his room. But they could find no ring!

Suddenly the mouse knew where it must be. The goldsmith must have hidden it in his mouth for safekeeping. So he tickled the man's nose with the end of his tail till the goldsmith sneezed in his sleep. Out popped the ring, and the animals pounced on it. The mouse leaped onto the cat's back, the cat leaped onto the dog's back, and the dog began the long, weary swim back home. So very tired was the dog that he nearly lost the ring in the waves. But just in time the cat caught it in her mouth. Then she, in turn, nearly dropped it, but the mouse caught it on his tail, and they all made it safely to land.

Meanwhile, poor Ali was in prison, and the royal executioner was sharpening his sword, preparing to cut off Ali's head. But even as the sword was being raised for the terrible blow, the mouse dropped the ring into Ali's hand.

"Wait!" he cried. "I can return all as it was."

And in almost no time at all, the palace with its gardens were back where they should be, and the Princess Salima was back where she should be, too, in her happy husband's arms.

III.

The Quest

A quest can take many forms. It may be an urgent journey to the dark realm of Sauron to destroy a ring of evil power, as it is in *The Lord of the Rings*. But in folktales and myth, the quest is more often a hunt to find something of worth. That something may be a holy artifact, as it is in the Arthurian legend of the quest for the Holy Grail, or it may be a secular goal, such as the gaining of a magic charm or the rescue of an enchanted princess or prince. No matter what the objective of the hunt, though, quest stories can be found in the folklore of every culture.

The Quest for the Grail

———— A Tale from Arthurian Legend ————

It happened that King Arthur and his knights sat at the famous Round Table of Camelot and were at peace—and restless with that peace. There seemed to be no further great deeds to be done, no goal towards which the knights could turn their skills.

All of a sudden, a lady on a white palfrey came riding into the hall, and did honor before King Arthur. "I seek Sir Lancelot, Sire," she cried. "I beg that he come with me."

No knight could refuse a lady's plea, most certainly not the gallant Lancelot. He rode with that lady to an abbey, where he found a young man of such a fine mix of elegance and modesty the youngster seemed the very essence of the perfect knight, though he had yet to attain that rank. His name, Lancelot was told, was Galahad, and he had been raised and taught by the wise Naciens of Carbonek.

When he heard that name, Lancelot paled in shock. There were but two shames within his heart. One was his secret, desperate love for Arthur's queen, Gwenivere. The second was the memory of a brief, mysterious encounter with the Lady Elaine, who afterwards had never revealed to him that she was pregnant with his child. Instead, she had slain herself soon after her baby's birth—the baby who had been reared in Carbonek. This fine youngster, then, was none other than Lancelot's son, and the knight had been summoned here to see Galahad's own knighting. Most gladly did Lancelot see that come to pass, but when he tried to persuade the newly-made knight to go with him to Camelot, Galahad at first refused.

"I am not yet ready," he told his father. "But come to Camelot I shall."

Now, within Camelot, at the Round Table where sat Arthur's knights, there was one chair left unoccupied because the mysterious message engraved on it in letters of gold warned that only the purest of men could sit there. And which knight would dare to make that claim? Since the chair was so potentially dangerous, it was known as the Siege Perilous. When Lancelot returned to court, however, he learned that the message had changed, promising now that the purest of men was about to arrive.

But before he and King Arthur could try to puzzle out the meaning, a knight came hurrying to the king with news of a wonder. "A great stone floats on the river, Sire, as though it were as light as wood. And in that stone is stuck a sword gleaming in the sunlight with a hilt of gold."

Arthur tensed, remembering, no doubt, the sword he had drawn from a stone on the day of his crowning. "Let us go see this wonder," he said.

When he and his knights had descended down to the riverbank, they found the stone floating in the river, just as they had been told, and the gleaming sword shone as brightly as the sun. Words were inscribed on that blade which said, "Only he at whose side I should hang shall take me from this stone, and he shall be the finest knight in all the world."

Arthur glanced at Lancelot. "That title surely belongs to you."

But Lancelot, thinking sadly of his love for Queen Gwenivere, shook his head. "The honor cannot be mine."

So Arthur turned to one after another of his knights. But

not a one of them could draw that sword from that stone. At last, deeming the task hopeless, they reentered Camelot. But no sooner had they seated themselves once more than there came a blast on the horn that signified a visitor. Into the hall came an old man clad in white, none other than Naciens the wise hermit who had tutored Galahad, and with him came the fair young knight himself. Fully clad as befitted his knightly status was Galahad, but no sword hung in the scabbard at his side.

"You be quite welcome," King Arthur told Naciens, "and this young knight with you."

But all those who stood near the Siege Perilous gasped, for now the golden letters read, "This is the seat of Sir Galahad."

"This place is surely yours," said the king in wonder. "Now, come, young sir. There is a marvel for you to see." He brought Galahad to the sword in the floating stone and told him, "All the other knights have tried their hand at releasing this weapon and failed."

"That is no marvel," Galahad said gently, "for this adventure is not theirs but mine." With those words, he reached gently out to the sword, and pulled it from the stone as easily as if from a scabbard. "This is the blade that has done much harm but shall now do only good. This is the blade that once belonged to Sir Balin, he who slew his own brother, Balan and sorely wounded King Pelles, my own grandsire, a wound which has never healed and never shall till I find him."

They all returned to the royal palace, since it was by now the dinner hour. But no sooner had all seated themselves than all light fled and a fierce blast of thunder shook the very walls. The brightest, purest of sunbeams cut through the gloom, and there into the hall came the Holy Grail, covered with fairest white samite, but no one could see who bore it. No sooner had the Grail been carried throughout the hall than it vanished once more, leaving the knights sitting in silent awe.

"Now, praise be to God for that fair vision," King Arthur

breathed at last.

Sir Gawaine, Arthur's own nephew, sprang to his feet. "By my faith, this vision was surely a sign to us. I here vow that tomorrow I shall set forth on a quest to find the Holy Grail, and never shall I return here until I have seen it more openly than it appeared to us."

"I so vow," the other knights cried. "And I."

Only King Arthur seemed sad at heart. "The Round Table has been completed for such a little while. I fear this is the last time I shall see the full flower of knighthood together, for surely many shall die in the quest."

And in the long months that followed, the king's sorrowful words proved all too true. Many knights did fall along the way, from battle or mischance. Others wandered on, hunting the Grail in vain, and underwent more strange adventures than can possibly be recounted here.

But during their journeyings, three fair knights, Sir Galahad, Sir Percival and Sir Bors came to ride together.

How Sir Percival became a knight was a tale almost as strange as that of Galahad, for Percival, though he was born of noble blood, had been hidden away in the forest by his mother, who had lost her husband and eldest sons to knightly wars and who had come to hate the very thought of knighthood. Raising her last son in humble surroundings, she believed, would keep him safe. But that was not to be his fate, for one day Percival chanced to see a knight riding through the wood and knew in that instant he, too, must rise to such a rank. It had been no easy task for a boy raised almost as a peasant, but Percival had overcome all odds, and here he was at Sir Galahad's side this very day. One sadness only held Percival's heart: he had all too briefly loved the Lady Blanchefleur, but she had mysteriously vanished from him, and though he ever longed to find her, he had never seen her again.

So the three knights rode on a great while till at last they came to the castle of Carbonek, the castle wherein was lodged King Pelles, the Maimed King, he whose wound would not heal. There they were greeted by an old man (some say he was Naciens the Hermit, some say he was even more than that) who took them before King Pelles. And to their great joy, the knights were told they were, indeed, near to fulfilling their quest for the Grail.

But first Eliazar, son to King Pelles, brought forth a sword that had been broken into three pieces. This was the very blade that had wounded Joseph of Arimathea, he who had brought the Grail to Britain.

"Which of you may make this sword whole again?" Eliazar asked.

First Percival laid his hand on the broken blade, then Bors did the same, but the sword never stirred. "This is for you to accomplish," Percival told Galahad.

And as soon as Galahad touched the broken blade, the three fragments became one once more.

Then it was that a clear, mighty voice called out, "Let all those who ought not to sit at the table of the Lord arise and depart hence."

So it was that all but King Pelles, his son, and the three knights departed. As these few remained at table, the hall at once blazed with light. And in came a strange, wondrous procession, lead by a white-clad old man dressed as a bishop. There were those who might have been mortal maidens or angels who bore into the hall two burning candles and all the holy elements of a full Christian Mass. But one bore a spear which dripped with never-ending blood. And one who came behind carried into the hall the Holy Grail itself. Percival nearly started from his chair in wonder, for surely it was his own lost Blanchefleur who was the bearer of the Grail.

The mysterious bearers placed their burdens down on an altar. The spear hung over it, but Galahad, moving with quiet certainty, stepped forward and took it down. He touched the point to King Pelles' wound so that the mystic blood dripped into it—and at once the wound was healed as though it had never been. Then it was that Galahad and the bishop together said Mass over the Grail, and the old man revealed himself as Joseph of Arimathea, he who had first brought the Grail to Britain.

"But it may no longer stay here on mortal Earth," he told Galahad.

And Galahad, purest of all the knights, said his farewells to his comrades, gave them greetings to bear to his father, Sir Lancelot, and quietly gave up the mortal life so he might accompany the Grail to the Hereafter.

Some tales say that Sir Percival, overwhelmed by the wonder of what had just occurred, gave up his life as well. Others tell of how he took holy orders. Still others, though, say that the Grail bearer was indeed his lost love, the Lady Blanchefleur, and that the last mortal act of Sir Galahad was to wed them. Those tales add that Percival and Blanchefleur went on to rule Carbonek together wisely and well, living their lives according to the highest, happiest of standards.

But the full fellowship of King Arthur's Round Table never did come together again, at least not in the mortal world.

Cupid and Psyche

———— A Tale from Ancient Greece ————

Once there lived a king with three daughters, the youngest of whom was named Psyche. Psyche was fair, so very fair that men began to worship her almost as though she were the Goddess of Love, Venus, herself.

Venus grew terribly jealous of this mortal girl. "Shall I, I, have my honors taken away by a little fool of a human?" she cried in rage, and had her son, handsome young Cupid sent to her. "Look," said Venus, "down there in the mortal world. Do you see that maiden, that Psyche? I wish you to see to it that she falls in love—and falls in love most shamefully!"

But Cupid, gazing and gazing at the human girl, knew he could never harm her. For as he stared, he fell most passionately in love with her, and dreamed only of ways in which he could win her heart.

Psyche, meanwhile, was far from vain about her beauty. Instead, she despaired of it, because she knew no man loved her for herself; men only came to wonder at that loveliness that was the merest chance. So overwhelmed were they by her beauty that not one man wished to marry her. And so poor Psyche sat alone.

Her father despaired as well, and at last sent for an oracle to see what his too-beautiful daughter's fate might be. To his horror, the oracle proclaimed, "Let the maiden be placed upon a mountain peak adorned for a wedding—or for a funeral. For he who takes her from that mountain top shall surely never be a mortal man."

And so, amid much weeping, Psyche was dressed in the finery that might be her wedding gown or burial shroud, and taken to the loneliest of mountaintops. There she was left alone, not sure whether to fear or hope. Would he who came be kind? Or would he be a monster who would rend her apart?

At last, exhausted, Psyche slept. And in her sleep, Zephyrus, the gentle breeze, carried her down to a flowery little meadow. When Psyche woke, she found herself beside a flowing fountain. Beyond that fountain stood a wondrous palace, all of gold and silver and sweet-scented cedar wood.

"Can this be the home of some deity?" she wondered, and moved warily forward. No one harmed her, no one even appeared to her, and Psyche entered the palace, wandering through this room and that, seeing more and more beautiful things.

A voice spoke suddenly from empty air. "Welcome, mistress," it said. "All that you see is yours to enjoy."

And a second voice added, "Rest now, if you would. Know that we are all your servants."

So Psyche rested on a bed that appeared as if from nowhere, and ate a feast that appeared as if from nowhere, and listened to sweet music from musicians she never saw. And gradually her fears were lulled.

But at last night fell. Now she must meet her bridegroom. And new fear started up in Pysche's heart as she remembered the oracle's prophesy. Would that bridegroom be a monster? Would he rend her limb from limb? She could see nothing in the darkened bridal chamber, nothing at all.

"Be not afraid," said a man's voice, and the sound of it was so gentle and filled with love that all the terror fled from Psyche, not to return. But when she would have reached for a lamp so that she might see her bridegroom's face, he stopped her.

"No. There is only this one prohibition: You must not try to see my face."

Wondering, Psyche agreed. In the morning her mysterious husband was gone before she woke, and she spent the day still in wonder, waiting for his return. In the night, they were joyous together as any other couple who had fallen deeply in love.

And so the time passed. One thing only kept Psyche from total happiness, and that was the fact that she'd heard not one word of her family. "They are well," her husband assured her. But then he added, "Beware your sisters."

"Beware!" Psyche cried in confusion.

"I feel it in my heart that if you ever speak with them, they will be the source of much grief to you, to us both."

But meanwhile, Psyche's sisters were wondering what had become of their sister. True, true, they had never really loved her—they, who were, in their mortal way, as jealous as Venus—but she *was* their sister, after all. And so one day they went wailing and weeping to the mountain. Zephyrus, soft-hearted Zephyrus, heard their sorrow and carried them gently to the palace, where Psyche met them in the doorway. What could she do? Warnings or no, she could hardly refuse to speak to them, or let them see the wondrous home in which she lived.

Her sisters grew even more jealous. They were wed to ordinary men, living in ordinary homes. Why should their youngest sister have all this splendor? "But you hardly speak of your husband!" they said as if truly worried. "Who is he? What does he look like?"

Pysche reluctantly admitted she had never seen his face, and her sisters recoiled in horror. "We knew it! We knew it! He's a monster, not a man, and he's just waiting till you least expect it so he can devour you!"

Psyche only laughed. But that night, long after her sisters

had left, she wondered. And at last the seeds of doubt they'd planted took fruit. She waited, heart pounding with suspense, till at last her husband slept, then lit a small oil lamp and, with hands that shook a bit, held it up.

Oh, the wonder she saw! Cupid lay asleep before her, so handsome no mere words could ever describe him, so handsome that Psyche, dazed with delight, bent to kiss him. But some drops of hot oil fell on Cupid's shoulder, and he started up with a wild cry of pain.

"My mother wished me to curse you with a shameful love," he told her, "but instead I fell in love with you myself. But now you have broken our joy together. I must flee, I must flee *now*!"

With a thunder of immortal wings, he was gone, and all around Psyche the wondrous palace faded as well. Left alone, she wept for a time in despair, then got slowly to her feet. She would find him again, this Psyche vowed, and set out on her journey.

Long did Psyche wander. At last she came to a river; so weary and forlorn was Psyche that she wished to hurl herself into it and end her loneliness. But Pan, horned, goat-footed Pan, god of the wild places, Pan who was playing his reed pipe by the river's bank, saw her and pitied her. "Don't let the water have you," he urged. "Go on. A god, and the son of a goddess, can only be won by courage."

So Pysche quested on. She came to a temple to Ceres, goddess of the harvest. "But no one has tended the shrine for some time!" Psyche said in disapproval, and set things to rights. And Ceres appeared before her.

"Kind-hearted Psyche, I would help you if I could. But Venus still hates you, and I can do nothing but urge you on."

"How can I possibly hide from Venus?" Psyche wondered. "Surely I can not."

And so, terrified by her own daring, she quested on till she had reached Venus's own home. So startled by this mortal girl's daring was the goddess that she failed to slay Psyche outright.

"So, Pysche," she cried mockingly, "you have come to pay a visit to your mother-in-law. Now we shall see exactly how dutiful a daughter-in-law you can be."

She took Pysche to a great heap of grain. "Do you see this grain? There are seeds of wheat, oat and barley all mixed together. It is to be your task to separate them, each type from each—and the task must be done by sunrise!"

Poor Psyche! No one human could have done that task. But the ants took pity on her, since they were even of lowlier status in the house of Venus. "Let us help Cupid's wife," they decided, and quickly had the three grains separated into three neat piles.

When Venus saw the neat piles of grain in the morning, she was furious. "You never could have done this deed without help!"

Psyche, wisely, said nothing.

"So now," Venus said after a moment, "since you found my first task so simple to perform, I have a second task for you. Do you see that torrent? On the far side of it are my golden sheep. I wish you to bring me strands of their gleaming wool. And this you must do before the night comes on!"

Psyche went down to the torrent. But how could she cross? And how could she possibly take wool from those sheep?

The reeds at the river's edge stirred and spoke. "Cupid's wife, hear us, heed us. Wait till evening falls. The torrent will still and the sheep lie down to rest. Strands of their golden wool catch in the lower branches of the trees. It will be an easy thing for you to glean that wool from those branches."

So it was. But when Psyche brought the gleaming strands to Venus, the goddess was even more furious than before. "Who aided you? You *must* have had help! But I have a third task for you, and this, you shall not find so simple to perform. Do you see the peak of that distant mountain? Do you see the stream that rushes down its side? Bring me a flask of that water. Go!"

Psyche climbed the mountain. But the water that had looked so innocent from afar glinted with strange light when seen so near. And—oh, terrible!—on either side were hideous serpents. "Beware," they hissed. "Beware."

But one of Jupiter's own eagles came soaring down. "Foolish girl!" it shrieked. "Did you think to take the Stygian water that makes even the gods wary?" It snatched the flask from her hands, darting easily between the serpents, and filled it with water from the stream's very source. "Take this to Venus. Now go!"

Psyche brought the flask to Venus. And if the goddess had been furious before, she was triply angry now. "I have one more task for you, daughter-in-law, one final task. You must take this tiny casket to Persephone. Ah yes," she continued with a smile, seeing Psyche start, "to Persephone, wife of Hades, ruler of the Underworld. Tell Persephone that Venus wishes as much beauty from her as will suffice for one day's use. Go!"

But the very stones of the palace whispered to Psyche, "Do not go empty-handed. Take with you bits of barley bread and hold within your mouth two coins. Speak to no one, stop for no one. When you reach the River Styx, Charon the Boatman will be waiting. Give him one of the coins, for that is his fee, and he will take you across that quiet river. When you reach the farther shore, you will find three women spinning. Say nothing to them, but take up the two small cakes you will find at their side. These shall be your passage back to the land of the living. When you reach the palace of Hades, you will find a terrible watchdog, three-headed Cerberus, guarding it. Give him one of the cakes and he will let you pass. After you have delivered your message to Persephone and wish to return, give Cerberus the remaining cake and again he shall let you pass. Give Charon the remaining coin, and he will see you safely back across the River Styx to the land of the living."

Psyche followed all that she had been told, and at last stood back among the living, not quite able to recall anything she'd seen in the Underworld, save that Persephone had been very lovely and her eyes had been very kind. But the tiny casket was in her hand, and Psyche looked down at it. "I wonder," she murmured. "What if I took just the tiniest crumb of what lies within? Would that make me just the smallest bit divine? And would that, oh, would that win me back my Cupid, my husband, my love?"

But when she warily opened it, what she found within the tiny casket was sleep, sleep so dense Psyche knew no more.

Now, all this while, Cupid had been wandering his mother's home, healing from the burning oil that had seared his shoulder, wondering how he would ever see his love again. At last, longing for Psyche, he took to the air in a rush of wings, and found her where she lay in enchanted sleep. Raging at what his mother had done, Cupid flew to the very peak of Mount Olympus and told the gods all that had happened. When he was done, mighty Zeus, master of all the gods, chuckled.

"There speaks the voice of one mad in love. And I think it only fitting that he be caught in the bonds of marriage with his love, mortal though she be."

So Psyche was brought before the gods and awakened from her enchanted sleep by their will. Zeus gave her a cup of the gods' own ambrosia to drink, and she became partly divine, partly of the company of the gods.

"Now you and Cupid shall never be parted," Zeus told her. "Now you and he shall live in joy forever, and no one shall deny you."

And so it was.

East of the Sun
and West of the Moon

A Tale from Norway

Once, long ago, there lived a poor man and woman who had so many children they had no hope of feeding them all. One cold winter night, as they sat despairing, wondering how they were all to survive that year, there came a rapping at the door.

"Some traveller must have lost his way," the poor man said. "I'll invite him in; the night is far too cold for anyone to be locked out."

But when the man went to see who was at the door, he gasped in horror, for there stood not a human but a great white bear.

"Good evening," said the White Bear, as courteously as any human.

"G-good evening to you, too," stammered the man.

"Will you give me your youngest daughter?" the White Bear asked, as suddenly as that.

"My daughter! D-do you mean to *eat* her?"

"I mean her no harm. And if you will give her to me, I shall make you and yours as wealthy as you now are poor."

Oh, but the poor father and mother were faced with a terrible choice! Could they trust the White Bear to do their daughter no harm? But how could they turn down the chance to become wealthy and save the rest of their family?

"Have I no say in the matter?" asked their daughter, young Karin. "Father, Mother, if I go with the bear, the rest of the family shall all live happily. The White Bear has sworn not to harm me, and I—I will believe him."

So Karin packed up her one spare dress and her one cloak, and said to the White Bear, "I'm ready."

"Climb up onto my back," the bear told her, and off they went. After they had travelled on into the night for some time, he asked her, "Are you afraid?"

"No," Karin said firmly.

"That's good. That's fine. Only hold fast to my coat, and there will be nothing to fear."

On and on they went, till at last they came to a great mound of a hill. The White Bear rapped on the side of it, and a door appeared and swung open. They entered, and Karin gasped to find herself in a wondrous castle, brightly lit with cheerful candles, their flames glittering off tables and chairs gleaming with gold.

"Climb down," said the White Bear, and gave Karin a little silver bell. "Ring this whenever you wish anything," he told her, and disappeared.

Well now, Karin was cold and tired and hungry after her long journey. Wondering a little, she rang the bell and said, "I would like something to eat."

Instantly, a great table appeared, spread with a fine dinner, finer by far than any dinner Karin had ever seen. She ate till she could eat no more, then rang the silver bell again and said, "I would like to sleep now."

Instantly she found herself standing at the doorway of a bedchamber which held a beautiful feather bed that looked so soft and welcoming Karin climbed into it and was asleep almost at once.

But no sooner had she fallen asleep than Karin woke with a start. A man was climbing into the bed beside her, but there was no light in the room by which she could see him. "Who—who are you?" Karin asked.

"I am the White Bear," he said wearily. "By night I may cast off my bear shape and sleep as a man. You need have no fear; I swore I would not harm you, and so I shall not."

"May I not see your face?"

"No," he said, and not a word more did he say. Not a move did he make to touch her, either, and at last Karin's weariness overcame all else, and she fell back into deep slumber.

When morning came, there was no one beside her. Karin rang the silver bell and was given a nice hot bath and clean, pretty clothes to wear. Then she went looking for the White Bear.

A bear he was, as though he had never been a man, and every bit as polite as ever. He was a fine person, bear or no, with whom to talk, and he and Karin soon were chatting together like old friends.

So the days passed, though Karin never once saw what the White Bear looked like when he was a man; he kept no lights at all in the bedchamber, nor would he allow her to bring any with her.

But after a time, even though the White Bear was a fine companion and it was lovely to have all the food and warm clothing she wanted, Karin began to wonder what had happened to her parents, brothers and sisters. And she began to grieve because all this while she hadn't spared a thought for them.

"Don't grieve," the White Bear said. "There's a cure for this homesickness: I shall take you back there on a visit myself."

"Oh, how wonderful!"

"But you must promise me this one thing. You must not talk alone with your mother. I feel it in my heart that if you do so, you will bring ill fortune on us both."

Karin promised she would do no such thing, and off they went. Soon they were back where her parents' poor little hut had stood—but it was now a fine house, and her parents, brothers, and sisters were all well-fed and richly clad. They welcomed her home with cries of joy, and Karin was so glad to be back home that she soon forgot all about what the White Bear had warned. She let her mother take her aside for a private talk, and soon Karin was telling the woman all about her life with the White Bear, how charming he was, and how he turned into a man every night.

"But I have never seen him. No matter how hard I plead, he will let me bring no light into the bedchamber."

"Oh no!" her mother cried. "What if he becomes a troll? You must learn the truth, my dear! Take this bit of candle with you, hidden in your sleeve. Tonight, when he is safely asleep, you may light it and see who shares your bed."

It sounded harmless enough to Karin. Sure enough, when she and the White Bear were back in their castle bedchamber, she waited till he was sound asleep then, with hands that shook a bit, lit the candle.

He was no troll, no monster at all! The White Bear was a prince, so handsome Karin couldn't keep from bending to kiss him. She did it ever so gently, not wanting to wake him, but a drop of hot wax fell from the candle and he woke with a cry.

"What have you done? Why have you disobeyed me?"

"I—I'm sorry."

"Oh, Karin, had you waited only one night more, one little night more, I would have been freed. You see, my stepmother cast a spell on me so that I am a man by night but a bear by day, and your patience would have broken that spell. But now I must return to her, to her castle that lies East of the Sun and West of the Moon, and wed the bride she chooses for me. Farewell."

With that, he vanished and the castle vanished, and poor Karin was left lying in the forest all alone. But after she had wept a little and sighed a little, she got to her feet and set out to find him. She walked far and she walked long, and at last Karin came to where a strange old hag sat playing with a golden apple.

"Good day to you, old mother," Karin said politely. "Do you know the way to the castle that lies East of the Sun and West of the Moon? I am going to find the prince who was a bear."

"Well now," said the hag, "if you know about him, perhaps you are the girl who should win him. Yes, yes, you are," the hag added, peering at Karin. "How interesting! I don't know how to find the castle, though, so take my horse and ride to the home of my next-door neighbor. Maybe she will know the way. But take this golden apple with you."

Off Karin rode. The neighbor might have been next-door, but next-door was a long, long way to go. At last she reached a second hag who looked just as strange as the first. This one was playing with a golden carding-comb. "So you're the girl looking for the castle that lies East of the Sun and West of the Moon, the girl who's to win the prince who was a bear. How interesting! I don't know how to find the castle, though, so take my horse and ride to my next-door neighbor and ask her. But take this golden carding-comb with you."

So off Karin rode to the next-door neighbor, who turned out to be a third hag just as strange as the other two. This one was playing with a little golden spinning wheel. "So you're the girl who's to win the prince who was a bear. How interesting! I don't know how to find the castle that lies East of the Sun and West of the Moon, either, though. So why not take my horse and ride to the East Wind. He might know. Take this golden spinning wheel with you."

Off Karin went to the East Wind, and a long, long journey it was. But when she got there, the East Wind, who was tall and slender with wide yellow wings, shook his head. "I have heard of that castle," he said, "but I have never flown over it. Come, we shall go to my brother, the West Wind."

He carried her safely as a baby in its mother's arms to the house of the West Wind. But the West Wind, who was tall and slender with wide red wings, shook his head, too. "I have never flown over that castle, either. Come, we shall go to our brother, the South Wind, for he is stronger than either of us and maybe he's seen the castle that lies East of the Sun and West of the Moon."

Off they flew to the house of the South Wind. He was twice as tall as the other winds, and broader, too, and his wings were gleaming silver. "I have flown over many strange lands," he told Karin, "but I fear I have never seen the castle that lies East of the Sun and West of the Moon. However, our brother the North Wind is the greatest and strongest of us all. Maybe he knows where to find the castle you seek."

Off they flew to the house of the North Wind. He was taller than all the other winds, and much broader, and his great wings gleamed like a starry black sky. "What are you doing here?" he roared.

Karin said as firmly as she could, "I am looking for the castle that lies East of the Sun and West of the Moon, so I may save the prince who was a bear."

"Oh, so *you* are the one!" the North Wind roared. "Yes, I know very well where that castle lies, and it is far, indeed. Once I blew a leaf right over it, but after that I had to rest for a full day before I could manage even the softest puff. But if you wish, I will see if I can take you there."

So he tore off into the sky, taking Karin with him. On and on he raced, while far below him, the world was shaken by the storm of his passing. But bit by bit the fury of his flight began to slow, then slow some more. At last he and Karin tumbled down to the ground, right by a stern castle on a crag. "There . . . is the castle . . . that lies East of the Sun . . . and West of the Moon," the North Wind panted. "Go find your prince while I . . . take a little nap."

But no one would let Karin into the castle. So she sat out-side, under a window, and began to play with the golden apple. It gleamed and it glittered, and soon it caught the attention of Long-Nose, the bride who had been chosen for the bear prince. She was just as cold as his stepmother, just as greedy, for she was a troll, just as the stepmother herself was a troll. And when greedy Long-Nose saw the golden apple, she called down, "How much do you want for that pretty trinket?"

"It is not for sale for gold," Karin said.

"What do you want for it, then?"

"I will give you the golden apple if I may spend a night at the bedside of the prince who lives here."

"Done!" cried Long-Nose.

But that evening she gave the prince a special potion to drink, and when Karin came to sit at his bedside, he would not wake for all her pleading.

The next day, Karin sat beneath the window and played with the golden carding-comb. Long-Nose was caught by the glitter and called down, "How much do you want for that pretty trin-ket?"

"I will give it to you if I may spend a night at the bedside of the prince."

"Done!" cried Long-Nose.

Again she gave the prince that special potion to drink, and when Karin came to sit at his bedside, he would not wake for all her pleading.

A third day, Karin sat beneath the window, and this time she played with the little golden spinning wheel. Long-Nose stared. If she had wanted the pretty golden apple and the golden card-ing-comb, she wanted this glittery toy even more. "How much do you want for that pretty trinket?"

"Let me spend the night at the bedside of the prince."

"Done!"

But what Long-Nose didn't know was that some of the servants, who were good-hearted folk, had seen Karin pleading with the prince to wake, and heard her weeping. And they told this to the prince. That night, when Long-Nose came with her special potion, he only pretended to fall asleep. When Karin came to his bedside and begged him to waken—he did. There was a joyous reunion then, to be sure.

"I will not have that Long-Nose for a wife were she the last of women!" said the prince. "You are the one I would wed. But there is one last test to be passed by you, my dear, before my stepmother's wicked spell is gone from me."

That morning, the prince declared to one and all that before he married Long-Nose, she must wash the drop of candle wax from his shirt—the candle wax that had dripped on it when Karin had first seen his face. Long-Nose scrubbed and Long-Nose rubbed, but the wax would not be moved. She gave it to her troll servants, but they could not remove the wax, either.

"A fine lot you all are!" the prince cried. "Why, I fancy even that girl who sits by the window could do a better job of laundering!"

It was Karin who sat there, of course, and Karin who entered. "Can you wash this shirt clean?" asked the prince.

"I think I can," she said.

And almost before she'd begun, the wax floated away, leaving the shirt white and unstained.

"This is the wife for me!" cried the prince.

The spell broke. The stepmother and Long-Nose and all their servants turned into the ugly creatures they really were, and off they fled, shrieking, into the wilderness.

And what of the prince and Karin? They freed all the good souls who had been kept captive by the trolls. They took all the gold and silver the trolls had stolen. And then they went as far they could from that castle that lay East of the Sun and West of the Moon, back to the living, happy world.

The Red Swan

——— A Tale from the North American ——— Chippewa People

There were three young men who were orphans, and so they hunted for themselves with none to help them. One day they went out, all three, to hunt whatever game each could find the best.

The youngest of the three was named Odijibwa, and as he searched long and hard for game yet found nothing, he was drawn by a strange reddish glow and a sweet singing. Following the sound, Odijibwa came to a lake, on which swam a beautiful red swan. Odijibwa shot arrow after arrow at the swan, but somehow all his arrows seemed to miss. At last he had only three left, three medicine arrows that had belonged to his father. Odijibwa drew his bow with care and fired a medicine arrow at the swan—and hit her cleanly.

To Odijibwa's amazement, the swan took wing as though this arrow, too, had gone wide. He hurried after her, sure she must be sorely wounded and wouldn't fly too far.

But fly she did, and run he did, determined not to lose the swan or the precious arrow. At last Odijibwa came to a small lodge, in which sat an old man who welcomed him inside. "Sit down and rest, young man. You must be very weary. Sit and eat."

Odijibwa was glad to sit and rest. But he nearly sprang to his feet in surprise when the old man said, "My kettle with water sits near the fire." For with those words a kettle appeared. The old man placed one grain of wheat and one blueberry into the kettle—and they grew into a fine meal.

If anyone would know how to find something as strange as a red swan, it would be this magician. But when Odijibwa told him the story, the old man shook his head. "I know nothing about this swan. Go on as you have begun, and soon you will come to my brother. Perhaps he can help you."

So Odijibwa went on. And soon he had come to another old man who also had a magic kettle and a magic way of cooking food. But he, too, knew nothing of the red swan.

"Go on as you have begun," he told Odijibwa, "and soon you will come to my brother. Perhaps he can help you."

So Odijibwa went on. Soon he came to a third old man who also was a magician. "You have chosen a difficult path," he told Odijibwa. "But if your guardian spirits protect you, you may still succeed."

"You know about the red swan?"

"She is no swan at all, but the kinswoman of a magician. He once bore a fine scalp, a scalp set with wampum, but when the daughter of a chief fell very ill, he gave up his scalp to her so the magic in it would cure her. But her tribe will not return that scalp, and so he sits powerless and in pain, waiting for someone to aid him. The red swan had been trying to bring heroes to him to help him."

"I cannot turn aside now," Odijibwa decided, and went on. At last, after a long and weary way, he came to the magician's lodge. Sure enough, an old man sat within, groaning, his head bare and bloody. There was no sign of the red swan, but Odijibwa saw that the lodge was partitioned by a screen, and thought he heard rustlings behind the screen.

Despite his pain, the old magician made Odijibwa welcome. Then he sadly told the young man how he had come to lose his scalp. "I did those people a kindness," he said, "but they betrayed me. And now they treat my scalp shamefully, and I have no power to retrieve it. Tell me, young Odijibwa, have you had dreams?"

By this, Odijibwa knew, he meant visions of power. He had, indeed, some dreams, and told those dreams one by one to the old man, not knowing what the magician wanted to hear. At first the old man only groaned in despair, saying each time, "That is not the one." But with the very last dream, he cried, "You are the hero I need! You can bring me back to health. Will you help me and win the red swan for your own?"

"I will," Odijibwa vowed, "and place the scalp back on your head with my own hands."

The old man cast a spell over him. Off Odijibwa went to the enemy tribe, stalking them as carefully as ever he had stalked game. There hung the scalp on a post, and the people were dancing fiercely about it.

Quickly Odijibwa called on the old man's magic. He became a hummingbird, whirring up to the scalp. But the people heard the sound of his wings, so he hastily turned into a fluff of down instead, falling onto the scalp. Turning into a hawk, he tore the scalp free and flew off with it, dodging the arrows of the angry enemy.

At last Odijibwa had outflown them. He flapped back to the old man's lodge and turned back into a young man. Hastily he dropped the scalp onto the magician's head, and it instantly grew right back where it belonged. The old man sprang to his feet—but now he looked like a handsome young man.

"Thank you, my friend!" he cried. "You have restored me. You have returned my strength and life to me."

"Thank you," said another, sweeter voice, and a beautiful young woman stepped from behind the partition. "I was the red swan who brought you here, and this magician you have saved is my brother. You and he shall be friends forevermore. And I shall be your wife, if you will have me."

"I will," vowed Odijibwa. "I will, indeed."

And so it was.

Courtesy of Warner Bros. Copyright ©1994 Warner Bros.

Part Five

"That's All, Folks!"

A hunter decides he's going to catch him a rabbit, and stalks through the forest with rifle at the ready. But the rabbit he finds has no intention of being caught, and sets off an ever-escalating series of tricks. The startled hunter finds his gun tied neatly into a knot or chases the rabbit through a hollow log—only to find himself, no matter how many times he runs back through that log, racing out over the edge of a cliff with no rabbit in sight. The end is inevitable: No matter what the increasingly frustrated hunter tries, the rabbit outwits him. At last the hunter gives up, leaving the rabbit cheerfully triumphant.

While the above isn't from any one cartoon, it should be easily recognizable as the general plot for a Bugs Bunny story. Bugs and the other characters who live in his wildly surreal world were created for the Warner Brothers studio in the late 1930s, and have gone on to receive worldwide recognition around the world. No matter what the cartoon or how seemingly inescapable the peril, the basic character of Bugs remains the same: he's brash, confident, and full of whatever tricks are needed for him to win out.

In short, he's a classic Trickster. A Trickster figure in world folklore may be a clever human who survives by quick-thinking ruses, but he or she is just as likely to be found in animal form: in North America, the classic trickster of the Pacific Northwest is Raven, in the Southwest, Coyote, and in the Northeast and in parts of Africa, Hare, while in West Africa and the Caribbean he is Ananse the Spider. But in all the Trickster's many forms he remains a force for chaotic change, the sort of mischievous fellow who says, "I wonder what would happen if I did *this!*"

Raven Steals the Sun

—————— A Tale of the Haida People —————— of British Columbia

Before things became as they are, the world was dark, darker than the blackest normal night. There was no light at all—save in the lodge of one strange old man. He hid the one great globe of all light in a cedarwood box, and kept it to peek into from time to time.

Raven it was who grew heartily sick of the darkness, because it meant he and all the other beings kept bumping and blundering into things. And he decided to do something about it. He listened here and listened there to bits of whispers on the wind, and learned in his clever way of the old man and the cedarwood box and the light within the box. Off Raven flew through the darkness to the old man's lodge, and perched on the roof to hear what more he might hear.

"The box is mine," the old man crooned, "the light is mine. The box and light are mine, and none else shall have them, never, never."

"We shall see about that," Raven muttered.

But deciding to steal the light was one thing, puzzling out a way to do it was another. There was no easy way into the lodge; no one could pass without the old man's permission. And such permission he would never give a stranger.

Raven was not the sort to give up on a challenge. He would

win that light, no matter how difficult it might prove or how long it might take!

Now it happened that the old man had a daughter, and one dark, sunless day, she went down to the river to gather water in her bucket of tightly woven reeds. As she raised the bucket, Raven turned into a spruce needle and dropped lightly into the water. As the girl raised the bucket to her lips, she drank Raven down. And not long after, she found herself most mysteriously with child. Neither she nor the old man knew how this could be, but in the right amount of time she gave birth to a son, a glossy-haired, bright-eyed son—a son who was Raven-in-human-form.

The old man was quite delighted with his unexpected grandson, playing with him and crowing over him and giving him everything and anything the quickly-growing baby wished. This was just as well, because the human-Raven would give a loud, harsh yell like the raven's cry if he weren't given what he wanted then and there.

And one day Raven began to yell and cry and carry on, and nothing would calm him, nothing quiet him. "I want the light!" he screamed. "I want to play with the light!"

The old man sighed. He didn't want to share the light with anyone, not even his grandson. But he could deny that grandson nothing. Besides, all this yelling was making his head ache! So he carefully brought the cedarwood box out of hiding. Opening it, he gave the great blazing globe of light to Raven.

"At last!" Raven cried in triumph. Changing shape so swiftly he was a feathery blur, he took flight, the light clasped firmly in his claws, completely ignoring the startled shout of the old man left behind.

Unfortunately for Raven, he had a rival, Eagle. Up till now, Raven had been able to avoid him in the darkness. But now Eagle clearly saw Raven in the blaze of light, and soared after him. His wings were bigger and stronger than those of Raven, and he wasn't weighted down by the globe of light. At last he overtook Raven, his talons outstretched. Frantically, Raven lightened his burden, breaking off a big chunk of light and tossing it away. It stuck in the heavens.

And so was the sun created.

For a little while, Raven kept ahead of Eagle. But now Eagle was gaining on him again. Frantically, Raven broke off a smaller chunk of light and tossed it away.

And so was the moon created.

For a little while, Raven kept ahead of Eagle. But now Eagle was gaining on him again.

"Do I have to give the whole thing up?" Raven cried.

But Eagle's outstretched talons looked very sharp. And so, with a sigh of regret, Raven threw away the last chunk of light. It broke into a hundred pieces.

And so were the stars created.

As for Raven, now that he was no longer burdened, he escaped Eagle with ease. And perhaps he couldn't help but take a little pride, even though he'd lost the golden prize, in the newly-made beauty all around him.

The Theft of Sun and Moon

A Tale of the Zuni People
of New Mexico

At the very beginning of things, neither sun nor moon were in the sky. The Kachinas, the spirit people, kept them, safe and secret, in a box that they opened whenever they wished some light. Without the sun, the world was always dark. Without the moon, there were no seasons; the world was never cold nor warm, never white with snow nor green with leaves.

Coyote thought this was a sorry state of affairs. He liked change, did sly Coyote—most certainly, since he was a clumsy hunter in the darkness shrouding the world.

"Ho, Eagle Chief," he called, "let us form a hunting partnership. Two hunters should do better than one."

Haughty Eagle looked down at Coyote and laughed. What, he, the keen of eye and mighty of wing, make a pact with a flightless ground crawler? But he remembered that Coyote, the sly one, could steal an eagle's meal, even in the darkness. Better to keep Coyote in the open, where he could play no pranks! So Eagle agreed to the partnership.

But even so, Coyote caught nothing but bugs. "Bah! How can anyone do any decent hunting in all this darkness! Tell me, Eagle, you who fly so high, have you ever seen any light in your travelings?"

"Why, yes, from time to time I have seen a flickering of light in the west, where the Kachinas live."

"Then west, we shall go."

Eagle soared lightly in the winds. Coyote, wingless, had to struggle through desert and mountain, river and mud. But he would not give up, not he!

There at last lay the camp of the Kachinas. Coyote and Eagle hid and watched. Eagle stared at the Kachinas' sacred dances. But Coyote stared only at a strange, dark box. When one of the Kachinas opened it a crack, golden light poured out. When one of the Kachinas opened it halfway, silver light poured out.

"That's what we want," Coyote whispered. "We must steal that box!"

"All you think about is theft!" Eagle whispered back. "I will go and ask the Kachinas if they will let us borrow their box of light."

Coyote watched as Eagle approached the Kachinas and demanded the box of light. He watched as the angry Kachinas threw stones to chase Eagle, bruised and squawking, back into the sky. But while all the Kachinas were chasing Eagle, Coyote the sly slid silently into their camp, caught up the box of light in his jaws, and scurried away.

But the box was heavy. Coyote's jaws were getting tired. Eagle swooped down to join him. "Here, give me the box. I can carry it more easily in my talons."

He snatched it up and flew away. Coyote ran after him, panting. "Hey, Eagle Chief! Let me carry the box again!"

"No, no, you will spoil everything. You only want to see what's inside."

Coyote yelled up at Eagle, "Whose sides ache from the Kachinas' blows? Not mine! Who stole away the box with never a bruise? Not you! Now, let me have the box."

The box was heavy. Eagle swooped down again. "Take it. But don't open it!"

But as Eagle soared up into the sky once more, Coyote studied the box. And curiosity began to burn and burn within him. Could the sun and the moon really be inside? Surely there could be no harm in opening the box just a bit.

A ray of golden light shot out and hit him right in the eyes! Coyote yelped—and let the lid fly open. In a blaze of gold, the sun flashed up into the heavens.

The first day had begun.

"Well now," Coyote said, admiring his gray coat in the sunlight. "That's not bad, not bad at all."

He watched the sun move across the sky till it was out of sight and darkness came again.

Eagle came flapping hurriedly back. "What have you done? You've let the sun escape!"

"It will return," Coyote said placidly.

"No, no, you've spoiled everything!" Angry Eagle lunged at Coyote. Coyote dodged—but as he did, he knocked over the box. The moon came shooting out and flashed up into the heavens. High rose the moon, higher yet, and the world grew chill. Leaves dropped from the trees, and an icy wind blew.

The first season had begun, and it was winter.

"What have you done?" Eagle shrieked. "You've brought cold into the world!"

True enough. But Coyote, ruffling his fur, only grinned. Why, things had worked out better than ever he'd planned! For he had brought day into the world, and night. He had brought winter, spring, summer, fall. He had given the world variety, never-ending changes enough to please even the wily gray trickster himself.

The Greatest Liar of Them All

—— A Tale of the Apache People ——
of Arizona

Coyote was going along one day when he came to a camp of men just sitting around, waiting for him.

"Coyote," they said, "we hear that you are the greatest liar of them all."

Coyote only shrugged. "How would you know such a thing?"

"Oh, everyone knows it. But how do you tell such great lies? Why does everyone always believe you? Come, show us how to lie."

Coyote shrugged again. "It was no easy thing to learn how to do. I had to pay a great price to learn how to lie so well."

"What price did you pay?"

"One horse, my finest buffalo horse." By that, he meant a horse well-trained to run in close among the buffalo so his rider could make many kills.

"What, like this?" asked one man, and led forth a fine horse, his best buffalo horse.

Coyote studied the horse, who sidled nervously at the scent of him. "Yes, this is exactly the sort of horse I mean. It was with one like him that I paid for my power to lie."

"But will you teach us to lie?" the men asked impatiently.

Coyote pretended to think it over. "Let me try to ride this fine buffalo horse. If he doesn't buck, I will explain my power to lie."

That sounded like a good bet to the men. After all, a buffalo horse is trained to be nice and mannerly. Coyote got up on the horse's back—but he dug in with his claws. Naturally, the horse began to buck, and Coyote leaped off.

"He needs a blanket between him and me," Coyote said. "That is surely the problem."

So the men put a thick saddleblanket on the horse. Coyote mounted again—but his claws were sharp enough to prick right through the blanket. And of course the horse began to buck again. Coyote leaped off.

"He still wants something more on his back. A good saddle, I guess."

So the men saddled the horse with their best saddle. They gave Coyote a fine riding crop, too.

"I shall try the horse one more time," Coyote said. "If he still bucks, I won't be able to tell you the secret of my power."

He rode the horse a little distance away, just out of reach of the men, then stopped. "This is the secret of my power," Coyote said. "I trick people into giving me things. Like a blanket. Like a riding crop. Like a good saddle and a fine buffalo horse."

And with that, Coyote rode away, and the men could do nothing to stop him.

A Bagful of Tricks

A Tale of the Uigur People ———
of China

Once there was and once there was not a padishah, a great
ruler, who heard of the tricks played on the
high-and-mighty by the Effendi Nasreddin. "I have heard this
fellow is able even to trick a padishah. Can such a thing be?"

"It is true, Your Majesty," his ministers warily assured him.
"This Nasreddin may be of common blood, but he is truly clever
enough to trick anyone, even a padishah."

"That's impossible!" raged the padishah. "What, a—a
nobody be more clever than a ruler? It cannot be so!"

To prove his point, the padishah disguised himself as a common man and rode off to the village of the effendi. There, he
greeted Nasreddin, who was sitting peacefully in front of his
house, with, "It is said that here there lives a most clever man,
the Effendi Nasreddin."

"So it is said."

"I have heard amazing tales of his cleverness—so amazing
that I doubt they can be true. Can his fame for trickery possibly
be justified?"

"I believe that it can," said the effendi, getting to his feet,
"for Nasreddin I am. What can I do for you?"

"I have heard much about you," said the padishah. "I have
heard that you can trick anyone and everyone. But I am here to

warn you that today you shall not win your little game. For no one born has ever been able to fool me."

"So, now!" The effendi scratched his head. "You are a difficult opponent, I can see that. For you no common trick will do. No, I must first go home and get my special bagful of tricks. Unless, of course, you are afraid of that bag?"

"Nonsense! Get whatever bag you wish—but be quick about it!"

"Well now, my home is a good distance from here. If you would lend me your horse, I could be there and back again in almost no time. Otherwise, I would have to walk and walk and—"

"Never mind! Here is my horse. Now go get your bag of tricks. And hurry back here as quickly as you can ride. I am eager to test your cleverness!"

Effendi Nasreddin bowed low, then leaped into the saddle and rode off as swiftly as an arrow from the bow. The padishah stood impatiently waiting.

And waiting.

And waiting.

Night fell. At last the truth struck the padishah: Nasreddin was not coming back.

"He tricked me!" the padishah admitted. "He did just what he set out to do—the Effendi Nasreddin has tricked the padishah!"

Pedro the Tricky

A Tale from Spanish New Mexico

Once there was a young fellow named Pedro, but he was such a clever one folks all called him Pedro the Tricky. Nothing was safe from his eyeing, for once Pedro had decided he wanted something, why, that something was as good as his. It was said he could trick the food right off the rich man's table and the pants right off that rich man's self! And half the time whichever man that Pedro had cheated had not the slightest idea of how the trick had been done.

Well now, fame of Pedro the Tricky spread beyond his little village. And one day another man who fancied himself a tricky fellow came riding into town. As luck would have it, the first man he came across was none other than Pedro himself.

"I am looking for Pedro," the stranger began without a greeting, "Pedro, known as the Tricky."

"Are you?" Pedro drawled.

"I've heard he's a pretty clever fellow."

"Have you?"

"I'm considered a pretty clever fellow myself."

"Are you, now?"

By now, the man was beginning to get more than a touch annoyed at these lazy answers. "Yes, I am! And do you know what I think? I think this Pedro cannot possibly be as clever as people say. In fact, I don't think he's so clever at all!"

"Well now, I might disagree with that," Pedro said, "because I happen to be Pedro the Tricky. And if I don't look as clever as people say right now, it's because I happen to have left all my tricks back at home."

"Then get them!" the man said eagerly. "I wish to see if you are anywhere near as clever as I."

"I don't know . . ." Pedro whined. "The day is so *very* warm, and my house is so *very* far away. It would take me all day just to walk there, and another day to walk back again."

"Ride, then!" the man cried impatiently.

Pedro shrugged. "How can I? I have no horse."

"Aie!" The man sprang down from his own horse. "Take mine. Only go on, hurry! Go get your tricks!"

Pedro, with a great sigh of reluctance, climbed into the saddle. But then he kicked the horse sharply in the sides and galloped off—only to stop a short distance away. "Congratulations!" he yelled back. "You've just been cheated by none other than Pedro the Tricky. And tricky is very much what I am!"

Laughing, Pedro the Tricky rode away.

Spider, Reader of Thoughts

————— A Tale of the Asante People —————
of Ghana

In the beginning days, the Sky God had three sons, Night, Moon, and Sun, who lived in three separate villages. The Sky God knew only one of his three children could inherit—but which of the three would it be? He prepared a royal stool for whichever of the three should prove the most worthy, and said aloud as he did so, "Who knows my thoughts?"

Ananse the spider was never one to keep quiet about anything that might be of use later on, so he claimed, "I do. I know them."

"Do you, indeed?" the Sky God asked. "Then you already know I wish my sons brought before me."

"Of course I do!" cried Ananse, and hurried off before he could be questioned.

But once he was out of sight, Ananse slowed to a stop. "Now what am I to do?" he wondered. "I claimed to know the Sky God's thoughts, yet I don't know even one of them."

Still, Ananse knew, he could hardly admit to having lied to the Sky God. So he used his quick, clever mind and plucked feathers from all the birds he could reach and stuck the feathers onto himself. Flying back to the Sky God's village, Ananse perched in a tree where everyone could see him, and waited. Sure enough, the people all stared. What manner of bird was this? No one knew.

Soon the Sky God came near the tree and glanced up at the disguised Ananse. "If clever Ananse were here, he would surely know the name of this bird. Never mind. I have decided that Sun is the one I wish to make a chief, but the test must be fair. That is why I have sent Ananse to bring my sons to me. I have pulled up the yam known as 'Kintinkyi,' and whichever one of those sons can tell me its name shall be given the royal stool."

Off Ananse flew. First he stopped in the villages of Night and Moon and told them, "Your father wishes you to go to him." Then he flew on to the village of Sun. Ananse had already decided it would be a very wise thing to be on the winning side, so when he told Sun, "Your father wishes you to go to him," he added, "after we have a little chat."

And when he and Sun stood away from the others, Ananse said, "Your father has prepared a royal stool, and wishes to give it to you. But before you can claim it, you must pass a test."

"What is this test?" asked Sun.

"Your father has pulled up a yam, and you must know which one it is."

"How can I possibly do that?" Sun wondered. "My father once told me the names of all things, but that was so long ago I have forgotten much."

"You need not worry about remembering things long ago," Ananse said with a grin. "Its name is Kintinkyi."

Off Sun went to the Sky God's village, along with Night and Moon. The Sky God greeted them and told them, "I have prepared a royal stool for one of you, the one who can name the yam I have pulled. Night, you are the eldest, so you shall go first. What is the name of this yam?"

Night had no idea. "It is named Pona," he said.

The Sky God turned to Moon. "You are my second oldest son. Now it is your turn."

Moon had no more idea of the right name than had Night. "The yam is named Asante," he said.

The Sky God turned to Sun. "You are my youngest son. Now it is your turn."

Sun stood in silence a long time, as thought he were thinking deeply. At last he said, "When I was very young, I used to walk with you, my father, as you told me the names of all things. And I have not forgotten this one. The name of the yam is Kintinkyi."

"That is correct," the Sky God said, and the tribe all shouted their applause. He turned to his other sons and told them, "You, Night, show you have paid no heed to any of my lessons. So, even though you are my eldest son, only dark deeds shall be done during your reign. You, Moon, have also forgotten my lessons, so only children shall play during your reign. But you, Sun, did not forget my lessons, so you shall be chief, and all matters to be settled shall be heard during your reign. And the rainbow shall encircle you whenever any try to challenge you, and show your people when the rainclouds gather that the waters will not flood and drown them all."

The Sky God turned to Ananse. "And as for you, Ananse, since you are so clever, all those words that were once known as 'The Sayings of the Sky God,' shall now be known as 'The Sayings of Spider.'"

And so clever Ananse gained both the Sky God's words and the friendship of Sun.

The Spider Pays His Debts

———— A Tale of the Hausa People ————
of Nigeria

One thing Ananse the Spider hated to do was pay debts. In fact, he would borrow from this animal so he wouldn't have to repay that animal. But at last the terrible day came when he had borrowed from every animal in the forest. So he thought and he plotted, for he had no money, none at all, with which to pay what he owed.

And all at once the Spider knew what he could do to get out of this ridiculous fix. He sent out word that if all his creditors came to him the very next day, they would receive payment—but only if they arrived in the proper order.

Sure enough, the first creditor to arrive the next morning was Hen. "Come inside my hut," Spider told her in his most friendly manner. "Wait, I will go outside and prepare you some food."

He went outside. There, just arriving, was Wildcat. "I wish repayment," he snarled, "and I wish it now."

"And you shall have it," Spider said. "The repayment is waiting inside my hut. Go and take it."

Wildcat entered, and found Hen waiting there. He pounced on her, and ate her up.

Meanwhile, outside the hut, Dog had just arrived. "I want my repayment," he growled.

"Of course you do," said Spider. "It is waiting for you inside

186

my hut."

Dog entered, and found Wildcat waiting there. He leaped on Wildcat and ate him up.

While this was happening, Hyena arrived. "Where is my repayment?" she whined.

"Inside the hut. Go and see."

Hyena entered, and found Dog waiting there. She sprang at Dog and ate him up.

Meanwhile, outside Spider's hut, Leopard had just arrived. "I am here for my repayment," he hissed.

"Good! It is waiting for you inside the hut."

Leopard entered and found Hyena waiting there. He jumped on her and ate her up.

Just then, the last of the creditors, Lion, arrived at Spider's hut.

"I know, I know," Spider said, "you want repayment. "Well, it is there, inside my hut."

Lion dashed inside. He found Leopard waiting there, and they began to fight. As they fought, clawing and spitting and snarling, Spider sneaked inside and dashed pepper into their eyes so they couldn't see to chase him. He hit them both with a heavy club, and killed them both.

And that was the way Spider settled all his debts.

Rabbit and Antelope Dig a Well

——— A Tale from the Bakongo People ———
of Angola

Once in the dry season, the time of thirst, Rabbit and Antelope agreed to dig a well together so they would always have water to drink. It would be hard, dusty, hunger-making work, so they both brought something to eat with them. But Rabbit brought only a few scraps, while Antelope brought more food, better food, nice, sweet, lovely food.

"Let us eat it now," Antelope said, "so we will have plenty of strength with which to dig."

"No, no," Rabbit protested, "Let us hide our food away so we can eat it when we're both hungry and tired."

This sounded like a wise idea to Antelope, so he agreed. And they hid the food away. But no sooner had they reached the spot where they wanted to dig their well, than Rabbit cried, "Listen! My children are calling me. I must go to them."

"I hear nothing," Antelope said.

"Yes, yes, I hear them! They are calling me. I will be back as soon as I can."

And Rabbit dashed off—straight to where he and Antelope had hidden the food. He ate as much as he wanted, then went leisurely back to where Antelope was digging.

"Well?" asked Antelope. "Which child was calling you?"

"Oh, it was little Unfinished," Rabbit said, and began to

work. But digging a well was hard work. After only a short time he cried, "Listen! My children are calling me again. I must go to them."

Off he raced—straight to the hidden food. Rabbit ate as much as he wanted, then went back to where Antelope was digging.

"Which child was calling you this time?" Antelope asked.

"Oh, it was little Half-Done," Rabbit said, and began to work. But even though Antelope had done most of the digging, Rabbit soon became weary. And he cried, "My children are calling me yet again. I must go to them."

Off he raced—straight to the hidden food. This time when Rabbit ate as much as he wanted, there was nothing left but the empty pots. Rubbing his full stomach, he went back to where Antelope was digging.

"Which child was calling you this time?" Antelope asked.

"This time it was little All Gone," Rabbit said.

By now Antelope was very hungry and very tired. "Let us go eat our food," he told Rabbit.

But when they got there, of course Antelope found nothing but the empty pots. "What has happened?" he cried. "Where is our food?"

"Oh, some wild beast must have stolen it," Rabbit said, pretending to be angry, and stalked off for his home.

But Antelope thought and thought over what had happened. "Little Unfinished," he said slowly. "Little Half-Done. Little All Gone. What kind of strange names are these? Not children's names, surely, not children's names at all. Rabbit did it! Rabbit ate all our food!"

So Antelope plotted his revenge. He cut a piece of wood into the shape of another rabbit, smeared it all over with sticky birdlime, and set the figure so it blocked the path to the well.

Sure enough, Rabbit came to drink from the well, and found a strange rabbit blocking his path. "This is a private well!" he cried. "What are you doing stealing our water?"

The strange rabbit said nothing.

"I asked you a question!" Rabbit cried. "Answer me!"

The strange rabbit still said nothing.

"Are you trying to insult me?" Rabbit asked sharply. "Answer me at once or I—I shall hit you!"

The strange rabbit still said nothing. Angry Rabbit smacked the stranger right in the face—and his hand stuck there.

"What are you doing? Let me go or I will hit you again!"

The stranger held fast. Rabbit hit him again—and his other hand stuck fast. He kicked the stranger, and his foot stuck fast. He kicked the stranger again, and his other foot stuck fast. The more Rabbit struggled, the more of him got stuck. At last he was completely caught in the birdlime.

And that was when Antelope came down to the well to drink. He took one look at Rabbit hanging stuck to the figure and began to laugh. "You tricked me," he said. "And I—oh, I have most certainly tricked you in return!"

The Stolen Figs

—————————— **A Tale from Chile** ——————————

Once there was an old man named Felix, who owned a splendid fig tree that every year grew a rich crop of nice, sweet figs. Felix would stand guard over his tree when the figs ripened, to be sure that no thieves stole his fruit.

But two thieves decided this would be exactly what they would do: rob old Felix no matter what he did.

"But how are we to do this?" one thief wondered. "Old he may be, but he's a quick fellow with a shotgun."

"Ah, but who can shoot a ghost?" the second thief asked with a grin.

And so, when night fell, the two thieves met near the fig tree. They had covered themselves with white cloth from head to foot, and as they approached the tree, they moaned, "Figs. Juicy figs. When we were alive, figs were our favorite food."

"But now that we're dead," they added, "we are hunting different game. We are hunting old Felix."

"Hunting me?" Felix exclaimed in horror. And without waiting a moment longer, he dropped his shotgun and headed off for his house at a run. The two thieves gathered as many figs as they could hold, laughing so hard they nearly dropped the lot.

The next morning, old Felix went in search of his shotgun. Surely it would still be there, he reasoned. For what good would a mortal weapon be to ghosts? As he hunted, his next-door neighbor, a woman who made pottery for a living, asked him what he was doing.

"Oh, I'm hunting my shotgun. And trying to figure out a way to keep ghosts away from my fig tree—and me!"

The potter was a clever woman, more clever than any two fig thieves. "I think I have an answer to your problem," she said with a grin.

That night, when the thieves returned for another harvest of stolen figs, they found someone there before them. "Look here, friend," they said boldly, "this is *our* tree. Go find some other tree to rob."

But the figure said never a word.

"What a rude fellow this is! Come, man, offer us one of your figs and call it quits."

The figure never moved.

"Well? Say something, curse you! Say something, can't you?"

Never a movement, never a word.

"Enough of this!" cried one thief, and gave the figure a good smack. But to his horror, he found himself stuck to the figure. "Hey! Help me!"

The other thief tried his best, but soon he, too, was stuck, and stuck fast to the nice, sticky tar figure the potter had made. All the yelling the two thieves were making brought old Felix out of his house on the run.

"So, now!" he cried. "Ghosts, are you? Hunting me, are you? I'll give you hunting, you thieves!"

He whapped them with his cane, a blow for each fig stolen. And only after old Felix was satisfied the thieves had paid in full did he call for the potter, who greased them till they could pull free and stagger off.

And, not at all strange to say, neither of them ever desired even the smallest taste of a fig again.

The Bolt of Cloth

—————— A Tale from Germany ——————

One day when Till Eulenspiegel—Till Owlmirror—was strid-
ing through the marketplace, a fine bolt of blue cloth caught
his eye and fancy. What a handsome tunic that cloth would make!
But what a handsome price the merchant would surely ask for it!

Pay for the bolt? Till grinned to himself. No need for something as boring as that!

So, after two secret stops with certain folk lingering in the
shadows, Till swaggered up to the cloth merchant and said,
"That is a fine bolt of cloth. So very green!"

"Green!" the merchant said in surprise. "The cloth is blue!"

"Tsk. You must have been staring into the dye vats for far
too long."

"I *beg* your pardon!"

"What else could it be? The fumes have obviously turned
your brain so badly you can't see that the cloth is green."

"My brain is fine," the merchant snapped. "It's your vision
that's defective. The cloth is *blue*."

"Green, I say."

"Blue!"

"I say it is green," Till said hotly, "and I am willing to wager
on the matter. Here, now, I have it: If two men agree with me
that the cloth is green, why then you shall give me the bolt. But
if the two men agree with you that the cloth is blue, I shall give

you the entire contents of my purse. Is it a wager?"

The merchant never hesitated. No matter what this lunatic claimed, the cloth was most certainly blue! How could he possibly lose? "A wager," he said, and shook on it.

Till gestured to a passing man. "You, sir, would you help us settle a wager?"

The man shrugged. "What is your wager?"

"Why, my friend here claims this cloth is blue. I say it is green. Which is the true color?"

The man stared at the merchant as though at a madman. "What sort of strangeness is this? The cloth is most surely green."

"Green!" the merchant cried. "How can you say such a stupid thing? The cloth is blue!"

But the man had already walked away.

"Go on, ask someone else," the merchant prodded Till. "Hurry."

So Till stopped a second man. "Pray help us settle a wager, good fellow. Tell us the color of this cloth. Is it blue or green?"

"Are you two feeble wits?" the man asked. "Of course the cloth is green!"

"No!" the merchant roared. "It is *blue*! The cloth is *blue*! Blue, blue, blue!"

"It is green as the very grass," the man said coldly and stalked away.

What could the bewildered merchant do? If one man had said "green," he might have been able to shrug it off, but when *two* men agreed... Almost sobbing, he handed over the bolt of cloth to Till, who slung it over one shoulder and sauntered off, whistling cheerfully.

But once out of sight of the merchant, Till tossed a few coins to the two men who'd sworn the cloth was green—the two men he had recruited before challenging the merchant.

And off Till Eulenspiegel went with his bolt of cloth—the nice, blue bolt of cloth.

Little Kandek

A Tale from Armenia

Once, long ago and far from here, there lived a little girl named Kandek. Now, Kandek's father was a farmer. And every day the girl would go out into the fields to bring him his lunch. Every afternoon she would go back home again, stopping at the big old apple tree to pick herself an apple.

But one day, while Kandek was climbing up into the tree, an old, old woman came up to it.

"Little girl," she called, "good little girl, give me an apple!"

"Hold out your hands, good woman," Kandek answered politely, "and I will toss an apple down into them."

"No, no, my sight is too poor, I could not see it. Kind child, come down and give me an apple."

So little Kandek climbed down to the ground. Aie, but the old woman smiled—and her teeth were sharp as knives! This was no woman at all, but a witch-ogre, a monster in disguise! Before Kandek could run away, the witch-ogre caught her up and stuffed her into a sack.

"Tonight I shall eat well," crowed the witch-ogre as she slung the sack over her back. "Tonight I shall feast on tender little girl!"

But Kandek kept her wits about her. Carefully she cut a hole in the sack with her little paring knife. She slipped out and stuffed rocks back in.

"How heavy you've become, little girl," the witch-ogre complained. "*Too* heavy!"

She discovered the rocks. She dumped them out, caught little Kandek, and stuffed her back into the sack.

But Kandek kept her wits about her. She slipped out of the hole she'd cut, and stuffed dry branches back in.

"How bony you've become, little girl," the witch-ogre complained. "*Too* bony!"

She dumped out the branches, caught poor Kandek, and stuffed her back into the sack. But this time the witch-ogre tied up the hole in the sack! Quickly she hurried home to her hut and shook out little Kandek onto the floor.

"Now I shall eat you!" the witch-ogre cried.

Kandek still kept her wits about her. "But if you eat me raw," she argued, "I shall give you a bellyache. You must cook me first." She yawned and pretended to be very sleepy. "Go gather wood. I shall take a nap."

The witch-ogre didn't want a bellyache. She looked at Kandek. But Kandek lay still and didn't move, no, not even when the witch-ogre poked her with a sharp finger. "Asleep," the witch-ogre muttered. "Good. Now I need not tie her up while I build my cooking fire."

She left to gather firewood. Little Kandek opened her eyes. But she couldn't run away, no! The witch-ogre was right outside. Instead, quick as thought, little Kandek scrambled up into the rafters of the roof, far overhead. There she hid.

The witch-ogre returned, arms full of wood. "But where is the little girl? She must be here. I smell the smell of human flesh."

She searched here and she searched there. Little Kandek hid up in the rafters and held her breath. But then the witch-ogre looked up.

"Aha! I see you up there, my little bird. Come down."

"Oh, no!" said Kandek.

"Come down, I say!"

"Oh, no!"

"Then I shall climb up after you," cried the witch-ogre. She brought a ladder. But it was too short. She put a chair on the table and climbed up on that. But it was still too short.

"You will never eat me," little Kandek sang. "You will never reach me! Only a pile of dry old branches can reach me."

"Dry branches, is it? Wait, wait, little girl, I'll have you for my dinner tonight!"

The witch-ogre piled up branches and more branches and still more branches. She began to climb, up and up, as the pile of branches creaked and cracked beneath her weight. Now she could reach Kandek!

But little Kandek still had her wits about her. She reached down and pulled one of the branches out of the pile. And the whole pile began to sway and crack, crack and sway. Down it went! And down went the witch-ogre with it, tumbling all the way down to the floor.

"I'm free!" cried Kandek.

Quickly she scrambled down from the rafters, sliding down the posts that held them up. She hurried away. And soon little Kandek was safely back in her father's fields.

What of the witch-ogre? She moaned, she groaned, she opened her eyes.

"That girl had magic!" the witch-ogre gasped. "She picked me up and threw me to the floor—It *had* to be magic! Aie, and she's just a little thing! The grown men and women must be even stronger! Maybe *everybody* in this land has magic! Oh no, oh no, that's too much magic for me!"

The witch-ogre took to her heels in fright. Did she ever stop? Who knows? But whatever became of her, one thing is sure: She was never seen in those lands again!

The Serf and the Swamp-Things

———— A Tale from the Ukraine ————

O nce, in the long ago that never was, there lived a serf named Ivan. Now being a serf meant being the next closest thing to being a slave: a serf could not own land or leave his master's land, either. Ivan was weary of being a serf and wanted only one thing, and that was to be free. But his cruel master, Lord Alexei, only laughed at him. Ivan was a good, honest worker. Lord Alexei didn't want to lose him!

"Bring me a hatful of gold," he told Ivan. "Then I will free you."

A hatful of gold? His soft felt hat, worn and torn with age, was the only thing poor Ivan owned. Where could he find even the smallest of gold coins? As he hung his head in sorrow, Lord Alexei added coldly:

"You have one other chance to be free. Chase the swamp-things out of the haunted swamp on my lands, and I will free you."

The swamp-things were terrible monsters. They ate any people foolish enough to go into their swampy home, and stole their treasure. No one could ever chase them out of the swamp, and Lord Alexei knew it.

But Ivan, though he had no gold, had a treasure much more important: his wits. So he thought for a time and pondered for a time. All the stories told how dangerous the swamp-things were.

But not one story said anything about the swamp-things being clever!

Ivan went down into the haunted swamp and sat beside a dark, dank pool. There he started to dig up mud and mold it into bricks. He had molded no more than three when—whoosh! Up out of the dark, dank pool rose the swamp-things' ugly heads, all full of sharp, sharp teeth and fiery eyes.

"What are you doing, foolish man?" they cried.

Ivan never flinched. "Why, I'm building my castle here," he said.

"We let no one build here!" the monsters screamed. "We shall eat you!"

"First one of you must wrestle me," Ivan told them calmly.

The swamp-things laughed like a cold wind whistling. The strongest of them clambered out of the pool, ugly as a great grey rock with teeth. Ivan shook his head.

"You?" he said scornfully. "Why, I wouldn't even work up a sweat against such a puny thing! Go wrestle old Granddad over there instead."

Furious, the swamp-thing leaped at what he thought was Ivan's grandfather. But it wasn't a man he landed on, it was a great black bear—a very angry bear! The bear whammed the swamp-thing and slammed the swamp-thing, and tossed him back into the pool with a terrible splash.

"I'm not going back out there," the swamp-thing whispered. "If his old granddad is so strong, he must be even stronger!"

But when the swamp-things poked their heads up out of the water and saw Ivan building his mud bricks, they hissed in rage.

Ivan glanced up. "What, you again? Go away. I am building my castle."

"No man builds anything in our swamp!" they screeched. "We shall eat you!"

"First," Ivan said calmly, "I challenge one of you to a whistling contest. He who sends the other flying with the force of his whistle wins."

A swamp-thing, blue and hairless as a frog, sprang up out of the pool. "I am a master whistler!" he boasted, and blew so hard trees bent and the birds were blown out of their nests.

"Very nice," said Ivan when the air had quieted again. "But now it's my turn. Cover your face, swamp-thing, or the force of my whistle might break your nose."

The swamp-thing hastily covered his face. Ivan took a deep breath—and pushed the swamp-thing with all his might. So mightily did he push that the thing went sailing into the pool with a splash.

"Did you see that?" the swamp-thing whispered. "His whistle was so strong it knocked me right into the water!"

The leader of the swamp-things swam up from the muddy bottom. The others had been ugly, but he was so ugly the birds were too frightened to sing. The others had been fierce, but he was so fierce his eyes were red-hot flames. In his scaly hand he clutched his great iron staff. Oh, that was an ugly pole, all bent and twisted—but the swamp-things thought it was beautiful. When he saw Ivan peacefully building his mud bricks, he hissed in fury and slapped the water with his staff so hard a wave splashed up and broke against the trees.

"I challenge you to a contest!" he shouted at Ivan. "We shall each hurl this staff in the air. And the one who hurls it the highest wins!"

The swamp-things all shuddered. "What if something goes wrong?" they whispered. "What if we lose our beautiful, beautiful staff?"

Ivan heard that whisper. So did their leader. But the thing continued angrily, "If you win, you shall build your castle. If I win—I shall eat you!"

"Fair enough," said Ivan calmly. "You go first."

The swamp-thing snapped his sharp teeth together and threw the iron staff into the air. Up and up it flew, till it was nothing more than a tiny black dot against the cloud-covered sky. Then down it came, crashing through the trees. The swamp-thing caught it in his sharp-clawed fist and laughed.

"There! Can you beat *that?*"

He handed Ivan the staff. Ivan tried and tried, but he couldn't even lift the heavy pole off the ground! He saw the swamp-thing's teeth gnash together in hunger, and thought quickly.

"Oh yes," Ivan said as calmly as he could. "I could beat that throw with only one hand. But I warn you, if I throw this staff up with all my strength, it will catch in the clouds up there. And then it will never, never come down again."

The foolish things believed him. What, their beautiful iron staff stay stuck in the clouds forever? "Oh no, not that!" they cried out in horror.

"Dear, sweet, gentle man, let us keep our staff. Build your castle."

"Well now, I don't think I want one any more."

"What *do* you want?"

Ivan remembered the stories he had heard about the swamp-things. He remembered how they were said to eat people—and steal their treasure. "I want only one small thing," he said. "A little gold. Just enough to fill my hat."

The swamp-things laughed with relief. To them, gold was sharp and shiny and ugly, something they stole only because humans seemed to like it so much! They eagerly filled Ivan's hat with shining coins. Heart racing with excitement, Ivan thanked them, and went off to find Lord Alexei.

Lord Alexei was furious. He didn't want to lose his serf. But he didn't want to lose the gold, either! At last, after muttering and shouting, shouting and muttering, he gave up.

"You are a free man," he told Ivan. "I swear it before these witnesses. Now, give me that hat!"

"Not so fast," Ivan said. "You said, 'Bring me a hatful of

gold.' You didn't say anything about actually giving it to you!"

Oh, Lord Alexei was truly furious now! But what could he do? He had freed Ivan in front of witnesses. And all of them agreed that the soft felt hat did, indeed, belong to Ivan—as did its contents.

And so everyone was left with something. The swamp-things had their beautiful iron staff.

Lord Alexei had a haunted swamp. And clever Ivan had the best thing of all, finer than any iron staff, finer than any gold: He had his freedom.

Granny and the Thief

A Tale from China

Once, long, long ago, old Granny was working in her garden. Suddenly: clink! Her hoe struck something hard.

"What's this? A coin? A little copper coin!"

Granny grinned at her good luck. Taking the coin home with her, she put the coin at the bottom of her small rice jar for safekeeping. The next morning, she took out half of the rice to prepare her meal. But what was this? At the end of the day, she found that the jar was full to the brim with rice once more!

"The coin is magic! Why, it must be the one the wizard gave great-great-Grandfather Li long ago, lost all these years. And now I've found it again."

Granny laughed out loud at her good luck. From that day on, she knew she would never have to worry again about going hungry. And she was happy to share her rice with anyone else who needed food, too. That made everyone happy.

Almost everyone. Word of the magic coin spread, as such things do. But the story changed in the spreading, as such things also do. By the time it had reached the ears of cruel Tiger the thief, the people were whispering that old Granny had found a magic coin that hatched a new pile of gold every day.

So Tiger hurried down to visit Granny. Oh, he was a fearsome sight, all knives and fierce stares! "I want your magic coin!" he told Granny. "I want your gold!"

"Gold!" Granny cried in surprise. "I don't have any gold! All I have is one small copper coin that produces rice. Do you want any rice?"

"Don't lie to me, old woman. I know you have gold. And I want that coin! Give it to me now, or I'll—"

"Dear me," said Granny mildly, "here comes Farmer Weng down the road to visit me."

There wasn't any Farmer Weng. But Tiger didn't know that. And for all his cruel looks, Tiger was a coward. He snarled and ran away.

"He'll be back," Granny said to herself. "But I can't let him have the magic coin! He would just throw it away as soon as he learned it didn't make gold. And if there's ever a drought and the crops fail, my friends and I will truly need that coin! No, he cannot have it!"

But what could one old woman do against the terrible Tiger? She was all alone here on her farm, with no one to help her. "Let me think," said Granny. And all at once she gave a little snort of laughter. "Very well, then. Let Tiger come. I shall teach that thief a lesson!"

That day, Granny sat most of the morning sharpening and sharpening her good steel sickle. She spent most of the afternoon catching a fierce little crab and a noisy little frog. The crab went into the water bucket in her house. The frog went into a box at the side of her bed.

"A good start," Granny said.

She placed the heavy bolt from the door against the head of her bed, and balanced her good, sturdy hammer on the ledge over the door.

"Even better!" said Granny.

She hid the bellows from the fireplace in amid the ashes. She strewed handfuls of hard little uncooked peas all over the floor. And then Granny sat in her small chair in the corner, waiting for Tiger.

And, sure enough, with the night came the thief. He pushed warily at the door. It swung open.

"What's this? The old woman has forgotten to bolt it!" Tiger peered inside. It was dark in there. Old Granny must be asleep. Tiger knew he must be very quiet.

He tiptoed in. But he tiptoed right onto some of the hard, uncooked peas. And—wow! They shot out from under his feet! Down went Tiger on his face with a crash!

"What happened? Who pushed me? It's so dark I can't see anything!" But there wasn't a sound.

"The old woman is still asleep." Then, who had pushed Tiger? He decided to get a spark from the fireplace so he could see. The thief bent over to blow on the coals to get a little flame burning. But as he did, Tiger put his hand down right on the hidden bellows. And—whoosh! They blew a cloud of ashes right in his face!

Coughing and choking, Tiger groped his way to the water bucket. But as soon as his fingers touched the water—Aie! The crab reach up and nipped him!

"There's a devil in the water! A devil blew ashes at me!"

Tiger forgot about washing. He would just take the magic coin and run! But where was the coin? By the old woman's bed?

Tiger tiptoed forward. But in the darkness, he didn't see the box with the frog in it. He tripped over the box, and the frog began to croak loudly, "Creak-crack! Creak-crack!"

A devil's voice! Tiger staggered back against the bed. And—oh! The heavy door bolt fell down from the head of the bed and smacked him sharply across the shoulders!

"The devil hit me! He's after me!"

Tiger forgot about gold. He ran for the doorway. But he stopped on the slippery peas again and crashed right into the door. And—aie! The hammer fell off the ledge and came plunging down to rap Tiger right on the head! He sat down with a thump.

"More devils! They're all around me!"

He heard a laugh. Granny stood up slowly. And Tiger saw that in her hand glinted and gleamed a sharp steel sickle.

"She's a witch! She wants to kill me!"

Tiger scrambled to his feet. He threw open the door and ran off into the night. Yelling in terror, he ran and ran and ran—and for all anyone knows, he is running still.

Granny blew on the coals till she had a nice fire going. She set the frog and the crab free, put the hammer and the bolt and the sickle back in their proper places, and swept up all the slippery peas. She looked at her rice-jar with the magic coin in it, and smiled.

"That's that," said Granny to herself, and went peacefully to bed.

The Orphan and the Miser

———— A Tale from the Tadzhik Republic ————

Once, long ago, there lived a wealthy merchant named Dilshod. But though Dilshod was wealthy, he was also so greedy that he never spent as much as a single copper coin if there were a way to avoid it. Each time he hired a servant, why, that merchant would find some way to trick the servant out of his or her wages. Soon word spread throughout the city. No one would work for Dilshod. No one wanted to be cheated!

"Your miserly ways will ruin us!" wailed the merchant's wife.

But Dilshod only smiled. "I will find us a new servant. He will serve us willingly for years—and all it will cost us is the price of his food. Watch."

So Dilshod went to a young orphan boy. Hafiz was that boy's name, and he was kind as he was poor, and clever despite his youth. He and the merchant's daughter, young Sureya, had often smiled shyly at each other in the marketplace. But orphan boys and merchant's daughters never get the chance to meet.

Dilshod pretended to study Hafiz. "Hmm, yes. I like the looks of you, indeed I do. In fact... Mmm... Yes. I do believe that someday I might even want you for a son-in-law. Come to work for me now, and when you and my daughter are of age, you shall wed her and be my heir. How does that sound to you?"

That sounded wonderful to poor Hafiz! Gladly he went to work for the merchant, and asked no wages of him. Gladly he toiled, dreaming of the future. And as the years rolled by, he fell deeply in love with Sureya, and she with him. Their hearts sang with joy at the thought that soon they would be wed.

But the days came and the days went, and not a word did Dilshod say about that. And one night Sureya heard her parents talking about the rich old man they meant for her to marry! In tears, she went to Hafiz, and in anger he went to Dilshod.

"Sureya and I are to wed!" he said. "You vowed it!"

"Marry my daughter?" Dilshod cried, pretending to be horrified. "You, an orphan? A mere servant? Nonsense."

"But you promised—"

"I promised nothing! Come with me to the judge. We shall settle this matter."

But the judge, alas, was Dilshod's cousin. When he heard Hafiz's plea, he only shook his head.

"Did you get this agreement on paper, young man? Were there witnesses? No? Shame on you, trying to cheat a fine, upstanding merchant. I order you to leave this city at once! Merchant Dilshod, what wages shall you pay this young scoundrel before he leaves your service?"

Dilshod pretended to think. "A sack of wheat should be enough. No, half a sack. Just the wages such a lying, ungrateful young man deserves!"

"Lying!" gasped Hafiz. "Ungrateful!"

But then, choking on his anger, he stopped and thought. And suddenly Hafiz smiled to himself. He bowed humbly before Dilshod and the judge. "There's only one problem, good merchant," he said meekly. "Your wife knows nothing of this. What if she refuses to let me have the wheat?"

Dilshod shrugged. He was very comfortable sitting here drinking tea with his cousin the judge. He didn't want to hurry home, particularly not over such a small matter as this. "If my wife looks out her window," Dilshod said, "she can see me sitting here. I will wave to her to let her know everything is fine."

"Why, that's wonderful," Hafiz said, biting back a laugh. He hurried back to the merchant's house and whispered to Sureya, "Will you marry me, come what may?"

"Of course I will!" Sureya whispered back.

Hafiz quickly told her his plan. Sureya fairly danced for joy. "Nothing of my father's will I take," she decided. "But these jewels are mine, and these I *will* take."

"Now come, my love, hurry," Hafiz said. "Hide over here in the courtyard where your father, back there with the judge, can't see you."

Sureya hid. Hafiz strolled to the center of the courtyard and called up to Dilshod's wife. She came to the window, frowning.

"What do you want, servant?"

"Your husband has told me to wed your daughter and take her away with me."

"*What!*" the merchant's wife shrieked. "You can't—He wouldn't—He would never let our daughter go off and marry a—a nobody like you!"

"There is your husband with the judge, good woman. Please, ask him yourself."

It was a long way to shout. Besides, the merchant's wife didn't want the whole city knowing her business. So she gestured fiercely to her husband, is this right?

Dilshod, of course, thought she was asking if Hafiz should have the half sack of wheat. He smiled and nodded.

That was too much for his wife. "Have you gone mad?" she screamed. "You can't mean it!"

Now *that* was too much for Dilshod. How dare his wife shout at him—and before the judge and the whole town, too! "I do mean it!" he yelled back. "Give the young man what he asks!"

"But—"

"Go on! *Give Hafiz what he asks!*"

What could the merchant's wife do? Bewildered and furious, she waved Hafiz and Sureya away. By the time Dilshod came home and found out what had happened, it was, of course, far too late. The two young people were safely wed and far away.

And since they had Sureya's jewels and Hafiz's clever wits, and their own strong love, they lived happily all their days.

How Corn Came to the People

A Tale of the Yaqui People of Arizona

Once, in the long-ago days, the people and the bird-and-animal-folk were friends and could speak with each other. But in those days, the people knew nothing about planting crops.

"Come," said proud Eagle to the men-folk, stretching out his golden wings. "I will teach you how to hunt."

But the men-folk had no wings. They could not soar in the air or dive down on prey like Eagle.

"Come," said cheerful Blackbird to the women-folk. "I will teach you how to gather bugs and berries."

But Blackbird was much smaller than any of the people. It took only a few mouthfuls of berries to feed him. The women-folk could not gather enough bugs and berries to feed all the people.

And so the people were always, always hungry.

One day, the bird-and-animal-folk held a great council meeting.

"We must do something to help the people, or they will starve," Blackbird began.

"They have no wings," Eagle said scornfully. "Why should we help such weak creatures."

"It's true they have no wings," said Blackbird. "The people have no claws, either, or fangs, or fur. But they can sing sweet people-songs and tell us wonderful stories."

The bird-and-animal-folk thought of those wonderful stories. They thought of those sweet people-songs, and agreed, "The people are our friends. We must help them."

"I know!" said Blackbird. "Let us give them the gift of corn."

"But—but only Yuku the Rain God keeps the corn seed," murmured shy Deer. "Everyone knows how greedy he is. He loves to gather treasures, and never, never parts with any of them. Yuku will never give up even a single seed of corn to the people."

"Why, then I shall steal some corn for them!" Blackbird cried.

With that, he flew off to the great house of the Rain God. There he fluttered about and pretended to do nothing, till Yuku forgot all about him. But as soon as Yuku's back was turned, Blackbird snatched up a bag full of corn seed in his beak and flew as fast as he could fly to the people.

And that was how corn first came to the people.

Ah, but back in his great house, Yuku the Rain God was counting his treasures. What was this? One of his bags of corn seed was missing!

"A thief was here!" he cried in anger. "The people are always hungry. They must have stolen it. But the corn will never grow for them! I shall hold back the rain, and that corn will wither and die!"

When the bird-and-animal-folk saw that no rain fell, Blackbird sighed.

"I shall fly back to Yuku," he said. "I shall ask him to set the rain free."

But when Yuku saw Blackbird flying towards him, the Rain God only laughed.

"The feathered one wants me to set free the rain. But that I shall never do!"

Instead, the Rain God set free the wild storm winds. They tossed and tumbled Blackbird from the sky, back to the bird-and-animal-folk.

"I—I can't fly in those strong winds," he gasped.

"Then I shall go!" cried Roadrunner. "I don't fly, I run!"

But when Yuku saw Roadrunner speeding towards him, the Rain God only laughed.

"The running one wants me to set free the rain. But that I shall never do!"

Instead, the Rain God set free the fierce lightning bolts. They flashed and crashed down at Roadrunner till they made him run away as fast as he could run, back to the bird-and-animal-folk.

"I—I can't go on!" he panted. "The lightning is too fierce for me!"

"What can we do now?" cried all the bird-and-animal-folk. "The people need the rain. We need the rain! How can we ever get Yuku to set it free?"

They all fell silent.

"I think I know," said a tiny, creaking, croaking voice.

Everyone looked around. Who had spoken?

It was Frog, one of the smallest of the animal-folk. "I do know what to do," she said, "I, and my brothers and sisters."

When Yuku saw Frog hopping towards him, the Rain God only laughed.

"The hopping one wants me to set free the rain. But that I shall never do! Now, how shall I deal with her? Shall I let the storm winds blow her away? Or shall I send the lightning bolts flashing down to—But what is this? I saw only one frog. Now there are two! No matter, no matter, the lightning will still—Wait, I was wrong. There are three frogs—no, four! No! There are frogs all over!"

"Greedy Yuku," croaked the frogs. "Greedy, greedy Yuku."

Their creaking, croaking voices filled the air.

"Stop that!" shouted Yuku, hands over his ears. "Go away!"

But the frogs would not go away. "Greedy Yuku," they said.

"Greedy, greedy Yuku."

Their creaking, croaking voices filled the air till Yuku could hear nothing else. "I must stop them!" he yelled. "But—but there aren't enough winds to blow all those frogs away! There aren't enough lightning bolts!"

"Greedy Yuku," croaked the frogs. "Greedy, greedy Yuku."

"Enough!" screamed the angry Rain God. "I—I will drown them! I'll let the rain drown them all!"

And so Yuku set free the rain. Down it plunged! Floods and floods of water fell from the sky.

But the frogs didn't drown. Oh no, frogs love water! All the frogs went splashing and swimming happily away.

"Oh no," gasped Yuku, "I set free the rain. I've been tricked!"

What could Yuku do? He was too proud to admit he'd been tricked by lowly little frogs. He could only smile and nod and pretend he had meant to set free the rain all along!

So it was that the rain fell once more. So it was that the corn could grow. And so it was that, thanks to the bird-and-animal-folk, the people never went hungry again.

Notes

The notes that follow provide source information and folkloric background on each of the stories. The books cited are cross-referenced in the book section of the Further Reading and Viewing list beginning on page 243 with full bibliographic information.

Part One

1. "To Boldly Go . . ." (p. 13)

These words are taken from the opening lines of each *Star Trek* episode: "...to boldly go where no man has gone before." *Star Trek: The Next Generation*, the spin-off television show that began in 1987, reflected the changing world by, among other things, updating this line to "...where no one has gone before."

Star Trek is, indeed, a phenomenon unlike anything ever known to television or the movies, having created, to date, three different but related television series—*Star Trek* (1966-69), *Star Trek: The Next Generation* (1987-94) and *Star Trek: Deep Space Nine* (1993 -present)—with a fourth in preparation; six motion pictures, again, with others in the works; and well over a hundred books and magazines. In addition, several conventions devoted to *Star Trek* fandom are held around the world every year (dates and addresses can be found in such magazines of the science fiction world as *Locus* and *Science Fiction Chronicle*).

2. Jason and the Argonauts (p. 15)

Jason fits neatly into a traditional category of hero: the man of royal or noble birth who is raised ignorant of his true heritage. See Part III for other examples.

Chiron, Jason's centaur tutor, has a story of his own. A wise, immortal being, he was friendly to humans, helping both as a scholar and as a revered physician. Unfortunately, not all centaurs were as civilized. During the marriage of Hercules, drunken centaurs tried to abduct his bride. In the resulting conflict, Chiron was accidentally wounded by one of Hercules's arrows. Such a wound could never heal, and Chiron, in constant pain, prayed to be turned mortal so he might die. His prayer was granted, but he lives on as the constellation Centaurus.

The most complete version of the adventures of Jason and the Argonauts (and the one on which this version is primarily based) can be found in The *Voyage of Argo*, by the poet Apollonius of Rhodes, who wrote his epic tale sometime about the third century B.C.E.* The complete story goes from adventure to adventure like a modern television series, with each adventure making up a separate "episode." A version of the story of the *Argo* was turned into a movie, *Jason and the Argonauts*, in 1963, with special effects by Ray Harryhausen. While it's an entertaining movie, it does make several startling changes, turning Medea, for instance, into a gentler, less magical heroine than the coldly efficient sorceress of legend.

The story of Jason, in addition to fitting the theme of a heroic crew of sailors venturing into the unknown, also belongs to the more general category of the quest tale. For more on the quest, see Part IV.

3. The Fool of the World and the Ship that Flew (p. 24)

This type of tale, in which the young hero gathers an unusual group of companions with magical powers, is very common in Europe, particularly in Eastern Europe. The magical ship is a relative to other magical flying objects, such as the carpets of Near Eastern lore, and the mysterious old man who helps Ivan the Fool has his counterparts in equally mysterious old men and women who turn up in folktales from around the world and who often test the hero or heroine by asking to share food. Sometimes these helpful elders are specific people, such as the Prophet Elijah, who turns up in some Jewish folktales, or the Greek goddess Hera, who turns up in the story of Jason and the Argonauts. Sometimes they are, instead, specific types of people, such as Cinderella's fairy godmother. Sometimes, though, these magical helpers don't have a specific identity. Instead, they seem to exist in the stories just to give the hero or heroine a chance to show their basic kind natures—which isn't of such small importance!

This tale is known to the author. A similar version can be found in *Russian Fairy Tales*, collected by Alexandr Afanas'ev.

4. The Children of Puna (p. 32)

While this tale fits within the basic theme of a questing group of sailors, it is a less common and more heroic variant, one in which the companions are undergoing their quest not for any personal gain but to put an end to a danger that is menacing their people.

Rata—also known in Hawaiian legendry as Laka—is listed as an

---

* C.E. and B.C.E. stand for "the Common Era" and "Before the Common Era." They are secular alternatives to A.D. and B.C.

ancestor in several ancient Polynesian clans; he may actually have been an historical personage, possibly not from Hawaii but from Samoa (the birthplace of his wife, Aparkura) or one of the other more southerly islands of the Pacific. There are many tales telling of the building of his canoe with the aid of the supernatural beings known as Menehune and of his struggles with various sea monsters.

The author's version of this legend is based on variants found in *Legends of Hawaii* edited by Padraic Colum and *Hawaiian Mythology* collected by Martha Beckwith.

5. The Seven Semyons (P. 38)

This tale, like that of the *Fool of the World*, (see note 3), concerns a crew of comrades gifted with bizarre, magical abilities. It also includes a folklore motif known as the "Master Thief" type of tale. The Master Thief is so skillful he can steal an egg right out from under a nesting bird—or the pants off an officious official! Semyon the Thief, like all his fellow folkloric thieves, is amoral but rather likeable, a master of his craft and such a smooth talker and actor he never gets punished for his deeds (or misdeeds).

This tale is known to the author. As with *The Fool of the World and the Ship that Flew*, a similar version can be found in Afanas'ev's *Russian Fairy Tales*.

6. The Story of Sampo (p. 42)

This story, part folktale, part myth, comes from the world of the *Kalevela*, the collection of ancient folk ballads that has been called the Finnish national epic, although it was only put into its present form by Elias Lonnrot in the nineteenth century. The figures here are very definitely larger than life and much older than the nineteenth century: Vainamoinen, the ancient wizard, is one of the older beings, not really human at all, having stayed in his mother's womb till he was an old man born with full knowledge of magic, while Ilmarinen, with his mastery of the forge, resembles the legends of smith-gods such as Vulcan. Both of them may originally have been gods rather than heroes, though no trace of their worship remains.

Vainamoinen was probably one of J.R.R. Tolkien's inspirations for his own not really human hero-wizard, Gandalf, who plays such an important role in *The Lord of the Rings*.

There are many "how and why" or "pourquoi" tales from around the world explaining how various parts of the natural world came to be, among them several stories in which a magical mill, such as the Sampo, turns the seas to salt.

7. The Journeys of Maeldon (p. 48)

The tale of Maeldun (or Mael Dun, Maildun, Maelduin, or even Maoldun) dates from perhaps the ninth or tenth century. More episodic even than the tale of Jason and the Argonauts, it includes a long catalog of islands with wonders the heroes visit without undergoing any adventures, almost as though they were tourists! Such listings of wonders were quite popular in Irish tales of the period. What makes this sailor-hero tale unique is that when the hero finally reaches his goal—which is, of course, revenge—he no longer wants to claim it.

This version is the author's own somewhat condensed version of the original, which is much longer and more episodic, including a lengthy catalog of wonderful islands. One good translation of the complete story can be found in *Old Celtic Romances* by P.W. Joyce.

Part Two

8. "It's a Bird, It's a Plane . . ." (p. 55)

The complete phrase, "It's a bird, it's a plane, it's Superman!" was exclaimed by many characters in the Superman movies, television shows, and comic books upon sighting the superhero in flight.

Although characters with superhuman strength have been around since the dawn of literature—the half-divine Hercules, who has his own cycle of tales but is also a supporting character in the story of Jason and the Argonauts, featured in Part I, is one example—it was writer Jerry Siegel and artist Joe Shuster who first came up with the idea of a specific hero known as Superman. They had a difficult time selling that idea to comic book publishers, but Superman finally did appear in Action Comics in 1938, and was given his own comic book, Superman Comics, in 1939. A highly-popular character, he has also appeared in newspaper comic strips, a radio series, several television series, an animated cartoon series, and several movies.

The theme of an abandoned child rescued from the waves is an extremely popular one; versions have been collected from countries as far apart as Ireland and China, and from times as far separated as the nineteenth centuries B.C.E. and C.E.!

For stories about other heroes who grew up ignorant of their true origins, see the tales of "Jason and the Argonauts" and "The Journeys of Maeldun" in Part I and the tales of heroes with supernatural helpers in Part III.

9. Sargon the Mighty (p. 57)

Sargon of Akkad was a perfectly real historical character who ruled over the kingdom he founded by force of arms, the land of Akkad—now part of Iraq—during the Second Millennium B.C.E. He really did, unlike the standard type of "hero raised ignorant of his noble origin," come from humble (or, depending on the version of the story, totally unknown) origins, but why the folklore motif of the baby rescued from a river was attached to him, or whether it actually did happen to Sargon, is unknown. The story of his childhood and rise to power was, at any rate, a popular story in Akkad, and was told in various versions or written on clay tablets right down to the eighth century B.C.E.

This retelling is based on the translated texts found in *The Sargon Legend: A Study of the Akkadian Text and the Tale of the Hero Who was Exposed at Birth* by Brian Lewis.

10. The Story of Moses (p. 59)

The story of Moses, the parting of the Red Sea, and the Exodus of the Jews out of Egypt is (or should be) familiar to almost everyone. This particular version of his early years is the author's own combination of texts from the Holy Scriptures, Exodus 1:8-2:20 and the Babylonian Talmud, Sotah 12a-13b. The names of Moses's mother and sister come from the Talmud. Although archaeological excavations have not yet found written proof of Moses's existence, it seems very likely that there was a historical figure behind the story. The Exodus has been roughly dated to somewhere between ca. 1450 and 1250 B.C.E., and the Pharaoh of the Exodus might have been either Rameses II or Seti I. Since Moses's mother might well have been aware of the earlier story of Sargon, which was certainly being told in the First Millennium B.C.E., she might have copied the idea of the little boat woven from rushes and smeared with pitch to rescue her baby, though of course this is pure speculation.

This is the author's own retelling of the Old Testament story.

11. The Two Babies Cast into the Water (p. 61)

The opening elements of this story, with the three sisters daydreaming about their husbands-to-be and the youngest winning a royal mate through her dreams of supernaturally beautiful children, are not at all unusual, turning up in Russian, Albanian, and other Eastern European tales. Pushkin made use of it in his "Tale of Tsar Saltan," which includes the theme of the baby—and in his story, the mother as well—being cast away in a floating chest. This story was turned into an opera, "Tsar Saltan," by the Russian composer Nikolai Rimsky-Korsakov. In the story of Perseus, mother and baby are also cast into the sea in a floating chest.

An intriguing aspect of folktales is that often not everything in a story is explained. Why does the tree sing or the bird talk? Who is the strange old man who gives the children his wise advise? No one knows. The motif of a boy or girl whose smiles, tears or footsteps result in marvels is also common in world folklore. Various characters are said to weep gems or have gold drop from their very words or have flowers spring up where they tread. In the converse of these tales, the nasty counterpart of the protagonist—who usually is an evil stepsister who torments the heroine and then disobeys various magical prohibitions or the rules of common courtesy—winds up with various unpleasant marvels that parallel the wondrous ones, such as having toads drop from his or her words.

This retelling of a Polish folktale (sometimes known in English as "About Two Babies Cast Onto the Water") is based on several versions, including that found in *The Glass Mountain: Twenty-Six Ancient Polish Folktales and Fables* by W.S. Kuniczak.

12. Grandfather Wisdom (p. 66)

This is a very popular tale in Europe; almost identical tales have been collected in France (where a devil takes the place of Grandfather Wisdom) and Germany (where an ogre is the golden-haired peril). Magical beings visiting a newborn baby with special wishes also turn up in other tales, including, of course, the various forms of "Sleeping Beauty." The motif of a young man on a quest who carries the questions of those in need is a widespread one as well, turning up in stories from countries as far apart as France and China.

This retelling is based on various Czech versions. This is the most common title in English for the tale. See *The Water Sprite of the Golden Town: Folk Tales of Bohemia*, by Zdenka and John Paul Quinn.

13. The Children of Ahmad Aga (p. 75)

Here is yet another version of the theme of a new mother falsely accused of witchly behavior because her child has been stolen away and replaced with a beast, in this version a dead snake. What makes this Turkish tale different from most variants is that the children have no desire at all to abandon their foster parents to seek out their father and claim an inheritance. The evil wife and her sorceress accomplice are totally forgotten!

This retelling is based both on the author's memory and on a version included in *The Sargon Legend* by Brian Lewis.

--- **Part Three** ---

14. ". . . In a Galaxy Far, Far Away" (p. 79)

The complete phrase, famous to everyone who has seen the first *Star Wars* movie, is the beautifully evocative, "Once upon a time in a galaxy far, far away," which are the first words to appear on the screen as the movie begins.

George Lucas, creator of the *Star Wars* universe, was a student of mythologist Joseph Campbell and is a lifetime fan of science fiction and fantasy. It's not at all surprising that several characters play mythic roles in addition to their roles in the story itself. For instance: Luke Skywalker is, of course, the hero ignorant of his origins, Obi-Wan Ben Kenobi is the helpful sage, Luke and Princess Leia are the hero and heroine separated at birth, and Han Solo is both a trickster and the hero who escapes through his cleverness.

15. The Story of King Cyrus (p. 81)

Cyrus, like Sargon and Moses (see Part II), was a perfectly real historical figure who lived between 599-530 B.C.E. He overthrew King Astyages, founded the Achaemenid Dynasty in Persia (now Iran), and ruled from 549 to 530 B.C.E. over an empire that included part of what is now Iraq. His father was Cambyses I, Prince of Persis, rather than the nobody of the folktale; his mother may have been the daughter of King Astyages. How did the folktale about his childhood as a boy ignorant of his heritage get attached to him? No one knows.

This story is known to the author. A fairly complete version is summarized in *The Sargon Legend* by Brian Lewis.

16. Percival: The Backwoods Knight (p. 85)

Percival (also known as Parsifal, Perceval or Parzifal) is one of the more famous knights of King Arthur's Round Table, with several medieval romances and even an opera by Richard Wagner, *Parsifal*, written about his adventures. He has his earliest incarnation as the Welsh Peredur, who is involved not with the Christian Grail but with earlier pagan grails. Later, more familiar versions, mostly dating from the twelfth to fourteen centuries, add the mysterious Blanchefleur and the element of the veiled cup—which is, of course, the Holy Grail. (See note 28 for more about the story of the Quest for the Grail and Percival's reunion with the Lady Blanchefleur.)

One of the most international figures in folklore is that of the Divine Fool, the man who is so totally innocent of the world and its ways that he reaches a nearly holy state. Percival, in some versions of his story such as Richard Wagner's opera *Parsifal*, takes on this role.

The author's retelling is a compilation from many sources, including *Le Morte D'Arthur* by Sir Thomas Malory and *The Romance of Perceval in Prose* translated by Dell Skeels.

17. The Boy with the Straw (p. 91)

There are many folktales throughout the world in which a character starts out with something relatively valueless and cleverly trades his way up to a true treasure—in this case, all the way to a throne. As is often true in the frequently illogical world of folklore, no explanation is available for the sudden magical transformation of sword to snake or painted birds to live ones!

This retelling is based on a folktale recorded in *Folktales of Japan* by Keigo Seki and collected by him from Kubomori Sashi of Okierabu Island, Oshima-gun, Kagoshima-ken.

18. The Boyhood of Finn (p. 94)

This is the author's combination of some of the many folktales told about Finn (or Fionn) mac Cumhail (sometimes rendered as Cool). He is a highly-popular figure in Celtic folklore, turning up both as the central figure in a whole cycle of heroic and magical tales set at the court of possibly historic High-King Cormac of Ireland, and as a weirdly-distorted, parodied figure in various less heroic folktales. While it's not impossible that there was a historical Finn, possibly dating to about the second century C.E., there isn't any actual evidence of his existence. What we do have, since he was such a popular character, are a good many conflicting stories about every stage of his long, varied, often magic-touched career.

Regarding Finn's two protector-tutors, wise women and warrior women are not unusual figures in Celtic folklore. Whether or not there actually were female druids has been a matter of much debate, and it's not always clear from the various folktales about the childhood of Finn whether his tutors really were druids, but there most certainly were women warriors both in fiction and history. The real-life Queen Boudicca held the Roman legions at bay for several years, while in the world of folklore, another great hero of Celtic lore, Cuchulain, was trained by a powerful woman warrior, Scathach, who was considered the finest fighter and tutor of fighters in Ireland.

This is the author's own compilation and retelling based upon many versions of this tale. For another version, see *Old Celtic Romances* by P.W. Joyce.

19. Cap O' Rushes (p. 99)

"Cap O'Rushes" is a variant of one of the most popular world tales: "Cinderella." In fact, more than six hundred variations have been collected from virtually every culture in the world. In a good many versions, including "Cap O'Rushes," the heroine is a far stronger character than the rather pallid, helpless heroine familiar to most Americans through the Disney cartoon and many watered-down fairy tale books. Cap O'Rushes and her folkloric sisters are characters able to accept temporary setbacks without flinching and are fully determined not only to survive but to triumph.

The opening segment of this story, in which the three daughters are asked how much they love their father and the youngest mentions "as meat loves salt," is an old folkloric theme, and has its parallel in stories from lands as far apart as Ireland, India, and Russia; it was also used by Shakespeare in Act One of *King Lear*.

This is the author's retelling of a popular English folktale. The tale can be found in several collections, including *English Folktales* edited by Joseph Jacobs.

20. Donkey-Skin (p. 104)

This is, of course, another variant on the story of "Cinderella." Like her counterpart, Cap O'Rushes, Donkey-Skin is a beautiful girl who takes on an ugly disguise to protect herself, and like Cap O'Rushes, she is a clever, determined young woman who, once she is over the shock of being on her own, manages very nicely. Donkey-Skin's mysterious godmother fits the theme of the sage as helper, appearing in the story long enough to give the girl the magical items she'll need to triumph, then disappearing from it completely.

Many of the versions of this tale include the motif of the three (or more) beautiful gowns which must be given to the heroine by her father as a condition of their marriage. As for the threat of incest that drives the heroine out into the world, in some versions, the father is described as having gone so mad from grief he can't tell mother from daughter, but in a good many he isn't given any such excuse. Some variants, like this one, drop him from the story altogether once his daughter is safely out of his reach, while others place him at his daughter's wedding feast, where he repents and weeps over the crime he almost committed. Some less-forgiving versions include a quick description of his locking himself in a tower and weeping himself to death over the loss of his potential wife.

Why was a donkey-skin picked for the heroine's disguise? It's impossible to say, but there may have been some elements of magical transformation in earlier versions; in the almost identical English tale of "Cat-Skin," the heroine has some oddly feline attributes while wearing that skin, such as shaking her ears, that suggest echoes of shape-shifting.

This is the author's retelling of a popular French folktale. Like "Cap O'Rushes," it can be found in many collections, including *Folktales of France* edited by Genevieve Massignon.

—————————— Part Four ——————————

21. "One Ring to Rule Them All . . ." (p. 111)

This is part of the evocative rhyme to be found at the start of *The Fellowship of the Ring*, the first book of J.R.R. Tolkien's *Lord of the Rings* trilogy, describing the magic rings—particularly the last, most perilously powerful—that are the focal point of the story.

J.R.R. (John Ronald Reuel) Tolkien (1892-1973) was primarily a philologist and a Don at Oxford University. It was his love of languages real and imaginary, together with his knowledge of Northern European epics and myths, that led him to the creation of a fantasy world in which to set the languages he'd invented. That world, of course, was Middle Earth. While *The Lord of the Rings* was first published in hardcover, it wasn't until the paperback editions appeared in 1965, (both in "unofficial" Ace editions—which were quickly removed from the market, and in the "official" Ballantine editions) that Middle Earth and its inhabitants became part of a publishing phenomenon that continues to this day. *Lord of the Rings* has gone through over seventy-five printings, with no end in sight, and virtually everything Professor Tolkien ever wrote, whether fiction or nonfiction, is in print in one form or another.

22. The Sword in the Stone: The Coming of Arthur (p. 114)

This is perhaps one of the best-known legends of Western civilization. Stories about Arthur can be found in every corner of Britain. They are familiar to almost everyone, and have been the basis for several motion pictures and many fantasy and historical novels. There almost certainly was an historical Arthur, even if he wasn't the romantic king of medieval story: He was probably Artos, a Celtic war leader who fought several battles against the invading Saxons in the fifth and early sixth centuries C.E., and who is listed in the Anglo-Saxon Chronicles as having defeated the Saxons at the Battle of Badon in 518.

According to legend, the sword taken from the stone is not the blade most commonly associated with Arthur, the famous Excalibur; instead, it's a nameless weapon that breaks soon after Arthur is crowned. With Merlin's guidance, the young king soon gains the more famous, less vulnerable sword from the magical Lady of the Lake. Unfortunately for Arthur, though, he makes a mistake that eventually becomes fatal: He does not retain Excalibur's scabbard, which would have protected him from all harm.

Arthur, of course, falls into the folklore category of the young hero raised ignorant of his true noble origins, just as Merlin falls into the role of the Wise Old Man or the Sage as Helper. But the story of Arthur is also inseparable from the equally worldwide motif of the sword in the stone or tree, the sword that can be freed only by the chosen hero. A parallel motif to that of the sword in the stone can be found in the story of Rama in the Indian epic *The Ramayana* and in that of Odysseus in *The Odyssey*. In both cases, the hero must draw a bow no other man can bend, Rama to prove his worth and win a bride, Odysseus to prove his identity.

This is the author's own compilation and retelling from a good many different version of the tale. See, for instance, *Le Mort D'Arthur* by Sir Thomas Malory.

23. The Sword is Broken: The First Part of the Volsung Saga (p. 118)

The story of Sigmund was first crafted by the Norse skalds, their bards, and written down in such compilations of mythological tales as the anonymous *Elder Edda* or the *Prose Edda*—a poet's handbook—of Snorri Sturluson, a twelfth century Icelandic poet. There is no one "authentic" version: some stories name Sigmund's sword Gram or Wrath, others give it no name, while in the Germanic version, the *Niebelungenlied*, it becomes Nothung or Needful. Sigmund is also known as Sigurd in some variants, and in some variants is slain not by Siggeir but by the warrior Hunding, who in these variants is the husband to Sigmund's twin sister. The version in this volume is the author's own shortening of the rather complex and sometimes confusing story.

Richard Wagner made his own use of the legend in his *Ring of the Nibelung* cycle of operas; in *Die Walkure*, his version of the story of Sigmund and Signy, whom he calls by the Germanic names of Siegmund and Sieglinde, the twins become doomed lovers, doomed primarily because Odin's wife, Frigga, is outraged at the twins' double sin of adultery and incest—she is, after all, the goddess of the marriage bed—and insists that they pay the supreme penalty. Even though he has been plotting for the offspring of Siegmund and Sieglinde to save the world of gods and men, Odin reluctantly agrees.

Like Arthur and the saintly Sir Galahad, Sigmund is the one man in his story who can free a sword no one else can move. Unlike the sword in the stone, the blade in this tale is the weapon of Odin himself, an object of desire even though it doesn't have any innate magical powers. In Norse mythology, Odin, father of the gods though he is, is a risky, perilous deity, a dangerous patron as likely to curse a man as bless him; at times he seems as much a god of Darkness as Light. He is said to have sacrificed his eye in exchange for the knowledge of runes of Power.

The main sources for the author's retellings of all three parts of the Volsung Saga were Snorri Sturluson's *Elder Edda* and *The Volsung Saga*, translated by William Morris.

24. The Sword Reforged: The Second Part of the Volsung Saga (p. 122)

The story of Sigurd—or Siegfried in the Germanic version of the saga—contains perhaps the most famous example in folklore of the sword that is reforged and returned to power. Tolkien, of course, made use of the motif in *Lord of the Rings*: When Aragorn, wandering the realm as a mere ranger, takes up his proper role as king, one of his first tasks is to reforge his shattered sword.

The motif of Sigurd gaining instant wisdom when he accidentally tastes the dragon's blood parallels, of course, the scene in which the Celtic hero Finn mac Cumhail gains wisdom through the accidental tasting of the Salmon of Knowledge (see note 18).

The waking of Brynhild with a kiss is, of course, a scene familiar to everyone who knows the fairytale of "Sleeping Beauty." Some cultures attached great power to the exchanging of breath—and thereby a portion of souls—that occurs in a kiss.

Richard Wagner also utilized the story of Sigurd, turning it into *Siegried* in his *Ring* cycle of operas. While both the Norse and the Germanic stories are fairly similar, in the opera the fatal combat that results in Brynhild's exile is that between Sigmund/Siegmund and Hunding. Wagner also turns the princely Sigurd into the rough-and-ready Siegfried, the boy raised almost alone in the forest, more at home with the wilderness than with human society; he has never, in the opera, even seen a woman till he and Brynhild fall instantly in love.

(See note 23 for sources.)

25. The Curse of the Ring: The End of the Volsung Saga (p. 130)

This is perhaps the strongest tale in folklore involving a cursed ring: No one who handles Andvari's ring, no matter how briefly, escapes his or her doom. Both the Norse and Germanic versions of the saga continue it on for several "chapters" after the deaths of Sigurd and Brynhild, following the ring as it brings out the greedy evil in man after man, leading to death after death till the final watery cleansing performed by the grieving Gudrun.

Richard Wagner used this portion of the Volsung Saga for his final *Ring* opera, *Gotterdammerung*, which is usually translated as *The Twilight of the Gods*. Although he follows the theme of the cursed ring closely, he deviates widely from the saga by making the funeral pyre of Sigurd and Brynhild a fire on the cosmic scale, paralleling the burning of Valhalla, a blaze in which the gods themselves are destroyed and a new world order based on love is created.

(See note 23 for sources.)

26. The Fairies' Goddaughter (p. 133)

This folktale shows a more benevolent type of magic ring, one given to a human for a kindness done to a fairy woman. The Fairy Folk are often considered as strictly part of Celtic lore, but they can be found in one form or another in every people's folklore. Like the fairies of Western Europe, these folk do reward a human who has helped them, but unlike their Celtic counterparts, they show no desire to keep the girl they've adopted as a changeling.

The motif of shape-shifting from human to animal as the result of an evil spell is another element common to world folklore. The heroine in this story "tames" the wild beasts back into human shape by "capturing" them with her human belongings.

This retelling is based on several similar Estonian tales, in particular "The God-Daughter of the Rock Fairies" in *Old Estonian Fairy Tales* by Fr. R. Kreutzwald.

27. The Ring of King of Djinn (p. 137)

Here is another tale showing a magic ring that isn't good or evil in itself, but is merely a tool. There's no real villain in the story—except for the greedy man tormenting the animals—but it's a clear example of "a kindness for a kindness." In some versions of this story, the protagonist has a peasant wife whom he forgets until the very end of the tale, when he's offered a monetary reward for returning the Sultan's daughter and suddenly rushes off to his first wife with the money.

There are many stories, from regions as widely separated as Great Britain and Central Asia, that feature a magical being who warns a human to claim as reward only a seemingly humble object, such as the ring the King of the Djinn wears or an apparently worn-out rug that's really a magic carpet.

The element of the helpful animals aiding their human friend by hunting for a lost magical object turns up in folktales all over the world; there are almost always three of them (three is a magic number in many cultures), often a dog, a cat, and a mouse.

This retelling is based on an Egyptian folktale translated by Inea Bushnaq in *Arab Folktales*.

28. The Quest for the Grail (p. 143)

There is no one definitive version of the tale of the quest for the Holy Grail, since, like many other legends, it was told and retold by many different people, all of whom added their own elements; it also incorporates several pieces of pagan stories, not all of which fit comfortably into their newer setting. In any form, the tale, which gained its most familiar, most Christian form in the twelfth and thirteenth centuries, is long and convoluted, particularly if all the various adventures of the knights, particularly of the saintly Galahad, are included. This version is intended to give only the most basic story, mostly from the late Medieval version of Sir Thomas Malory, and is the author's own condensation.

There are, of course, a good many folklore elements in this story. The Grail itself in Christian iconography is variously said to be the one from which Jesus drank at the Last Supper or that which caught his blood at the Crucifixion. But sacred grails, whether in the form of goblets or cauldrons, are a great deal older than Christianity, and are known to a good many peoples. For the pagan Celts, for instance, it took the form of the Cauldron of Plenty, the cauldron from which no one went away hungry, or the Cauldron of Life, which, in the Welsh tale of King Bran in the collection of Welsh myths and legends known as the *Mabinogion*, returns the dead to life. A grail almost always contains holy water or wine, often the Water of Life itself. An example of the Grail Legend used in popular culture can be seen in the Spielberg/Lucas movie, *Indiana Jones and the Last Crusade*, in which a drink from the Grail bestows immortality.

King Pelles is sometimes said to have been wounded not by a knight but by trying to take a weapon too sacred or magical for him to safely handle; the weapon inflicts a wound that will not heal. But the Maimed King, also known as the Fisher King, is a figure much older than the Arthurian King Pelles. In a good many cultures, the king and the land are one; if the king is wounded or loses virility, the land's fertility suffers as well. There have been some attempts in popular culture to show this older side of the story. The 1981 movie *Excalibur* shows the tie-in of king to land, and *The Fisher King*, both the book by Anthony Powell, and the 1991 movie made from the book, though set in modern times, makes blatant reference to the ancient story.

The motif of the sword in the stone turns up in the tale of the quest for the Grail almost as a parallel of the story of Arthur, though of course it has other parallels as well (see notes 22 and 23). The motif of the sword that is broken and reforged turns up in the Grail story as well, though it serves little purpose except to point up the holiness of Galahad (see note 23).

Percival is, of course, yet another hero raised ignorant of his true origins who rises to his true potential (see note 16).

This retelling is a compilation of the many—and often contradictory—versions of the Grail Quest. See *Le Mort D'Arthur* by Sir Thomas Malory.

29. Cupid and Psyche (p. 149)

This is a variant of one of the most popular folktales in the world: "Beauty and the Beast." In this particular type of tale, the enchanted hero disappears after the heroine breaks a prohibition—she either tries to see his human face although she's been forbidden to do so, or tries and fails to break the spell by burning his animal skin—and she must go after him. It is a very popular type of story, turning up both in this Classical Greek tale and in stories from all over Europe and Asia, from Britain to Russia (see note 34).

The evil stepmother or, in this case the jealous mother-in-law, who sets the heroine three seemingly impossible tasks turns up in many a folktale from around the world. Usually one of the tasks takes the shape of sorting some difficult items, feathers or, as in this story, grain; animal or supernatural helpers always come to the heroine's aid just in time.

The instructions for surviving the visit to the Underworld are interesting. Charon should be familiar to anyone who has studied Greek mythology as the boatman who ferries souls across the River Styx or sometimes the River Lethe, River of Forgetfulness; the coins placed on the eyes of Greek and later era corpses were his payment. Cerberus, too, should be familiar as the three-headed canine guardian of the Underworld.

Those three women who sit and spin just may be none other than the three Fates themselves. Three supernatural figures turn up in most tales of this type, though usually as willing helpers of the protagonist (see note 30).

The author has retold this story from many sources, including *The Golden Ass* by Apulenius and *World Tales* edited by Idries Shah.

30. East of the Sun and West of the Moon (p. 156)

Here is an example of how similar folktales from around the world can be. Once again there is a heroine who weds a nonhuman (or in this case an enchanted human) whose face she is forbidden to see and who, of course, breaks that prohibition, sending the hero flying and herself off on a quest to find and regain him. In almost all versions, the heroine is helped by three mysterious figures, sometimes described as hags, sometimes just as "old women." One thing they always have in common is magic; they almost always give the heroine three magical toys with which she bribes her way to the prince's bedside and breaks the enchantment binding him. Most of these stories also contain the motif of the shirt that only the heroine can wash clean.

This retelling is based on the tale by the same name found in *East O' The Sun and West O' The Moon*, George Dasent's compilation of Norwegian folktales made in the field by Peter Christen Asbjornsen and Jorgen Moe Asbjornsen in the nineteenth century.

31. The Red Swan (p. 164)

This Chippewa tale, which is about not one but two quests—one for the swan herself and one for the magician's stolen scalp—contains folktale elements familiar to folk stories the world over:

Every people who live in countries that harbor swans have tales of swan-maidens, shape-shifting young women who often take human lovers; other peoples have other shape-shifting young women, such as the crane-maidens found in some Japanese tales. Usually, as in this tale, the swan-maidens have control over their shape-changing; sometimes, as in certain Irish tales, the swan-shape is the result of a curse. The Russian composer Piotr Tchaikovsky used this theme of involuntary shape-shifting in his ballet *Swan Lake*.

The three old magicians who help the hero have their parallels in a good many other world folktales, although in most stories they are female characters, not male (see note 30).

The idea that hair has magical power is another common theme found around the world. A version familiar to many turns up in the Biblical story of Samson, whose superhuman strength lay in his hair.

This retelling is based primarily on the tale recorded by Henry Rowe Schoolcraft in 1838 and published in *Schoolcraft's Indian Legends*.

Part Five

32. "That's All, Folks . . ." (p. 169)

This is the classic ending to Warner Brothers' "Looney Tunes" cartoons, cheerfully delivered by Porky Pig.

When Bugs Bunny was first created as a Warner Brothers cartoon character, it's unlikely that anyone in the studio had the Trickster archetype in mind: cartoons of the 1930s were full of animal protagonists, and it's very possible that one of the inspirations for Bugs was the cocky Hare in Disney's "The Hare and the Tortoise." But Bugs is far closer to a classic trickster than to any earlier cartoon characters. Although his character has mellowed somewhat over the years, the earlier Bugs Bunny cartoons show him as being very close indeed to the totally unpredictable, amoral Trickster of folklore. A good many other cartoon characters bear at least a passing resemblance to the classic Trickster, from Woody Woodpecker down to today's favorite underachiever, Bart Simpson.

33. Raven Steals the Sun (p. 171)

Raven is the trickster-creator of the Pacific Northwest, selfish and noble at the same time. In the myths of the tribes that people the region from Alaska down through British Columbia, Washington State and Oregon, he is responsible for a good many creations, from this accidental creation of sun, moon and stars to that of many a natural earthly feature. It is he who is generally credited with having created both animals and people. In some myths Raven takes on the role of firebringer to humanity: Fire, in the folklore of many cultures around the world, is something that needs to be stolen from a selfish owner, just as the light has to be stolen in this story. A version that may be more familiar to many readers is the story of Prometheus, who was punished by the jealous Greek deities for giving fire, their plaything, to humanity.

The author has retold this story from several sources, including *The Raven Steals the Light* compiled by Bill Reid and Robert Bringhurt.

34. The Theft of the Sun and Moon (p. 174)

Here is Coyote, the classic southwestern Trickster figure, in his dual role as creator-by-chance and thief. Like Raven, he steals the box containing the sun and the moon, and like Raven, his antagonist/ally is Eagle. Which tale came first? Who can say? Did one influence the other? Very possibly. A great deal of trading went on in North America between the various tribes, and folktales often travel with the traders.

This retelling first appeared in *The World & I*, April, 1990, pages 646-8, in an issue devoted to the Trickster theme.

35. The Greatest Liar of Them All (p. 177)

This is a rather mild Coyote tale. In others, such as the previous story, the chaotic being is clearly someone of great, primal power, one who creates the world, peoples it, and steals fire for those people, while in still others he is a boldly bawdy character, so much so that some Coyote stories have been censored from folklore collections! At any given time, he is as much victim as trickster, getting humiliated or even killed again and again, though of course he, being the archetypical figure the Trickster is, can't stay dead for long.

This retelling is a compilation of several versions, including "Coyote Shows How He Can Lie" in Barry Holstun Lopez's *Giving Birth to Thunder, Sleeping with his Daughter: Coyote Builds North America*.

36. A Bagful of Tricks (p. 179)

Here is one of the mysteries of comparative folklore. It's not surprising that tales from different tribes in North America might have similar elements; the distances between those tribes weren't insurmountable and there weren't any massive bodies of water to cross. But how is it that the Apaches of Arizona have almost the same story, even though the protagonist is different, as the Uigur people of far-off Central Asia and China? Is a basic form of this tale as old as the crossing of the Bering Strait? Or is it an example of the universality of the folktale? No one can be sure.

A Trickster figure can be human instead of animal. The Effendi Nasreddin is the protagonist of a whole cycle of Uigur tales, the point of which usually is to see the pompous or unjust humbled, though sometimes Nasreddin does seem to simply be having fun with his cleverness. He is a familiar character in the stories of other Near Eastern cultures as well, turning up in tales from Turkey (where he is known as Nasreddin Hoca) all the way to China—not surprising, since the Uigur were once a nomadic people. There may be a real man behind all the stories, one who lived in the Turkish town of Akshehir a good many centuries ago; then again, there may not.

This is a retelling of a tale included in *The Effendi and the Pregnant Pot: Uygur Folktales from China* translated by Primrose Giglesi.

37. Pedro the Tricky (p. 181)

Here is yet another folklore puzzle. Which of these three variants (see also notes 35 and 36) came first? Obviously the Coyote tale can only date to the arrival of the Spaniards in the New World, and the reintroduction of horses that came with them. Does this mean that the tale of Pedro is earlier than that of Coyote? Are they the same age? And what of the Uigur tale of Nasreddin? Is that the oldest version of the tale? None of these riddles can actually be answered, but they are fun for students of comparative folklore to consider.

This is the author's slightly abridged version of a more complex trickster tale collected in New Mexico by Aurelio M. Espinosa in the first part of this century. Other tales of Pedro can be heard in the American Southwest, in Mexico, and in South America.

38. Spider, Reader of Thoughts (p. 183)

Ananse, the trickster spider, is a common protagonist in tales from West Africa, and since people, whether travelling voluntarily or because they have been enslaved, take their stories with them, he is also common in tales from the Caribbean. He is sometimes a figure of mythic importance, as in this tale, but in other stories Ananse is involved in less cosmic matters (see note 39).

The idea that the youngest of three sons should be the one to triumph (even though in this tale he needs a little help from Ananse) is a familiar one in European folktales. Many theories have been proposed to account for this, including one that assumes that the last-born son, rather than the first-born, would be the one to inherit from his father.

The author has retold this version from several sources, including *African Myths and Tales* edited by Susan Feldman.

39. The Spider Pays His Debts (p. 186)

This Hausa story features Ananse at his most coldly practical: It's not a "nice" story by standard moral ideals, but there's something embarrassingly satisfying at the idea of avoiding paying debts in such a tricky way. And this tale does show a very common side of the Trickster. He's always an amoral character and usually as self-centered and selfish as a young child, involved with his own well-being even if it means harming or even killing off anyone who gets in the way.

As with *Spider, Reader of Thoughts*, this retelling is based on several sources, including *African Myths and Tales* edited by Susan Feldman.

40. Rabbit and Antelope Dig a Well (p. 188)

Here is a definite ancestor of Bugs Bunny! Unlike Hare in the previous tale, Rabbit has no high motivations: he wants the most he can get for the least amount of work, depending on his wits rather than on honest labor.

Two very familiar folktale types are combined in this tale. The first is that of the two dissimilar animals who form a partnership in which one steals food from the other over a day or so, each time claiming he is going to see a child who has such names as "Half-Gone" and "All-Gone." Needless to say, the partnership, which turns up in various forms around the world, ends in disaster! The second tale type is best known to American readers from the "Brer Rabbit and the Tar Baby" story told by Joel Chandler Harris; the idea of a character attacking a statue covered with sticky material and getting stuck to it also turns up in European and American folklore (see note 41).

This retelling is based on similar tales found in *African Myths and Tales* edited by Susan Feldman and *African Folktales* edited by Paul Radin.

41. The Stolen Figs (p. 191)

This tale from Chile shows how nicely a folk motif can be transmitted from one culture to another. Whether or not the "Tar Baby" motif originated in Africa, it has become a popular image in other regions as well; this tale may have had its origins in stories told by slaves, or it may have travelled all the way from Spain (see note 40).

There are many folktales from Europe and Asia, as well as from the New World, in which would-be thieves are outwitted by their chosen victim. In one French tale of a farmer and two thieves attempting to steal some bacon from him, that bacon changes hands so many times even the three protagonists finally give up and share the booty!

This retelling is based on a version collected by Yolando Pino-Saavedra from Juan de Dios Diaz in Ignao, Valdivia in 1952 and included in *Folktales of Chile*.

42. The Bolt of Cloth (p. 193)

Here is an example of how a folkloric hero may belong to more than one culture and reveal different aspects to each. Till (or Tyl) Eulenspiegel is considered an amoral trickster in German folklore; a somewhat gentler one in Dutch folklore, puncturing the dignity of the pompous; and a downright heroic if still tricky defender of his native land in the Belgian province of Flanders. In the former tales, he has no genuine motives other than self-interest, but in the latter, he pulls his pranks on abusers of the common folk or on the Spaniards who menaced Flanders at the time of the Spanish Inquisition.

The idea of using trickery to confuse someone about the true color of a cloth or item of clothing is a common one in folklore, appearing in one form or another throughout Europe, Africa and Asia; in one version, a tricky fellow confuses two less intelligent folks by wearing a coat that is red on one side and blue on the other, then walking between the two of them so that they come to blows over, "The coat is red!" "The coat is blue!"

This tale is known to the author and dates at least to the six-teenth century. See *World Tales* edited by Idries Shah.

43. Little Kandeck (p. 195)

Sometimes the protagonist of a Trickster type of folktale isn't actively a Trickster at all, but merely someone who uses trickery to save his or her own life. Kandek is a clever little girl who has her coun-terparts in tales of equally clever youngsters from Europe, Asia and Africa. The heroine in the English tale "Molly Whuppy," for example, not only escapes from the sack of the giant who has captured her and her sisters, she tricks the giant into killing his own daughters instead. In the Bantu tale of "Demane and Demazana," a girl who's been caught in a sack by an ogre manages to leave a trail for her brother to follow.

This retelling is based on a story found, among other places, in *Armenian Folk-tales and Fables* by Charles Downing.

44. The Serf and the Swamp-Things (p. 198)

The theme of an ordinary man outwitting supernatural but far less clever foes through a faked contest of strength is another idea that crosses international story boundaries, an idea found in one form or another around the world. Particularly common are such tricks as squeezing the whey from cheese as if it were water from a stone or fool-ing the opponent into racing against a rabbit or wrestling a bear. The specific motif of the clever human against water beings is popular in Russia and Central Asia.

This tales is known to the author. A similar version is recorded in *Ukrainian Folk Tales* translated by Irina Zheleznova.

45. Granny and the Thief (p. 203).

This Chinese folktale is one of the few stories in which the trick-ster protagonist is a peaceful, elderly woman. But Granny is no less clever in defending her home against the would-be robber than the rest of the folks in this chapter!

In folktales from around the world, the thief, unless he is the pro-tagonist, is usually portrayed as someone who is foolish enough to be easily tricked by the person he's trying to rob. In a Jewish folktale from Middle Europe, for example, a man carrying his wages home through a forest is stopped at gunpoint. But the man calmly pretends his wife will never believe he was robbed unless there's some sign of a struggle, and tricks the robber into shooting off his gun till all the bullets are gone; the man then flattens the would-be thief with a punch and goes his way.

Stupidity on the part of the folkloric thief is true whether the thief is human or something else entirely. In some variations of this Chinese tale, the terrible robber, Tiger, isn't a man, but an actual tiger (though just as foolish).

The main source of this retelling is a Han folktale called "The Old Woman and the Tiger," a version of which is included in *The Water Buffalo and the Tiger: Folk Tales from China*.

46. The Orphan and the Miser (p. 207)

Misers in folktales exist to be tricked and taught lessons in humility, and the fellow in this tale is no different. The idea of orders accidentally or deliberately misunderstood is a common one in world folklore. Sometimes the hero, rather than being a deliberate trickster, is the innocent bearer of a letter that would mean his death if delivered; usually a good samaritan switches letters so that instead of being slain, the hero is granted a great reward, often including marriage to the daughter of the one who had ordered his death. Shakespeare used the theme of the switched letter to good effect in *Hamlet*, when the prince changes his own death warrant into a death warrant for the unfortunate, if treacherous, courtiers Rosenkrantz and Guildenstern.

This story is retold from one collected in the *Sandalwood Box: Folktales from Tadzikistan* translated by Katya Sheppard.

47. How the Corn Came to the People (p. 211)

It seems only right to bring this series of Trickster tales full cycle with a mythic "how and why" or "pourquoi" tale. Like in "Raven Steals the Sun" and "The Theft of Sun and Moon," a selfish deity or demi-god must be overcome for the benefit of the rest of the world or, in this case, humanity. There is no one trickster figure here; the unspoken moral is that even the humblest can be of worth. This is one of the few Trickster types of tales in which the Trickster figures, in this case the birds and animals, act out of pure altruism.

This is the author's retelling of a tale first gathered in the field by J.B. Johnson in 1940. Another version can be found in *Yaqui Myths and Legends* by Ruth Warner Giddings.

A Suggested Reading and Viewing List

Most people have favorite science fiction and fantasy movies and television shows, and some have favorite musical theater and opera productions. A list of recommended entertainment that uses folklore themes follows:

I. Movies and Television

Fantasy Movies

Donkey Skin (Peau D'ane), Orion Pictures (U.S. distributor), 1971. Directed by Jacques Demy and starring Catherine Deneuve, Jacques Perrin, Jean Marais and Delphine Seyrig. This is a French version of Perrault's tale of a princess who escapes her father— who wishes to wed her—disguises herself as a common kitchen maid, and wins herself a handsome prince; the story is, of course, a variant of "Cinderella" and is first cousin to the tale of "Cap O'Rushes." The special effects include some dazzling gowns and the script is charming and witty.

Jason and the Argonauts, Columbia Pictures, 1963. Directed by Don Chaffey and starring Todd Armstrong, Gary Raymond, Nancy Kovack, Honor Blackman, and Nigel Green.

This rather "Hollywood" British version of the epic tale softens the character of Medea to damsel-in-distress blandness, but does follow the basic story fairly well, and includes some good special effects from that genius of stop-action photography, Ray Harryhausen.

Indiana Jones and the Last Crusade, 20th Century Fox, 1989. Directed by Steven Spielberg and starring Harrison Ford, Sean

Connery, Denholm Elliott, Alison Doody, John Rhys-Davies, Julian Glover, River Phoenix, Michael Byrne, and Alex Hyde-White.

This third movie in the Indiana Jones trilogy sends Indy off on a quest with his scholarly father for nothing less than the Holy Grail, which in this version is an earthenware cup watched over by mystic guardians, which grants immortality to whoever drinks from it.

Willow, 20th Century-Fox, 1988. Directed by Ron Howard and starring Val Kilmer, Joanne Whalley, and Warwick Davis.

While this fantasy movie from the George Lucas stable far from matched the success of the *Star Wars* movies, it does contain some fascinating folklore elements, including that of the royal baby who must be rescued and reared by common folk.

Arthurian Movies

Excalibur, C.I.C., 1981. Directed by John Boorman and starring Nicol Williamson, Nigel Terry, Helen Mirren, Nicholas Clay, Cherie Lunghi, Corin Redgrave, Paul Geoffrey, Patrick Stewart, Gabriel Byrne, and Liam Neeson.

This is a visually fascinating, if eccentric, British retelling of the story of Arthur, from his conception through the quest for the Grail to his final battle with Mordred. It brings into play the mythic theme of the land's fertility as tied to the health of the king.

The Sword and the Stone, Walt Disney Productions, 1963. Directed by Wolfgang Reitherman, with the voices of Ricky Sorenson, Sebastian Cabot, Karl Swenson, and Julian Matthews.

Here is a flawed but entertaining, if highly whimsical and sometimes far too cute, animated version of the story of the boyhood of King Arthur, loosely inspired by T.H. White's book, *The Once and Future King*.

The Fisher King, Columbia/Tristar Productions, 1991. Directed by Terry Gilliam and starring Robin Williams, Jeff Bridges, and Amanda Plummer.

Although set in modern times and only marginally a fantasy, this movie, like the book by Anthony Powell on which it was based, with its bizarre mixture of down-and-out grittiness and ancient legendry, deal with the theme of the Maimed King, the

Arthurian King Pelles.

Monty Python and the Holy Grail, EMI/Python Pictures, 1975. Directed by Terry Gilliam and starring Terry Jones, Graham Chapman, John Cleese, Terry Gilliam, Eric Idle, and Michael Palin.

The title of this British movie pretty much sums it up: King Arthur meets slapstick in a story of wonderful silliness that still manages a few moments of genuine beauty and an unglamorized glimpse of the Middle Ages.

———————————— Science Fiction ————————————

Forbidden Planet, MGM, 1956. Directed by Fred McLeod Wilcox and starring Walter Pidgeon, Ann Francis, Leslie Nielson, Warren Stevens, Jack Kelly, Richard Anderson, Earl Holliman, George Wallace, and James Drury.

This intelligent science fictional retelling of Shakespeare's *The Tempest* includes (as, of course, does the original fantasy play) several folkloric themes, but it's also of interest both as a good science fiction movie and as the source of some of the ideas and gadgetry (such as the transporter) that inspired *Star Trek.*

Star Trek Television Series:

Star Trek, Paramount Pictures, 1966-69. Various directors, starring William Shatner, Leonard Nimoy, DeForest Kelley, James Doohan, Michelle Nicols, George Takei, and Walter Koenig, with regular appearances by Majel Barrett, Grace Lee Whitney and Mark Lenard.

Sometimes facetiously known as "Star Trek Classic," this is the series that started the whole Star Trek phenomenon. There had been earlier science fiction shows on television, but this was the first to show an interracial, interspecies crew, and mixed in with the adventuring, a good amount of tolerance for other ways and beliefs.

Star Trek: The Next Generation, Paramount Pictures, 1987-present. Various directors, starring Patrick Stewart, Jonathan Frakes, Brent Spiner, Marina Sirtis, and Michael Dom.

This spin-off series is set approximately 150 years in the future from the world of the first show, but continues in the same adventurous yet tolerant theme.

Star Trek: Deep Space Nine: Paramount Pictures, 1992-present. Various directors, starring Avery Brooks, Nana Visitor, Rene Auberjonois, Armin Schimmerman, Terry Ferrell and Siddig Al-Fasi.

Set on a space station in the same universe as ST:TNG, this show features even more intermixing of human and alien species in the struggle for equality and tolerance.

Star Trek motion pictures:

Star Trek: The Motion Picture, Paramount Pictures, 1979. Directed by Robert Wise, starring the regular cast from the original *Star Trek* television show, with the addition of Stephen Collins and Persis Khambatta.

Star Trek II: The Wrath of Khan, Paramount Pictures, 1982. Directed by Nicholas Meyer, starring the *Star Trek* television cast plus Ricardo Montalban, Kirstie Alley, Bibi Besch, Merril Buttrick, and Paul Winfield.

Star Trek III: The Search for Spock, Paramount Pictures, 1984. Directed by Leonard Nimoy, starring the *Star Trek* television cast plus Christopher Lloyd, Robin Curtis, Merrick Buttrick, and Dame Judith Anderson.

Star Trek IV: The Voyage Home, Paramount Pictures, 1986. Directed by Leonard Nimoy, starring the *Star Trek* television cast plus Jane Wyatt, Catherine Hicks, Robin Curtis, Robert Ellenstein, John Schuck, and Brock Peters.

Star Trek V: The Final Frontier, Paramount Pictures, 1989. Directed by William Shatner, starring the *Star Trek* television cast plus David Warner, Lawrence Luckinbill, and Charles Cooper.

Star Trek VI: The Undiscovered Country, Paramount Pictures, 1991. Directed by Nicholas Meyer, starring the *Star Trek* television cast plus Kim Cattrall, Christopher Plummer, Brock Peters, Kurtwood Smith, Rosana DeSoto, David Warner, John Schuck, and Michael Dorn.

While these movies never live up to the promise and excitement of the various television series, they give a tantalizing glimpse of what *Star Trek* could look like on a larger-than-television budget.

The *Star Trek* universe has left its mark on just about every level of modern society. T-shirts and buttons bearing such familiar slogans as "Beam me up, Scotty," and "He's dead, Jim" (or, since *The Next Generation's* starship captain is Jean-Luc Picard, "Il est mort, Jean-Luc") can be seen on the street or at science fiction conventions, while people who may never have heard of the Greek god, Vulcan, certainly recognize the name as that of Mr. Spock's home planet!

The Star Wars Trilogy:

Star Wars, 20th Century-Fox, 1977. Directed by George Lucas, starring Mark Hamill, Harrison Ford, Carrie Fisher, Alec Guinness, Anthony Daniels, David Prowse, Peter Cushing, and the voice of James Earl Jones.

The Empire Strikes Back, 20th Century-Fox, 1980. Directed by Irvin Kershner, starring the same cast as *Star Wars*, with the addition of Billy Dee Williams and the voice of Frank Oz.

The Return of the Jedi, 20th Century-Fox, 1983. Directed by Richard Marquand, starring the same cast as *The Empire Strikes Back*.

These three movies are crammed full of derring-do and way-out adventure, and they contain an amazing number of folkloric and mythic themes, from the boy raised in ignorance of his true heritage to the motif of the Wise Old Man. (This is no accident: at one time George Lucas was a student of mythologist Joseph Campbell.) *Star Wars*, like *Star Trek*, has had a tremendous hold on popular culture, creating a series of bestselling books and adding such phrases as "Use the force" to everyday speech.

Bugs Bunny, Warner Brothers, 1939-present. Various artists, starring the many voices of Mel Blanc.

There are so many Bugs Bunny cartoons to be seen on television, in the movies and on tape that a listing of them here would take up far too many pages! Most of them can't be—and shouldn't be—easily reduced to simple description, since they are all full of weird situations and settings, and wonderfully ridiculous sight gags, but any one of the cartoons will give the viewer a good image of Bugs Bunny as Trickster.

————————— Musicals and Operas —————————

Camelot, Lerner and Lowe, 1960.

This was a splashy, if not totally successful, Broadway musical, a retelling of part of the story of King Arthur, based on T.H. White's *The Once and Future King*, which focuses on the ultimately tragic love triangle between Arthur, Queen Gwenivere, and Sir Lancelot. The musical was turned into an also less-than-successful movie by Warner Brothers in 1967, retaining most, though not all, of the score.

Das Ring Des Niebelungen (The Ring of the Niebelung), Richard Wagner.

In this four-opera cycle, Wagner retells the story of the Teutonic gods, their eventual downfall, and the Volsung Saga.

Das Rheingold (The Rhinegold), 1869.

This "prelude" opera deals with the events surrounding the theft of the cursed ring of Andvari.

Die Walkure (The Valkyrie), 1870.

This second opera in the Ring cycle concerns the doomed love story of Siegmund and Sieglinde (the Norse Sigmund and Signe) and the breaking of the hero's sword.

Siegfried, 1876.

The third opera in the cycle is the story of the young hero who reforges the broken sword, slays the dragon, Fafnir, and goes on to wake and love the fallen Valkyrie, Brunhilde.

Die Gotterdammerung (The Twilight of the Gods), 1876.

In this final opera in the cycle, Wagner links the murder of Siegfried to the downfall of the gods and the birth of a new order based on love.

Parsifal, 1882, Richard Wagner.

This is Wagner's fantastical musical retelling of the story of Percival, the search for the Grail, and the healing of King Pelles, who here is replaced by Amfortas, King of Monsalvat.

II. Books

 Folktale Collections

There are literally hundreds of collections of folktales available in bookstores and libraries. The following are only a sampling of the wonderful worlds waiting to be discovered. Most of them are easily found in libraries or bookstores; some are more obscure but are worth hunting down for their stories.

Afanas'ev, Aleksandr. *Russian Fairy Tales*. Pantheon Books: New York, 1975. This collection of Russian tales collected in the 19th century and recently reprinted in English is one of the best and most easily found.

Apollonius of Rhodes, translated by E.V. Rieu. *The Voyage of Argo*. Penguin Books: London and New York, 1950. There are several other translations available of this classic adventure fantasy epic.

Beckwith, Martha. *Hawaiian Mythology.* University of Hawaii Press: Honolulu, 1970. This is an excellent overview of the subject, and relatively easy to find in paperback.

Bushnaq, Iner. *Arab Folktales*. Pantheon Books: New York, 1986. A good collection of tales from Moslem countries, this is another in the Pantheon Fairy Tale and Folklore Library.

Colum, Padraic. *Legends of Hawaii*. Yale University Press: New Haven, 1937. This is a literary collection but it remains true to the original stories.

Dasent, George Webbe. *East o' the Sun & West o' the Moon*. Dover Publications: New York, 1970. This is a reprint of an 1888 edition put together by Dasent from the collection of Norwegian folktales gathered by Peter Christen Asbjornsen and Jorgen Moe Asbjornsen in the middle of the nineteenth century.

Downing, Charles. *Armenian Folk-tales and Fables*. Oxford University Press: London, 1972. This entertaining anthology of retold tales has recently been reprinted in paperback in a U.S. edition.

Espinosa, Aurelio M. *The Folklore of Spain in the American Southwest: Traditional Spanish Folk Literature in Northern New*

Mexico and Southern Colorado. University of Oklahoma Press: Norman, 1985. This is a scholarly but fascinating study of the survival of Spanish folklore and folk customs in the New World.

Feldmann, Susan. *African Myths and Tales*. Dell Publishing: New York, 1963. This is a good overall look at sub-Saharan folktales in an inexpensive format.

_____. *The Storytelling Stone: Myths and Tales of American Indians*. Dell Publishing: New York, 1965. Another good overall survey in an inexpensive format.

Giddings, Ruth Warner. *Yaqui Myths and Legends*. Arizona University Press: Tucson, 1983. This is one of the few available collections of tales from these people.

Giglesi, Primrose, translator. *The Effendi and the Pregnant Pot: Uigur Folktales from China*. New World Press: Beijing, China, 1982.
This is a collection of humorous (and moral) tales about the Effendi Nasreddin, a popular character in folktales from Turkey, where he becomes Nasreddin Hoca, all the way through Central Asia and Iran, where he becomes the Mulla Nasrudin, to China. This book is only one in a series of English language Chinese folktales put out by New World Press, most of them easily found and inexpensively priced. For other tales of the Effendi, see the listings for Shah and Walker.

Jacobs, Joseph. *English Fairy Tales*. Dover Press: New York, 1967. Jacobs was a folklorist who made several collections of retold folktales such as this one and its companion book, *More English Fairy Tales*, also available from Dover Press. Ostensibly for children, these volumes also include some interesting notes on the tales and their parallels.

Joyce, P.W.. *Old Celtic Romances: Tales from Irish Mythology*. The Devin-Adair Company: New York, 1962. These are grand stories told in a dramatic, romantic style.

Kreutzwald, Friedrich Reinhold. *Old Estonian Fairy Tales*. Tallinn Perioodika: Tallinn, Estonia, 1985. This book is a little difficult to find in the United States, but copies can be located in stores specializing in Slavic imports. It's an interesting collection of tales including some regional stories.

Kuniczak, W.S. *The Glass Mountain: Twenty-Six Ancient Polish Folktales and Fables*. Hippocrene Books: New York, 1992. These are very readable retellings of classic folktales.

Lewis, Brian. *The Sargon Legend: A Study of the Akkadian text and the Tale of the Hero Who was Exposed at Birth*. American Schools of Oriental Research: Cambridge, Massachusetts, 1980. This is a scholarly work, and a little difficult to find, but it contains fascinating summaries of many variants of the tale of the child who was rescued from a boat or box.

Lonnrot, Elias, compiler, translated by Francis Peabody Magoun, Jr. *The Kalevala, or Poems of the Kalevela District*. Harvard University Press: Cambridge, 1963. Although the *Kalevala* is described as the national epic of Finland, it is actually a compilation of folk ballads arranged in coherent order as one continual story by Dr. Lonnrot in the nineteenth century. Full of tales of magic and high adventure, it was almost certainly one of the influences behind the creation of *The Lord of the Rings*; Professor Tolkien was well acquainted with the Kalevala, and the Finnish wizard-hero Vainamoienen is almost certainly an ancestor of his wizardly hero, Gandalf.

Lopez, Barry Holstun. *Giving Birth to Thunder, Sleeping with his Daughter: Coyote Builds North America*. Avon Books: New York, 1981. There are several editions available of this excellent collection of Coyote tales from the various North American tribes, but this is one of the easiest to find. There are dozens of other collections of tales about Coyote in print; a search through any bookstore with a sizeable Native American section will turn up several. This one, however, shows Coyote in all his many facets.

Malory, Sir Thomas. *Le Morte D'Arthur*. Penguin Books: New York, 1969, two volumes. There are many other editions of this famous work available; the first printing was in 1485! While Sir Thomas was far from a law-abiding citizen—*Le Morte D'Arthur* was written while its author was in prison for, among other things, cattle theft—he remade the legends of King Arthur into a literary whole in this work.

Massignon, Genevieve. *Folktales of France*. Translated by Jacqueline Hyland. University of Chicago Press: Chicago, 1968. The tales in this book were originally collected in the field, and are divided up by region.

Morris, William. *Volsung Saga*. Collier Books: New York, 1962. Although not everyone agrees on the accuracy of this translation by the nineteenth century author, it's perhaps the most easily found version of the saga.

Pino-Saavedra, Yolanda. *Folktales of Chile*. University of Chicago Press: Chicago, 1967. A fascinating collection of tales compiled by Chile's foremost folklorist.

Quinn, Zdenka and John Paul. *The Water Sprite of the Golden Town: Folk Tales of Bohemia*. Macrae Smith Company: Philadelphia, 1971. This is a collection of retellings that are readable and true to the tales.

Radin, Paul, ed. *African Folktales*. Schocken Books: New York, 1983. This is a good collection of sub-Saharan tales, and easy to find in bookstores.

Reid, Bill and Robert Bringhurt. *The Raven Steals the Light*. University of Washington Press: Seattle, 1984. This is a compilation and retelling of Haida tales about Raven, together with fascinating illustrations by artist Bill Reid.

Schoolcraft, Henry Rowe. *Schoolcraft's Indian Legends*. Michigan State University Press: East Lancing, 1991. An interesting nineteenth century collection of folktales and myths from the Chippewa and other tribes of the Great Lakes region.

Seki, Keigo. *Folktales of Japan*. Translated by Robert J. Adams. University of Chicago Press: Chicago, 1963. This is an anthology of tales collected in Japan, for the most part in the early years of this century.

Shah, Idris. *The Exploits of the Incomparable Mulla Nasrudin/The Subtleties of the Inimitable Mulla Nasrudin*, Two Volumes in One. Octagon Books: London, 1985. This two-in-one collection features tales both old and new about the Mulla, also known in Turkey as the Hoca and in China as the Effendi, and shows that he is very much still alive and well in the living world of folklore. For other tales about this popular character, see the listings for Giglesi and Walker.

_____. *World Tales*. Harcourt Brace Jovanovich: New York, 1979. The subtitle sums it up: "The extraordinary coincidence of stories told in all times in all places." A good collection of comparative folktales with some intriguing, sometimes downright bizarre, illustrations.

Sheppard, Katya, translator. *The Sandalwood Box: Folk Tales from Tadzhikistan*. Richard Sadler Ltd.: Buckinghamshire, 1971. Translated from *Die Sandelbolztrube*, Verlag Volk und Welt/Kultur und Fortschritt: Berlin, 1961. Although this book is not easy to find, it is a fine collection of folktales from what is now the Tadzhik Republic.

Skeels, Dell, translator. *The Romance of Perceval in Prose*. University of Washington Press: Seattle, 1961. This is not the easiest book to find, but it's a translation of an interesting French medieval version of the Percival story and worth a look.

Sturluson, Snorri. *The Prose of Edda*. Translated by Jean I. Young. University of California Press: Berkeley, 1954. This is actually a twelfth century handbook on poetry, but it contains a good summary of Norse mythology, including some of the tale of the Volsungs.

Sherlock, Philip. *West Indian Folk-Tales*. Oxford University Press: Oxford, 1987. Although Sherlock rather annoyingly doesn't give specific islands of origin for the stories he's retelling, this is still a good introduction to how easily Ananse the West Africa trickster made the transition into the stories of the peoples of the Caribbean Islands as well.

Walker, Barbara. *Watermellons, Walnuts, and the Wisdom of Allah, and Other Tales of the Hoca*. Texas Tech University Press: Lubbock, 1991. As the title states, this is a collection of some of the hundreds of Turkish tales about Nasreddin Hoca or, as the Uigur people call him, Effendi Nasreddin, and the Iranians Mulla Nasrudin. See also the listings for Giglesi and Shah.

Water-Buffalo and the Tiger: Folk Tales from China, The. (Second series). Foreign Language Press: Beijing, 1980. This is one of a series of small, inexpensive paperbacks. Although every now and then Communist propaganda slips in, these are, for the most part, excellent collections, fairly easy to find in the United States.

Zheleznova, Irina, translator. *Ukrainian Folk Tales*. Dnipro Publishers: Kiev, 1986. These are authentic tales, many of them with echoes of Soviet propaganda that don't detract from the fascination of the tales themselves.

--------------------------------- Fiction ---------------------------------

It is, of course, impossible to list every fantasy and science fiction book that contains folkloric motifs; a listing of fantasy novels relating to King Arthur alone could fill a volume! The following is intended merely as a starting place for readers interested in folklore-inspired novels.

Alexander, Lloyd. The *Prydain* series:

The Book of Three. Holt, Reinhart and Winston: New York, 1964.

The Black Cauldron. Holt, Reinhart and Winston: New York, 1965.

The Castle of Llyr. Holt, Reinhart and Winston: New York, 1966.

Taran Wanderer. Holt, Reinhart and Winston: New York, 1967.

The High King. Holt, Reinhart and Winston: New York, 1968.

    In this fantasy series full of wit and cleverly designed characters and based on Welsh mythology and folklore, Taran, the young hero, goes from lowly pigkeeper to hero and ruler.

Anderson, Poul. *The Broken Sword*. Ballantine Books: New York, 1971. This fantasy takes a great deal of its inspiration from the Norse sagas, and contains both the themes of the broken sword and of the young man raised ignorant of his true origins.

Bradley, Marion Zimmer. *The Mists of Avalon*. Alfred A. Knopf: New York, 1982. This is a feminist version of the Arthurian legend, as seen through the eyes of Morgan le Fay.

Cooper, Susan. *The Dark is Rising* series:

Over Sea, Under Stone. J. Cape: London, 1965.

The Dark is Rising. Atheneum: New York, 1973.

Greenwitch. Atheneum: New York, 1974.

The Grey King. Atheneum: New York, 1975.

Silver on the Tree. Atheneum: New York, 1977.

    In this series of contemporary fantasies ostensibly for young readers, the author makes intriguing use of various British folklore motifs as well making her own additions to the story of King Arthur.

Deitz, Tom. *Windmaster's Bane*. Avon Books: New York, 1986. Two young men from Georgia become involved in the world of Faerie through the gift of a magic ring.

de Lint, Charles. *Jack the Giant-Killer*. Ace Books: New York, 1987. The author uses the British and American trickster figure of Jack as a ritual title of the protagonist in this urban fantasy.

Garner, Alan. *The Weirdstone of Brisingamen*. Ace Books: New York, 1960. This evocative fantasy involves children from our world in magical adventures centering around a mythic bracelet.

Gilliam, Richard, editor. *Grails: Quests, Visitations, and Other Occurrences*. Unnameable Press: Atlanta, 1992. This is a collection of modern short stories based on the Grail theme.

Greenhalgh, Zohra. *Contrarywise*. Ace Books: New York, 1989.

_____. *Trickster's Touch*. Ace Books: New York, 1989.
These two fantasy novels give a fascinating look into the unpredictable mind and actions of a Trickster, and the effect such a being has on the deities and mortals with whom that Trickster interacts. Unfortunately, both books are currently out of print.

Lee, Tanith. *The Birthgrave*. Daw Books: New York, 1975.
In this science fantasy, the protagonist not only learns she is of noble birth, she learns she isn't even of the human race.

Lewis, C.S. *The Chronicals of Narnia.*

The Lion, the Witch, and the Wardrobe. The Macmillan Company: New York, 1950.

Prince Caspian. The Macmillan Company: New York, 1951.

The Voyage of the "Dawn Treader." The Macmillan Company: New York, 1952.

The Silver Chair. The Macmillan Company: New York, 1953.

The Horse and his Boy. The Macmillan Company: New York, 1954.

The Magician's Nephew. The Macmillan Company: New York, 1955.

The Last Battle. The Macmillan Company: New York, 1956.

Despite being labeled as children's books and having a heavily Christian accent, these seven books, which are full of folkloric references, hold enough magical wonders to appeal to any reader of fantasy. The third book in the series, *The Voyage of the "Dawn Treader,"* focuses on the theme of the heroic sailors on a quest, while the fifth book, *The Horse and His Boy*, concerns a young hero who was raised ignorant of his true worth coming into his own. C.S. Lewis was a contemporary and friend of J.R.R. Tolkien.

_____. *Till We Have Faces*. Harcourt Brace Jovanovich: New York, 1956.
Lewis reworks the myth of Cupid and Psyche into a fascinatingly complex fantasy novel.

Lisle, Holly. *Minerva Wakes*. Baen Books: New York, 1994.
A woman hunting for her kidnapped children discovers her

wedding ring is actually a ring of magical power.

McCaffrey, Anne. *Dragonflight*, Ballantine, 1968. Lessa, the heroine of this first book in the *Pern* series, fits neatly into the category of the hero raised ignorant of his true worth; she's first seen living in impoverished surroundings, very much like Cinderella.

McKillip, Patricia A. *The Riddle-Master of Hed Trilogy*:

The Riddle-Master of Hed, Atheneum: New York, 1976.

Heir of Sea and Fire, Atheneum: New York, 1977.

Harpist in the Wind, Atheneum: New York, 1979.

This fantasy trilogy centers about a young man's quest to solve a vital riddle about himself and his land. Unfortunately, it may be difficult to find save in bookstores dealing in used and out-of-print books.

Moon, Elizabeth. *The Deeds of Parksennarion*. Baen Books: New York, 1992. In this one-volume fantasy trilogy, a young woman rises from humble peasant to pure-hearted, gallant knight, questing for truth and justice.

Powell, Anthony. *The Fisher King*. Norton: New York, 1986. Like the movie made from it, this is an odd combination of fantasy and reality, a look at modern street life with an Arthurian overlay.

Pratchett, Terry. *Witches Abroad*. A ROC Book: New York, 1993. This is one of Pratchett's hilarious Disc World books. This volume takes on several folkloric themes, including the story of "Cinderella," and sets them all on their ears without losing the charm and power of the true folktale.

Sherman, Josepha. *The Shining Falcon*. Avon Books: New York, 1989. Based on Slavic folklore, the author's fantasy novel follows the quest of a young woman for her true love, who is transformed into the shape of a falcon.

Shwartz, Susan. *Grail of Hearts*. Tor Books: New York, 1993. Inspired in part by Richard Wagner's Opera *Parifal*, this fantasy novel is an intriguing interpretation of the Grail legend as seen through the eyes of Kundry.

Stewart, Mary. *The Merlin Trilogy*:

The Crystal Cave. William Morrow & Company: New York, 1970.

The Hollow Hills. William Morrow & Company: New York, 1973.

The Last Enchantment. William Morrow & Company: New York, 1979.

Stewart retells the story of Merlin in this historical fantasy trilogy that manages to combine what little is historically known of the period with the sense of wonder surrounding the Arthurian cycle.

Thomas, Roy and Gil Kane. *Richard Wagner's The Ring of Nibelung*. Warner Books: New York, 1989. This is a flawed but entertaining graphic novel version of the opera cycle, which in turn is based on the Norse and Germanic legends of Sigmund and Sigurd.

Tolkien, J.R.R. *The Lord of the Rings*. Houghton Mifflin: Boston, 1965. There are so many editions of this seminal fantasy trilogy and its "prequel," *The Hobbit*, that it's almost impossible *not* to find a set in a bookstore or library; they have gone through an incredible number of printings, and the trend shows no sign of slowing. Professor Tolkien's fantasy novels are now being taught in schools and are just as likely to be found in the literary section of bookstores as in the fantasy and science fiction section. Readers interested in the background of *Lord of the Rings* may want to search out Professor Tolkien's essay, "On Fairy-Stories," which has been included in many collections of his shorter work.

White, T.H. *The Once and Future King*. G.P. Putnam & Sons: New York, 1939. T.H. White here retells the story of Arthur from boyhood on in a sly, cynical, and often hilarious fashion. The book was the inspiration behind the Walt Disney version of the story of Arthur, *The Sword and the Stone*.

Other Books and Audiocassettes from August House Publishers

Cajun Ghost Stories

Performed by J.J. Reneaux

Winner of the 1992 Parent's Choice Award

Audiobook $9.95 / ISBN 0-87483-210-1

Cajun Folktales

J.J. Reneaux

"An excellent anthology ... The folklore is as spicy and interesting as their famed food."
—Publishers Weekly

Hardback $19.95 / ISBN 0-87483-283-7
Paperback $9.95 / ISBN 0-87483-282-9
Audiobook $12.00 / ISBN 0-87483-383-3

Listening for the Crack of Dawn

Donald Davis

Winner of the Anne Izard Storyteller's Choice Award

Hardback $17.95 / ISBN 0-87483-153-9
Paperback $11.95 / ISBN 0-87483-130-X
Double Audiobook $18.00 / ISBN 0-87483-147-4

Race with Buffalo

and Other Native American Stories for Young Readers

Collected by Richard and Judy Dockrey Young

Hardback $19.95 / ISBN 0-87483-343-4
Paperback $9.95 / ISBN 0-87483-342-6

Once Upon a Galaxy

The ancient stories that inspired Star Wars, Superman, and other popular fantasies

Josepha Sherman

Hardback $19.95 / ISBN 0-87483-386-8
Paperback $11.95 / ISBN 0-87483-387-6

Eleven Turtle Tales

Adventure Tales from Around the World

Pleasant DeSpain

Hardback $12.95 / ISBN 0-87483-388-4

AUGUST HOUSE PUBLISHERS, INC.
P.O. BOX 3223
LITTLE ROCK, AR 72203
1-800-284-8784